Japanese by Spring

BY ISHMAEL REED

ATHENEUM
NEW YORK · 1 9 9 3

MAXWELL MACMILLAN CANADA
TORONTO

MAXWELL MACMILLAN INTERNATIONAL
NEW YORK · OXFORD ·
SINGAPORE · SYDNEY

ISHMAEL REED

Japanese by Spring

Copyright © 1993 by Ishmael Reed

Atheneum   Maxwell Macmillan Canada, Inc.
Macmillan Publishing Company   1200 Eglinton Avenue East
866 Third Avenue   Suite 200
New York, NY 10022   Don Mills, Ontario M3C 3N1

Macmillan Publishing Company is part of the Maxwell Communication
Group of Companies.

Library of Congress Cataloging-in-Publication Data
Reed, Ishmael, 1938–
    Japanese by spring / by Ishmael Reed.
        p.   cm.
    ISBN 0-689-12072-9
    I. Title.
PS3568.E365J35   1993   92-36280   CIP
813'.54—dc20

10 9 8 7 6 5 4 3

Printed in the United States of America

*This book is dedicated to Junette Pinkney,
Pearl Alice-Marsh, Cheryl G. Eaves, Marc
Shaffer, Dr. Cuthbert Simpkins, Diane
Simpkins, A'lelia Bundles, Reginald Lewis,
Carol Christ, Bill Banks and Russ Ellis,
and to the African University of Oakland.*

Today, the alien barbarians of the West, the lowly
organs of the legs and feet of the world, are dashing
about across the seas, trampling other countries
underfoot, and daring, with their squinting eyes and
limping feet, to override the noble nations. What
manner of arrogance is this!
—Aizawa Seishisai, *Shinron*, 1825

The Japanese are likened to the American Indian in
their manner of making war. Our fighting men say
that isn't fair to the Indian. He had honor of a sort.
Moreover, even a dead Jap isn't a good Jap. His loving
comrades mine him and set him. . . . Yet, such are
the Nipponese. In death as in life, treacherous.
—*The New York Times Magazine*, February 13, 1942

It was at Fort Yukon that White Fang saw his first
white men. As compared with the Indians he had
known, they were to him another race of beings, a
race of superior gods.
—Jack London, *White Fang*

PART

One

●

chapter one

W hen Benjamin "Chappie" Puttbutt's mom and dad said Off to
the Wars, they really meant it. George Eliott Puttbutt was a two-
star Air Force general, cited and decorated for distinguishing himself
in two of the three great yellow wars, the wars against Japan, Korea
and Vietnam, and Ruby Puttbutt's star was on the rise as a member
of the United States Intelligence community. As a military brat
Benjamin knew the techniques of survival and so, after reading that
Japan would become a future world power, Puttbutt began to study
Japanese while enrolled at the Air Force Academy during the middle
sixties. It was the end of an upbringing characterized by regimen
and discipline. George and Ruby Puttbutt's idea of education was
similar to John Milton's. In his "Of Education," he recommends
that "two hours before supper [students] . . . be called out to their
military motions, under sky or covert according to the season, as
was the Roman wont; first on foot, then, as their age permits, on
horseback, to all the art of cavalry . . . in all the skill of embattling
. . . fortifying, besieging, and battering, with all of the helps of
ancient and modern stratagems, tactics, and warlike maxims."

* * *

That's not the only attitude they shared with Milton. With their continuous need for enemies, their motto could have been taken from Milton's panegyric for Cromwell: "New Foes Arise." Their favorite blues singer was "Little Milton." Their favorite comedian: Milton Berle.

Chappie had disappointed his family by being expelled from the Air Force Academy. The academy regarded him as a troublemaker, because he had tried to organize a Black Panther chapter among the few black cadets who were enrolled there, in the middle 1960s. At least that's what everybody thought. In those days he wore a big Afro. It was so big that once some blackbirds tried to make a nest in it. He'd finally received his MA from a small college in Utah, and after years of one- to two-year stands at different schools he'd settled at the English department at Jack London College. The deal was, that after three years of commuting between the African-American Studies department, between those who believed Europe to be the center of all culture and those who said that the center of culture was Africa, he'd receive tenure in the Humanity department. Those were the terms of the agreement he'd made with Jack London during his job interview at the MLA. He'd preferred that his tenure be in the Humanity department. He'd be on the winning side, or so he thought. He remembered the rich baritone laughter of his father when he had informed him that he had gotten a job teaching English and literature.

Breaking a tradition going back to the revolutionary war, when the first Puttbutt volunteered for service. Not exactly. In the photos of his ancestors in their military garb, which lined the wall of his father's Maryland den, one was missing. No Puttbutt served in World War II. His grandfather was missing. Didn't serve. Both his mother and father, when they were angry with him, would say, "You're just like your grandfather." Other than that, they never mentioned the man. His expulsion from the Air Force Academy prevented him from finishing Japanese. He got as far as the fifteenth lesson.

Benjamin "Chappie" Puttbutt III was now going to give Japanese another go. He had read one of those ads in the newspaper, "Japanese by Spring," and had signed up with a private tutor at the beginning of the spring semester, 1990, hoping that by spring of 1991 he would know enough to take advantage of the new global realities. He was talking that way now. Sounding like a graduate student in political science. All about global realities. Geopolitical this. Realpolitik that. Weltanschauung this. He was sounding like an edition of *Foreign Affairs*.

chapter two

I he ambulance carrying one injured black student was pulling away and heading toward the gate. Another student could be seen inside another ambulance. He was being administered oxygen by paramedics. Two others were being chased by a mob of white students led by the Bass boy. One tried to climb a fence, but he was pulled down by some members of the mob and pummeled. He screamed. There was blood everywhere. Robert Bass, Jr., president of the Amerikaner Student Society and the American Student Chapter of the Order of the Boer Nation, a nationwide organization of right-wing students, who were being bankrolled by old man Only and his friends, lifted the student from the pavement and punched him one more time. Flecks of blood flew from his face before he passed out. The other student had disappeared beneath a group of whites, who were attacking him with a baseball bat. The baseball bat and the nightstick had become the favorite weapons in the domestic war. Some-times those using the nightstick recited baseball metaphors when punishing some poor "suspect." The Los Angeles police who beat Rodney King boasted of having hit "quite a few home runs" on his head. "I haven't had a good game of hardball like this in a long time," one said. (The films of the King beating were similar to the scenes in nature films where hyenas circle and attack a prey while other scavengers approach and retreat.)

There was a television crew processing the scene. Nowadays, the TV crew was an essential body part of the mob. Seeing Benjamin Puttbutt, who had achieved notoriety for his magazine article in the *New York Exegesis*, denouncing affirmative action, the television crew headed in his direction. The reporters were shouting over each other, competing for his attention.

"Mr. Puttbutt, another black student has been beaten. What is your reaction to yet another attack on black students by white students?" Puttbutt walked briskly toward his office, the reporters following him, waiting for the answers to their questions. He didn't disappoint them. The reporters began scribbling in their notebooks and the TV cameras closed in on him.

"The black students bring this on themselves," he said, sucking on a menthol cigarette. Frowning to indicate gravity. Being careful not to leak any of the ashes on his blue blazer or gray slacks. "With their separatism, their inability to fit in, their denial of mainstream values, they get the white students angry. The white students want them to join in, to participate in this generous pie called the United States of America. To end their disaffiliation from the common culture. Black students, and indeed black faculty, should stop their confrontational tactics. They should start to negotiate. They should stop worrying these poor whites with their excessive demands. The white students become upset with these demands. Affirmative ac-tion. Quotas. They get themselves worked up. And so it's under-standable that they go about assaulting the black students. The white students are merely giving vent to their rage. This is a healthy exercise. It's perfectly understandable. After all, the whites are the real oppressed minority. I can't think of anybody who has as much difficulty on this campus as blondes."

"But one student, the one they sent to the hospital, suffered a fractured skull," a reporter said.

"Was he wearing one of those Malcolm X caps?" A white reporter volunteered that, yes, he indeed was wearing a Malcolm X cap.

"There. So you see. I was correct. He was confronting instead of negotiating. Why, this black separatism is tempting such reactions from the white students. These black students must cease their intellectually tawdry practice of playing to white guilt. They should do more to improve and develop themselves. That way, whites will respect them."

"But this has been the thirteenth black student to have been beaten over the last three weeks." Puttbutt didn't answer the last question. The reporters and camera crews dropped off and headed toward some other interviews.

He walked past the bronze statue of Jack London that stood in the middle of the campus. He paused for a moment to look up. London had his hands in the pockets of a navy pea jacket. The sculptor had captured what were called Jack London's boyish good looks . . . pompadour, raccoonlike shaded eyes. The apostle of the blond beast, the Nietzschean übermensch was a brunet just as his fellow blond beast admirer, Adolph Hitler. In the sculpture, a wolflike dog seemed attached to London's pants leg. London's solution to the Yellow Peril was outlined in a strange fiction entitled "The Unparalleled Invasion" (1910) in which Jacobus Laningdale, "a professor employed in the laboratories of the health office of New York City," works on a plan that will relieve the world of "the Chinese problem."

In 1975, President Moyer meets with Jacobus Laningdale for three hours. They discuss the increase in the Chinese population—by 1975, one billion and growing. With its industrial awakening generated by the Japanese invasion, China is a threat to the white world and does not heed its requirement that it reduce its population, and indeed scoffs at the West's concerns. Li Tang Fwung, described in the London story as "the power behind the Dragon Throne," replies to a convention of 1975 called in Philadelphia and including all Western nations to appeal to and threaten China about its soaring birthrate. He says, "What does China care for the community of nations? We have our own destiny to accomplish. It is unpleasant that our destiny does not jibe with the destiny of the rest of the world, but what would you do? You have talked windily about the royal races and the heritage of the earth, and we can only reply that, that remains to be seen. You cannot invade us. Never mind about your navies. . . . Our strength is in our population, which will soon be a billion. Thanks to you, we are equipped with all modern war machinery." After his speech London writes, "The world was nonplused, helpless, terrified." (In 1991, the US is so obsessed with the forty-billion-dollar trade deficit with Japan, which means that Japan is selling forty billion dollars more in the US than the US is selling in Japan, that the twenty-billion deficit with China is virtually ignored.) What does the world do? It adopts the plan concocted by Jacobus Laningdale. In a scene reminiscent of the B-52 dropping the atom bomb on Hiroshima, Jack London places an airship above the streets of Peking. "From the airship, as it curved its flight back and forth over the city, fell missiles . . . tubes of fragile glass that shattered into thousands of fragments on streets and house-tops." In this story, Jack London, Oakland's most prominent novelist, candidate for mayor in 1912, the man for whom Oakland's tourist draw, Jack London Square, is named, recommended the extermination of the Chinese: "every virulent form of infectious death stalked the land, wrought from bacteria, and germs and microbes and bacilli, cultured in the laboratories of the West that had come down upon China in the rain of glass."

After the Chinese are wiped out, a multicultural civilization is raised on its remains. "It was a vast and happy intermingling of nations

that settled down in China in 1982 and in the years that followed
a tremendous and successful experiment in cross-fertilization." Jack
London College of Oakland was named for the apostle of Anglo-
Saxon superiority. He swallowed the doctrine of development which
has polluted the earth and is destroying the ozone, posing a greater
threat to those whose lack of pigmentation makes them vulnerable
to ultraviolet rays than all of the Yellow Perils, Black Studies programs and Rap musicians combined. "There was no way to communicate Western ideas to the Chinese mind. China remained asleep.
The material achievement and progress of the West was a closed
book to her; nor could the West open the book." But even with his
faith in Anglo destiny, London was as miserable as most superracists
are. A bad husband and father. Given to petty outbursts. Paranoid.
He thought that the third world was mocking him. London thought
that the yellows, blacks and reds were laughing at him. Laughing at
Jack London, whose final solution for the Chinese was written in a
book called *The Strength of the Strong,* penned by a man who hung
out at the Piedmont baths among "beautiful" men. In the story
"The Unparalleled Invasion," China laughs at the West and, by
implication, Jack London. On page 88 of the story, "China laughs."
On page 91, "China smiled." On page 92, "China smiled," and on
page 92, "China smiled." On the same page, "China smiled," again.
In 1911, Jack London pined for a white man who would "wipe that
golden smile" off heavyweight champion Jack Johnson's face. Jack
London thought that "third world people" were laughing at him.
Laughing at the blond beast admirer's brunet hair. Laughing at his
addiction to heroin.

Another demonstration passed by. A more J. C. campus organization known as Faith of our Fathers, or the FF, was marching through
the campus and shouting their slogan, "We are Wiggers. We are
Wiggers," to indicate their status as white niggers. Everybody was a
nigger these days. Women, gays, always comparing their situations
with blacks.

• • •

Puttbutt was a member of the growing anti–affirmative action industry. A black pathology merchant. Throw together a three-hundred-
page book with graphs and articles about illegitimacy, welfare depen-
dency, single-family households, drugs and violence; paint the inner
cities as the circles of hell in the American paradise—the suburban
and rural Americas which were, in the media's imagination, wonder-
lands with sets by Disney—and you could write your way to the top
of the best-sellers list. Get on C-SPAN. It was the biggest literary
hustle going and Puttbutt decided that he was going to get his. He
had written a dozen or so articles about affirmative action. About
how your white colleagues don't respect you. About how you feel
stigmatized. About how you feel inferior. You know, the usual. All
of these speeches, op-eds and lectures, he felt, would get him where
he wanted to be. Would get him tenure. Hadn't his colleagues come
up to him after every printed interview he'd given to congratulate
him? To tell him that he said what many of them could only whisper?
To congratulate him for broaching a subject that was painful to
discuss? Being a military brat, a survivor and a loner, he was thinking of the only person in his life who counted. He was thinking
of himself. About how his ordeal from semester to semester would
end. He would have an opportunity to end his arrangement with
African-American Studies. Though its chairman, Charles Obi, was
cordial to him, the others made it clear that they didn't want him.
He was regarded as an Uncle Ben. Being in the English department
was a cup of tea in comparison to the muje that he suffered in the
Department of African-American Studies. To say that they weren't
comfortable with him would be an understatement. They made it
clear to him that they wanted a "club member," which was the
code phrase for those of similar ideology, and the ideology kept
shifting.

Though there were a few guys still wearing those nationalist pillbox
hats, and "Black is Back," or "Black is the Future" sweaters, dread-
locks, the defining ideology of the eighties was feminism. Puttbutt

was still a feminist. Memorized every mediocre line by Zora Neale Hurston. Could recite Sylvia Plath from memory. Could toss around terms like phallocentricity. Struggled to make sense of Catharine A. MacKinnon. But now their power was waning—the few black women who had joined the white feminist cause had walked out and formed their own organizations, and the California white men, like Rhett Butler, were deserting the Scarlett O'Haras, were leaving white women for Asian women. Some of those in the Department of Humanity who were to vote on his tenure were feminists and so he still had to be friends with them in case he needed their vote. They'd been trying to attract April Jokujoku, a firebrand radical lesbian ecologist activist to the campus. They were going to pay her three times his salary. Her poetry collected causes the way some people collect stray cats. His informant, Effie Singleton, who worked in African-American Studies and who knew just about everything that was happening on campus, told him that some of those women wanted to replace Puttbutt with her. But he had asked Marsha Marx, chairperson of Women's Studies, about these rumors and she had assured him that they had no basis in fact.

chapter three

An African professor named Kwaku Ladzekpo said that, when teaching, he had picked up from some white students that they felt more intelligent than him.

"Here I am, standing in front of a college class talking about my own culture, and some students would contradict me and say that they knew more about Africa than I did. I was dealing with a lot of eighteen-year-olds who were the products of the TV society and who basically believed that America was the greatest country to ever

be on the face of the earth." Professor Ladzekpo was right. And like
Professor Ladzekpo, Chappie never knew when he'd be tested. Other
black professors, no matter how many credentials they had, or how
much rank, would constantly complain about the racism they encountered in white classrooms and the lack of respect in the classrooms that were largely black. Not Chappie, as he was called. While
he constantly criticized black students, their study habits, their lack
of discipline, he, in the manner of other black neocons, never
criticized whites, and indeed blamed blacks for his rude treatment
from whites. (Though Chappie was called a neoconservative, neither the Neolithic Conservatives nor the Paleolithic Conservatives
would accept him. A speech he had made before the neocon think
tank, the Woodwork Foundation, had fallen flat. A reporter re-
counted that after Chappie Puttbutt had retold the story of how he
was once part of the Black Power movement, but left after they
discarded his "white comrades in the struggle," nobody applauded.)
If only African Americans—a phrase he hated—would shape up,
then the white students would be prepared for a man of his depth,
Chappie thought.

While the white students called their other professors Professor
this, or Mr. that, they called him Chappie. It took them about a
month to recognize him as a member of the human species. Chappie was always writing op-eds about how whites were confusing
him with members of the "underclass," which is what the media
were calling blacks nowadays. If the underclass worked hard and
achieved what he had, the white students would know better, he
felt. Wouldn't confuse him with them. Because they would all
be like Chappie. So this too was the underclass's fault. For not
trying to belong. For being marooned. For still hanging on to
"blackness."

Chappie's black days were behind him. He no longer suffered from
the double consciousness that Du Bois spoke of. The black part of

him had been completely annihilated. His photo could appear on a box of Wheaties and nobody would know the difference.

chapter four

Bass Jr. and his friends were giving him problems. Up until recently their contempt for him had been confined to sitting in the rear of the room glaring, their arms folded. But now they had been making ugly remarks about him and disrupting his lectures. On the last day of the semester he walked into his class of twenty students and was met with an unusual silence. They were staring from him to the blackboard behind him. He turned around and saw the source of their interest: "Dinner with Puttbutt. Bring your own watermelon." The Bass boy and his friend burst out laughing. The Bass boy was dressed in black leather. He wore a swastika armband, and his companion was wearing a sweater with the letters DEUTSCHLAND ÜBER ALLES and a ugly, aggressive Prussian eagle sewn on. Both had shaved heads. With the unification of Germany, the nazi nuts in the US had grown bolder. You couldn't get a street named for Martin Luther King, Jr., but there was no trouble in getting one named for Charles Lindbergh, a letter to the editor had complained. The national media were giving glowing tributes to Termite Control, neonazi and American representative of the Paleolithic South African Right, the Boer Order. Commentators on the payroll of the Woodwork Foundation were saying that Termite had begun an "honest" discussion of race. The posters for Termite Control's Traditional Values campaign showed the faces of big-nosed Jews with five o'clock shadow, and big red-lipped blacks, attached to the bodies of termites. He had placed second in a congressional primary in Southern California. Out of the corner of his eye, Puttbutt caught a smirk on the face of the blonde sitting to his right. On the first day of the semester she had asked him about his background.

"What are your credentials?" she asked, affecting a superior smile. In the 1960s, when he was a TA with a huge Afro and addicted to blackness, he would have grabbed his genitals, shook them and said, "Right here, bitch, these are my credentials." In the old days when he was a black militant firebrand and chairperson of the black caucus at the Air Force Academy, he would have told her to kiss his deguchi. But instead, he meekly told her to look him up in *Who's Who in America.* They listed all of the anthologies he'd complied and his best-seller, *Blacks, America's Misfortune,* and a critical study of a 1920s poet, Nathan Brown, his Ph.D dissertation. Puttbutt, a military brat, a loner, survivor, an Oniyèméji who dwelled on the margins, was isolated in another way. He was a New Critic in a department that included Miltonians and French theorists. Since Brown had lived out his life in exile and had become a popular poet in Europe, a household name in Rome, London and Paris, Puttbutt received many invitations to lecture abroad and made 20 percent of his income from these lectures.

chapter five

Recently, the two leading troublemakers in the class had gone beyond the watermelon joke. The incident that had created "tension" on campus was the cartoon of him that appeared in the right-wing campus newspaper, *Koons and Kikes.* One of the reasons the administrators at Jack London College were reluctant to discipline some of the right-wing students was because the students received full backing from right-wing corporations and law firms. Their main local supporter was Robert Bass of Caesar Synthetics, considered to be one of the most powerful men in Oakland, and the spearhead behind the failed plan to bring the Los Angeles Raiders back to Oakland.

He was the leader of the old guard alumni. Bass had also insisted that Jack London College be built away from the Oakland flatlands because he didn't want it to become a focal point of radical activity as had Merritt College on Old Grove Street, now Martin Luther King, Jr. Boulevard. Merritt had been a breeding ground for the Black Panthers, a group organized in the 1960s to oppose police brutality. The ethnic breakdown of Jack London was 48 percent white, 30 percent Asian-American, 10 percent Hispanic, 8 percent black and 4 percent "other." Some of the members of the alumni and the newspaper they advertised in felt that 8 percent was 8 percent too much, and the local newspapers were always carrying op-eds about how blacks were admitted without having the scholarship required for success. This in a country where most of the students couldn't locate the planet they occupied in the Solar System and where 80 percent of the population believed in the existence of the devil. A Carnegie Foundation for the Advancement of Teaching report surveyed 5,450 professors, who concluded that their students were "greedy" and "unprepared." Seventy-five percent said that the students they taught were "seriously unprepared in basic skills," and 18 percent said "colleges spend too much time and money teaching students what they should have learned in high school." A majority also said "there is more violence and alcohol and drug abuse on campus." Fewer black students were entering school than before. They were even denied the opportunity to mess up as much as the white students.

chapter six

He was having breakfast in the Faculty Club. Some of his black colleagues had risen in unison when he entered the room and walked out. The Afrocentric contingent began to mutter in Yoruba, "Aja Fun Fun ni. Aja Fun Fun ni." *White Dog* was a movie in which Paul Winfield starred. The movie was based upon a book by Romain Gary. It was about a dog who was trained to bite blacks, but whine and lap out of the hands of the whites. They apparently were disturbed by his remarks to the press about the most recent black student casualties.

He didn't worry about them. They had little power and what little they had was frittered away through backbiting and vicious feuds among themselves. The American-born Africans were fighting each other over identity, whether to be called black or African American, and the Swahili contingent, led by Matata Musomi, were fighting to keep the Yoruba out of the curriculum. All Puttbutt cared about was whether the white faculty was impressed with his position on the Bass Jr. problem, the affirmative action problem and all the other problems that seemed to be worrying white men to death. Problems that the California Association of Scholars outlined in their criticism of affirmative action and quotas, and such "nonsense" as "reeducating the faculty at sensitivity seminars." Stuart Miller, a member of the association, spoke for many when he said, "I would rather spend a year in the paddies planting rice." As soon as Puttbutt read of the group's existence in the *San Francisco Examiner*, he wrote a letter to the editor offering them his support.

* * *

Even though Dr. Crabtree, leader of the traditionalists, never spoke to him, his colleagues would often congratulate him on his position that blacks were their own worst enemies. They were always coming up congratulating him on his lonely stand. I just want to congratulate you on your lonely stand, they would say. How he was risking ostracism from blacks by saying things that were hard to say. Saying painful things. For saying the truth. For being courageous.

He spotted a TV crew, sound man, cameraman and a popular Japanese-American reporter heading toward his table. Even the faculty members who allowed nothing to distract them looked over in his direction where he dined on fettuccine and salad. Puttbutt's picture was in the local newspapers almost daily, and there were editorials congratulating him on his stand. Saying how brave it was of him to risk the label "turncoat" in order to say some painful things about race relations in the United States. For him to say things that were previously unspoken. That's what the interviewer wanted to know. Why wasn't he very angry with the Bass boy, a member of the Amerikaner Student Society, who had been such a bane to him? Calling his home at odd hours during the night; sending terrible things to him in the mail. And what about the cartoon in the student newspaper?

"Young Mr. Bass is feeling his oats," he told the reporter who was handing him what Lafcadio Hearn described as a "Japanese smile," one that concealed the face's true intentions. He was giving him his Tatemae side. "He'll get over it. Though many would say that our nation's campuses are potent with strife, I disagree. We blacks must buckle down so that the whites will respect us. Unless we do so, we will become like some of our less fortunate brothers and sisters; part of a permanent underclass. If there is anger directed at black students, then it's because they have caused this anger with their excessive demands." His colleagues in Humanity thought that he was so reasonable. So responsible. Though they never invited him to social occasions at their homes. He hoped that those who were about to award him lifetime security were listening. Would read these quotes. Would respect him. Would award him tenure. But why would he be concerned? Everybody knew that he was a shoo-in. That he was a team player. That whenever he was on campus there would be domestic peace.

But his students laughed at and mocked him. The know-it-all valley girl from Long Beach, Cherry Blue, the Nikkei-jin smart aleck, Muzukashii. Muzukashii always dressed like a Swiss mountain climber. Shorts, backpack, nerdy thick glasses, shirt buttoned to the top. He always joined Bass Jr. in trying to trip him up. They were always questioning his knowledge, always taking up the class's time with frivolous questions and arguments. Muzukashii was on the heavy side and made it a habit of looking to Bass Jr. and the other boy for a reward when he made an especially nasty crack to Puttbutt. Always talking, whispering and giggling when he tried to talk. Always staring at him with contempt. Always arriving to class late and noisily. Always intimidating the rest of the class with rude remarks and sarcasm and even physical threats.

Puttbutt's gum problems intensified during the semester when he taught. He experienced heart palpitations and insomnia. He got indigestion a lot and had to keep a box of baking soda on hand. But it could be worse, he always reminded himself. While Nathan Brown had died penniless, freezing to death on his way to pawn his overcoat in Chicago, Puttbutt was almost affluent, and with some of the dividends from the stock investments that his father had made on the advice of the defense contractors with whom he did business, Puttbutt lived a very comfortable life. A mark of his success was that he lived at the bottom of the Oakland Hills. On Ocean View near Broadway. But one day he would be up there. One day he would join Oakland's affluent political, intellectual and artistic aristocracy. Up there. But even now he had achieved a modicum of success. All of his neighbors were white.

Mercifully, it was the last day before spring break. During the months of May, June and July he'd do his annual tour of Europe. They loved him in Europe. He had canceled all but one appointment for that afternoon so that he could spend it packing for his European tour, but before going home, he had to see Dr. Obi, chairperson of the African-American Studies department. Dr. Obi still hadn't said whether he would be teaching there in the fall. His last semester with African-American Studies, he hoped.

The Bass boy walked by him, almost knocking him down.

"Mr. Bass, may I talk to you for a moment?" Bass told the other boy to go ahead. The boy, his fellow troublemaker, looked Puttbutt up and down with a sneer. The Bass boy was tall, thin and blond when he permitted his hair to grow. He had the blue eyes of the villain in 1940s novels by black writers. The sharp jaw and the sinister nose of the white villains drawn by *Muhammad Speaks* cartoonist 3X.

chapter seven

W hat is it, Professor?" The word "Professor" said sarcastically.

"I just wanted you to know that I have no hard feelings about that cartoon you drew of me in the student newspaper. The reason that you drew that cartoon is because you are rightly upset about the demands of black students. Their excessive demands and demonstrations. Their need to challenge instead of negotiate. Their victimization. Their need to feel that racism, not doubt, is the main obstacle to their success. Their demand for ethnic courses which are merely vehicles for spewing invective against white people." Bass Jr. and his companion smirked at each other.

"I wasn't interested in whether you liked it or not." Bass Jr. then got all up into Puttbutt's face. He and his companion balled their fists. Twenty years or so before, when Puttbutt was organizing the black students' caucus at the Air Force Academy, he would have decked the white boy, but these were the nineties. Diplomacy was in. Confrontation was out. Negotiation was in.

"Just wanted you to know that if Dean Hurt suspends you I'll do everything within my power to see to it that you're reinstated." Bass Jr. and his friend had a big laugh over that statement.

"I'm not too worried about it. My father owns this school. They don't have the guts to suspend me. So whatever a Hurt or nigger thinks doesn't worry me." Fighting words. But Puttbutt ignored them. He was right. His father, R. Bass, Sr., did own the school. He was its biggest supporter.

"By the way, you could have at least told me that you were going to be away from school for a couple of weeks." Puttbutt was so cool. So dignified. Besides, how would he look wrestling on the ground with a student. That's what they wanted. That's what they expected of him. His mother always said. She always insisted that he fight in a subtle, organized manner. The way she fought. With cunning. With maps and strategies. His mother was an authority on Clausewitz and Giap.

"I had something important to do. You know that I'm the head of my organization's South African refugee committee. I was in Jo'burg. Doing some business. Is there anything else?" Their plan was to exchange the "hardworking" Afrikaners for welfare people in the US, according to the local version of *Koons and Kikes*. Puttbutt had written an op-ed for a local newspaper arguing against the university divesting its money from South Africa.

"No. There's nothing." He started out, but then paused.

"By the way, Professor."

"Yes, Mr. Bass?"

"You know, the only reason I took this course was because of that requirement that your jungle bunny friends got through."

"There's no need for any derogation of a group of people, Mr. Bass." The N word would have ruffled some of these blacks who went around with a chip on their shoulder. Didn't bother Puttbutt. He didn't feel one way or the other about it. He agreed with S. I. Hayakawa, that it was only a word and as soon as you knew that words were merely just that, they didn't bother you. He had it wrong when he said that Puttbutt had gotten the requirements through, though. In fact, Chappie had opposed it.

"If we'd had it our way the thing would have never passed."

"I'm well aware of that, Mr. Bass." Bass swaggered out of the lecture hall, grinning and looking back, sneering at Puttbutt. Outside, he could hear Bass Jr. and his companion laughing and talking in stage plantation dialect. He felt as though he were suffocating. His chest felt stuffed. He felt lightheaded. He had to hold on to a desk to avoid passing out.

Outside, the students were congregating around the huge fountain that stood in the middle of the campus. Others were entering buildings where their classes were located. The campus was built in the sixties, and so everything looked fresh and new. He saw one of his colleagues from the English department walking toward him.

"How are you, Professor Crabtree?" he asked. As usual, his colleague looked right through him without saying a word. Crabtree was probably the unidentified "white male" professor whom the newspapers quoted as having said that blacks and Hispanics were lowering the standards of Jack London College. Puttbutt agreed. In an op-ed printed in one of several local right-wing papers, Puttbutt had congratulated him for having the courage to broach a subject that the liberals on campus were afraid to discuss. That he had succeeded in breaking the silence, broaching a taboo subject. Saying things that had been left unspoken. He thought that this would convince Professor Crabtree that he, Puttbutt, was responsible. That this would cause Professor Crabtree to become favorably inclined toward him. Professor Crabtree hadn't even bothered to reply to his letter.

chapter eight

Puttbutt was checking his mail in the Humanity department. There was a report from a sexual harassment meeting during which the subject of whether male professors should keep their office doors open or shut when interviewing female students had been discussed. Some mail inviting him to a conference about literature and gender. Somebody had their arm around him. It was Jack Milch, chairman of the Humanity department.

"Puttbutt, babe. Come on into the office. Got something to show you."

"Sure, Dr. Milch." He wouldn't have to wait for them to tell him. Milch was going to tell him now that his tenure was just about certain. That he wouldn't have to go through the torture of year-to-year appointments anymore. Inside his office, Puttbutt noticed that the entire walls were covered with photos of Anita Hill. Every inch. Covers of magazines with Anita Hill's picture. Newspaper clippings.

Dr. Milch showed him a photo of Anita Hill. Her hair was straight and buppie. Her eyes fixed in a permanent in-your-face glare. Her angrily painted lips jutted out like the front of a battleship. Yet there was beauty in her face. The photo had been autographed.

Dr. Milch was as wide as he was tall. About five feet seven inches. Sometimes you could see his belly button where the bottom of his shirt had become unbuttoned from the pressure of his weight. When he looked at you it seemed that he was facing you on an angle. Like someone looking into the wrong TV camera. He seemed to be looking over your shoulder. When the Thomas-Hill hearings were on, it was said that he had four television sets installed in his office. When Thomas defeated Hill in the national game show whose prize was the black man's genitals, it was rumored that Milch wanted to shut down the department for a day, only to be overruled by Bright Stool, who was on Thomas's side.

"You can't imagine how much I respect this young lady. Her courage in coming forward to expose this loathsome porno freak, Thomas." Dr. Milch was wearing a T-shirt with Anita Hill's picture on it. Milch was the department's expert on black feminist literature, but the Miltonians still had the real power. When the gender-whipped Milch, acting on behalf of the department feminists, attempted to curtail the power of the Miltonians (they claimed that Milton was a possible batterer because his wife Mary Powell, whom he'd married in June of 1642, went to visit her family after a few weeks and didn't return until 1645 [in those days when they said I'm going home to mother, they were serious]), Milch found out how much power the older Miltonians wielded. His moves were blocked and he almost lost his chairpersonship.

"She did show courage," Puttbutt said, relieved that the chairman had revealed his position so that he wouldn't have to guess before agreeing. Puttbutt supported Thomas. Some of the Northeast liberal blacks were vitriolic in their denouncement of the man. Some were sincere, Puttbutt knew, but others were embarrassed by his physiognomy, which they considered to be too "African." The same charge these types leveled against Garvey. It was also a class thing. When Thomas was at Yale, a sharecropper's son, his critics were driving sports cars and waving their parents' cash around. For them Thomas had the wrong "background." Later investigative reports from the *New Republic, Reason, Commentary,* and the *American Spectator* had revealed that Hill was a Manchurian candidate for the white feminists who had tailored her testimony. The portrait of Anita Hill in these reports came across as spaceshippy.

Puttbutt had heard Ishmael Reed say on the radio that since they were receiving most of their hits from feminists who had been at one time aligned with the traditional left, maybe black guys ought to join the Eagle Forum. These feminists were now aligning themselves with the right on the issue of pornography, and expressed a similar enmity toward black men. In fact, one could argue that not only did the Willie Horton campaign set the atmosphere in which a black man like Rodney King could be beaten but also the decade-long drubbing of black men by a feminist elite that had access to television, film and publishing. Ishmael Reed said somewhere that he agreed with Norman Mailer's assessment of Ms. magazine, the headquarters for black male antipathy, as a "totalitarian sheet." He had been attacked by one of their black house feminists in the January 1991 issue. She said that Ishmael Reed was "the ringleader" of black men who were opposed to black women writing about black male misogyny and that he was calling such black women traitors to the race. Ringleader Ishmael Reed has never called anybody a traitor to anybody's race and not only hasn't opposed black women writing about black male misogyny but published some of it. Robin Morgan, the editor, refused to accede to his request that his side of the story be aired. Since many prominent black women were accusing the feminist movement of racism, as black women had since the days of Sojourner Truth, who was booed and hissed by feminists at the Fourth National Women's Rights Convention in New York City in 1853, it was understandable that some would accuse this movement of singling out black men for their harshest criticisms. As in the case of Ishmael Reed versus Ms. there seemed to always be a powerful white feminist in the background, egging on those whom bell hooks referred to as black divas.

There was a report that Ms. Hill hadn't added the explicit sexual matters that Thomas was supposed to have discussed with her until after she had gone public with her charges of sexual harassment against Thomas. When Ishmael Reed read in the *New Republic* that Catharine A. MacKinnon met with Anita Hill before Ms. Hill testified, he figured that he knew what happened. He had followed Ms. MacKinnon's career since she was crowned intellectual leader of northeastern feminism at a conference called "The Sexual Liberals and the Attack on Feminism," held in New York, April 4, 1987. The conference was so anti-male that a woman who said that she liked men was booed. Black women walked out in protest against their being excluded from panels. (Whether Anita Hill–supporter Catharine A. MacKinnon joined them is not known.) During her speech Ms. MacKinnon spoke fondly of a position taken by a publication called *Rat*, with which Robin Morgan had been associated, that male ejaculation was an act of war. (The worst name that Robin Morgan could think of to call a feminist with whom she had a disagreement was "heterosexual.") Ms. MacKinnon's associate Andrea Dworkin believes that sexual intercourse is the ultimate act of oppression by men against women. Ms. MacKinnon was co-author with Andrea Dworkin of legislation that would censor pornography. It was being said that Ms. MacKinnon influenced Canada's criminal sanctions against pornography, pornography being anything material that subordinates and degrades women, that is, anything that MacKinnon and her followers deem pornographic. She is also a supporter of the McConnell Bill which says that "those who produce, distribute, exhibit or sell obscene material may be liable for damages if victims of sex abuse believe that this material helped instigate the crime."

It was Ishmael Reed's guess that Ms. MacKinnon used Ms. Hill to turn the Thomas hearings into a referendum on pornography. Ms. MacKinnon believed that a black man was guilty until proven guilty and through her contacts with profeminist elements of the TV networks' cultural elite she was able to hop from network to network, during the hearings, denouncing Thomas as a liar.

Ishmael Reed never thought he'd agree with Linda Chavez, but

Ms. Chavez was right when she said that feminists like Ms. MacKinnon had used some of the vilest stereotypes against Clarence Thomas in order to derail the nomination of Thomas. Phyllis Schlafly was also right when she accused Ms. MacKinnon of using dirty tactics against Thomas. Like the Indiana Klan feminists of the 1920s, Ms. MacKinnon, a law professor mind you, denied Clarence Thomas due process. The people, according to polls at the time—the majority of men and women, black and white—repudiated Ms. MacKinnon and her followers. But the mostly white media and professional feminists had rigged the will of the people so that by the time they finished with the matter, it seemed that Thomas had lost and Anita Hill had won. Even the producers of "Designing Women" and "The Trials of Rosie O'Neill" got in some jabs at the Supreme Court justice. Ishmael Reed had suggested that next time a black man and a black woman had a public row, UN observers should be called in so that the public sentiment as recorded in opinion polls wouldn't be flouted by feminists. Milch had gone into a funk of depression after Thomas had prevailed. Millions had tuned in to watch Mosina call the law on Mose.

Puttbutt looked to Milch's desk. Books by black women were piled up, including one by an author who had hit the black male bashing jackpot by writing a book that mixed and sampled all of the gender conflicts found in the former black male bashing books. He noticed a picture book of black women that had been composed by a photographer named Brian Lanker. Lanker said that he had been inspired to do these photos by his nanny, and by reading Alice Walker. Milch had spoken at every occasion about how a black nanny had nurtured him while his mother, an upper-middle-class cocaine junkie, spent most of her time asleep. Jack London and David Duke also had colored mammies. The book by the photographer didn't bother him. There were some books of poetry that did. April's books. Milch's eye caught Puttbutt's.

"Oh, those. She's quite a powerful poet. But Puttbutt, you have nothing to worry about."

"Really, Dr. Milch."

"No problem, Puttbutt, babe."

"Gosh, thanks, Dr. Milch." Puttbutt left Milch fondling and gazing at the photo of Anita Hill. Puttbutt began to whistle and to think about that house in the Oakland Hills.

chapter nine

He entered the African-American Studies department. On his way in, his former friend, Effie, who could usually be found at the Xerox machine, called him over. She gave him a big Arkansas smile. Her clothes didn't show off her figure. How did he know? He'd run into her as he jogged around Lake Merritt one day. Mite dake. She wasn't wearing as much clothes as she wore at work. Her clothes were modest. Chappie never went into details when describing women. The feminist movement had accomplished one thing. Eliminated the need for long and unnecessary and embarrassing descriptions of female anatomy in novels by men. He took a note to remind himself to suggest this as a topic for a future panel at the MLA. She told him the mood of the department. They'd just received a budget cut and some people would have to be laid off. The word is that they're going to bring in April Jokujoku to take your job, she'd said. April Jokujoku was always jumping on people about their "homophobia." Their "sexism." Their "racism." She was a good writer, but the publicity image distracted from the verse.

"But Marsha Marx has assured me that this is not the case, Effie."

"Whom do you believe, Marsha Marx or me?" Effie said. "You know you can't trust these white women." Effie gave him something to think about. If April received an appointment in Women's Studies, how long would it take before they gave her a job in the Department of Humanity? Crowding him out. He knew that these white departments, like many American institutions, could only tolerate one black faculty at a time, and that being the case, he was going to be that person.

He walked to Dr. Obi's outer office. The other secretaries stopped buzzing, which he took to mean that the prospects of his being rehired were not good. Crossina, Dr. Obi's "administrative assistant," finally acknowledged that he was in the room. Puttbutt told her that he had an appointment with Dr. Obi, whereupon she had a caffeine-induced panic attack and went ballistic.

"Dr. Obi does not exist in this department to serve you! He is a very busy man! I don't care if you do have an appointment!" She looked like the heroine of the nineteenth-century "passing" novels. Chesnut's *House Behind the Cedars,* or George Cable's *Grandissimes.* She definitely needed a protein injection, or a good stiff zucchini. The kind of black woman who took to sun lamps in order not to look "too white." Whenever somebody would complain about her rudeness, Dr. Obi would defend her. Rumors were that the darker Dr. Obi had a thing going with this yellow female. Somebody had nicknamed her Crossina Giddy.

Most of the people in the department were Francophobes and Anglophobes from the Islands, or from Africa. The chair, Charles Obi, spent most of his time begging President Stool not to decrease the department's budget and fending off the right wing who felt that the department should be closed down. Matata Musomi was the head of the Swahili contingent that had been imposed upon the department by those who ran the college. They were devoted to the British style. Matata treated the African Americans disdainfully. Just as Mexicans felt that they were superior to Chicanos, the Nihon-jin superior to the Nikkei-jin, some Africans felt themselves to be superior to African Americans, their "brothers" who were rounded up by women warriors and sold into slavery about the time of the Yoruba Empire's breakup. Sànyà, the owner of the African bookstore located near campus, had said that Swahili was a slave trader's language with a Arab vocabulary and a Bantu syntax. According to him, forces in the government had introduced Swahili into the American school curriculum so as to keep African Americans from the language of their ancestors: Yoruba. While the Swahili group treated him as though he were igbe, his African-American colleagues thought of him as a quisling, as a member of the black cultural and intellectual Vichy regime. But Puttbutt never complained about the digs and the harassment he received from the African-American Studies department. He was up for tenure and so any little infraction or a few bad student evaluations of his course could get him into the same kind of income level as the black writers he wrote his lectures about. Reading their works in coffeehouses or occupying dingy bohemian basements. Their works confined to little magazines that nobody read. Drinking themselves to death. Obscure and unloved. While he sat, waiting for his interview with Obi, he looked around the outer office. Next to Obi's picture was the obligatory photo of Malcolm X, mouth open, finger pointing, frowning. He'd become a sort of pop icon for the black diaper babies. A fashion accessory. The New York Times, which a few days after his death had carried a mean-spirited editorial regarding his "violent" life, published an enthusiastic review of the opera based upon his life. For the diaper babies he had been toned down and was now acceptable to publications that hated him during his life. He glanced at the magazines on the table. Most of them included articles about the black family. The establishment was insisting that blacks get married, while their own sons and daughters were experimenting with every possible sexual arrangement. He wondered about the sexual activities of daughters of the men who owned the conservative newspapers that lectured blacks about their behavior. He wondered about how they lived. He had read in Spy magazine that a Gothic bow-tie-wearing communist, who wrote as though black people had driven him out of his mind, and who was always lecturing blacks about their family instability, had had his clothes thrown out on the street after his wife discovered an affair he was carrying on with the daughter of the country's most powerful media jingo. A fundamentalist white preacher whose organization had received funds to hold a White House conference on the black family had conceived a child out of wedlock. And two of the main critics of blacks' personal behavior, a *New York Times* columnist and a New York senator, were among the biggest drunks in creation. A beauty queen told the press that a senator who was about to run for the presidency on an immorality-in-the-inner-city platform got more than a massage when he visited her in a New York hotel, and a former president, whose whole program had been welfare queens and big bucks, had been accused of date rape in an unauthorized biography about his wife. Old Nat Hawthorne said there'd be days like this.

Obi emerged from his office. He still walked with a street bob. His blackness had the iridescent beauty of a San Antonio grackle; his fifteen-hundred-dollar conservative pin-striped suits fitted him perfectly. His teeth were a brazen white and they looked as though he'd never had a cavity. His skin was clear and bore a sheen. He used some sort of expensive cologne. The kind of guy who used imported condoms: Kimonos. He talked as though his throat were growing cotton. He gave him a silky handshake.

"Hey, my brother," he said. "What are you doing here?"

"We had an appointment. You said that you wanted to talk to me."

"Hey. That's right. Come in." He followed him into his office. There was a wineglass on his desk with a lipstick smudge at its tip. You had to go to a place like Emporium Capwell's to purchase the kind of perfume that dominated the odors in the room. There was a portrait of W. E. B. Du Bois on the wall. Whenever Obi got drunk, he'd remind everybody that he had a Ph.D. from Harvard, but what he'd done with it few could tell, except that he was an academic fireman. Maybe that's why they gave him one. Going around the country to dampen the enthusiasm for Black Studies, while chairing a Black Studies department.

"Man, that was a beautiful way you handled those white boys. Beautiful. I had lunch with the President Stool today and he couldn't stop praising your name. Somebody with less class would have made a big deal out of it." The president, huh? Puttbutt had seen the president reeling across campus once. He lived in a huge house at the edge of the campus that resembled one of those from Jane Austin's novels.

"Revenge is counterproductive."

"Well said," Charles said. A mocking smile, because he knew the real reason why he hadn't taken the Bass boy to task was that he wanted tenure. Puttbutt had earned his tenure, not like these affirmative action types, playing on white guilt. He did it the old-fashioned way, he earned it. He was tired of anger, of petitioning, of forcing himself on white people. He was tired of revenge. He had grown up in a house of revenge. His father had always wanted to retaliate immediately against any harm brought to his country, his religion and to his family. In that order. His mother, too. Their world was divided between friends and foes. They had an enemies list that must have been a mile long. Chappie theorized that it was because they grew up in Mississippi, where people laid traps and bait for other people. It was in Mississippi that, while attending one of those black agricultural schools, they joined the ROTC. Obi smiled. It was one of two smiles that he owned. The other one was filthy. Used when currying favor from higher-ups. Used to lure women into sexually compromising positions, or so they said. A woman from the Women's Studies department had accused him of addressing her as "dear."

"Man, you one serious motherfucker," he said. "You never come to the black faculty cocktail parties, and the liberals in the Humanity department say that you don't mix with them. How do you expect to get ahead if you're not collegial? Stroking people. Writing thank-you letters. Sending people Xmas cards. Doing lunch. Visiting sick colleagues. Working out in the gym. Picking up the bill at the Faculty Club." Obi had his hands behind his head. He was leaning back in his chair. He was one of these aristocrats Stanley Crouch

was always writing about. Always trying to be street. But his dress
and style—busy—gave him away. Talked a lot of corny ghetto talk
when he communicated with the brothers, but his stuff published
in scholarly journals was unreadable.

"What did you want?"

"About the Bass boy. You had the right attitude, I mean in the
old days we would have busted the pisspot in the mouth. No matter
what his connections were. But we have to keep our cool. This ain't
the sixties. The times call for a more discreet strategy. I mean, if it
weren't for my efforts they would have closed down this department
a long time ago. But this corny beatnik dean is talking about suspending this kid. Maybe if you would talk to him."

"For what?"

"Don't get excited, now. Old man Stool and I thought, well you
were the one that the little fart Bass Jr. mailed the dead rat to.
You're not offended. Why should he be? Anyway, some of the
people in the department are a little upset about this arrangement.
You know the people don't like you. Your controversial stand on
affirmative action and your disparaging remarks about almost anything black. I'm always defending you." They were always making
it clear that they didn't want him and the only reason he was there
was to satisfy the Shiroi-jin. When he taught there last, they didn't
even provide him with an office. Told him that he could use a chair
in an office that was shared by two professors. Then to add to the
insult, they apologized to the professors for whatever inconvenience
his presence caused.

"They want to bring April out here. They said that if they took
you out of the budget they could afford her demands." She wanted
computer equipment, two secretaries, a bodyguard and a house in
the mountains, though her whole pitch was about the oppression of
underclass females in the ghettos. While the underclass women
were getting their subsistence budgets cut by white male politicians,
journalists, and think-tank black pathology gangsters, she, being a
talented tenth aristocrat, blamed the problems of her and her "diva"

buddies on white women and black men. She was one of the most
successful cause pimps in the business. Ecology. Animal rights. You
name it, and if there were speaking fees to it or other cash to be
made, there she was whining about the fate of the poor white mink.
She'd hypnotized these white women. Had them eating out of her
hand. Had a column in some "progressive" magazine that was full
of shifty-eyed and sleight-of-hand rhetoric.

"I've been opposed to their move from the start. I'm always
speaking up for you at the faculty meetings. I even got you the
budget you wanted for visiting lecturers. If you get Dean Hurt not
to suspend Bass Jr. I'm sure the whole thing about April will go up
in smoke."

"I'll talk to him," Puttbutt said. Obi's velvety, filthy grin, this
time.

"I knew that you were reasonable. Talk to this lame motherfucker. Tell him that this man Bass is putting ideas in the alumni's
minds. If he plays his cards right, he might end up being vice
president. Whitherspoon is getting old. Told me the other day that
all he wanted to do was to go trout fishing. A basketful of worms
and a bottle of sherry is all that he wants out of life. Early morning
delivery of the *Times*. Maybe teaching Shakespeare during the summer." Obi stood up and walked around the table. He put an arm
around his shoulders as he escorted Puttbutt out of his office. "You're
playing everything right. I'm talking to the head of the English
section of the Humanity department about that permanent appointment." When he said "English," he almost burst out laughing.
Probably thinks I'm queer, Puttbutt thought. "All you have to do
is get settled around here. And . . ." he paused as they stood in the
doorway. "The sisters said they appreciate your doing more women,
but that they wanted one of their own kind to teach. They also said
that when they said you should teach more women, that they didn't
have ancient Japanese women in mind." He taught from an English
translation of the Hyaku-jin: Lady Kii, Kinsuke Oye, Lady Sei, Lady
Ise, Koshikibu, Murasaki Shikibu, Izumi Shikibu.

• • •

As on some other campuses, the Black Studies department had become a satellite of the Women's Studies department. In the late seventies and eighties the sisters and their patron persons had bowled over everybody with their double-oppression pitch (April's was triple: woman, lesbian and black), but now the white man couldn't spend time worrying about whether he was going to favor them over Mose or whether he was going to sprinkle a little joy on some other group, and I do mean sprinkle. And some of the white women, who had discovered that they'd been chumped by some of the more blatant hustlers, those who grinned at them at book-signing parties, but talked about them like a dog behind their backs, were having second thoughts.

No wonder suicide was the second leading cause of death among white men, according to the *New England Journal of Medicine*, Puttbutt thought. Everybody was trying to put them on a guilt trip instead of paying their own way, Benjamin "Chappie" Puttbutt thought. Everybody was dissing them. "Dissing" being another word that had trickled up from the streets that middle-class black intellectuals were using to death. Dissing this and dissing that.

"Dr. Charles, could you tell me whether I'm going to be hired next semester. I'd like to know. I have plans. I submitted a syllabus as I was instructed, but I still haven't received a contract. My course isn't even listed in the catalog. I'm leaving for Europe in a couple of days and would like to know before I leave. The spring semester will be my last in this department. Surely, there shouldn't be any problem with your signing the contract."

"I'll call you tonight about the reappointment. Going to Europe, huh. Who arranged that for you?"

"I'm always getting invitations to go to Europe and to Asia and South America."

"Can't be any cash in it." Dr. Obi's eyes stood up on cash.

"That's what's wrong with the United States. Everybody has

their eyes on the profit margin." The words shot out before he had a chance to check himself.

"Well, what's wrong with that?" Dr. Obi had been president of the Maoist Student League in the sixties. Now, all he talked about was his Volvo and his summer house on the Russian River. The only thing that connected him with that former time was the last name he'd adopted, after dropping his slave name. The Nigerian critic Chinweizu had quipped that American blacks had dropped their slave names for the names of slave traders. The original Muhammad Ali was a slave owner, for example.

"Nothing. Listen, I'll hear from you tonight." Dr. Obi didn't call. It was the last day of the spring 1991 semester. On May 15, 1991, Puttbutt left for his European tour.

chapter ten

The tour that had begun in Italy in May was coming to an end. Puttbutt had to do Paris and London and then he'd be heading for home. It was raining as he left Orly Airport. It took a little negotiating but he and his fellow critics won. They had refused to leave the airport unless their hosts supplied them with separate limousines. His limousine was waiting for him. As his limousine began to head for Paris, he heard someone calling him. He looked to his right and saw a contingent of African-American writers. They were standing out in the rain, waiting for a bus that would take them to their Left Bank hotel. They were lucky if they got a room with a bath. The critics, on the other hand, were to be housed at one of the fanciest hotels in Paris, located on the Right Bank near the Champs-Élysées. He'd stayed at the hotel before. The lobby resembled one of those ornate rooms at the Palace of Versailles. The staff consisted of wigged waiters and doormen. The hotel personnel were required to dress in the period of the Sun King. He was to be the featured speaker at the Nathan Brown Centennial celebration; the writers had been brought along for entertainment. The chauffeur held the door open for him. He climbed in. He instructed the chauffeur to drive past the writers. They were shouting at him. They apparently wanted him to give them a lift. He asked the chauffeur to speed up. Some of the writers had recognized him, but he didn't wave. He pretended to be absorbed in *Le Figaro*, which had his photo on the cover. He looked back at the writers. They were boarding a bus. It was raining and they were getting soaking wet. Dr. Barbara Christian spoke of the Paradise Lost/Paradise Regained worlds of writers and critics. The "high world of lit crit books, journals and conferences, the middle world of classrooms and graduate students, and the low world of bookstores, communities, and creative writers."

chapter eleven

He'd addressed an overflow crowd the night before at Kent. Defended Nathan Brown against charges that were coming from across the Atlantic that Nathan Brown was a misogynist whose poetry was actually written by his wife. Received a splendid write-up in the *Independent* the next day. Now he was on the way to Heathrow in a cab driven by an Arab. Puttbutt didn't care all that much about Arabs. Especially after they'd kidnapped his mother. He hadn't heard from her in three years, after some group calling itself the Liberation of something or other had seized her. She didn't deserve being held hostage in some dingy hole in the Middle East.

The traffic heading to the airport was bumper-to-bumper. O shit-surei. He was going to miss his plane. When he got there, British

Airways was taxiing out to the runway, but when the airline superin-
tendent learned that it was he, Chappie Puttbutt, the black American scholar, hailed by right-wing columnist James Way as the second
Douglass, waiting at the gate, the plane was brought back so that
he could board. Boy did these Europeans love literature. It was hard
to believe that they and the white Americans were of the same
tribe.

Many hours later the plane was flying over that ugly stepsister of
California mountains. Mount Diablo, home of the Falcon Man and
the Eagle, "who created Indians everywhere."

chapter twelve

There was no limousine waiting for him at San Francisco Airport,
and instead of people fetching his luggage he had to fend for himself.
While he rode first-class on British Airways, when he got to New
York he had to transfer to an American airline. For some reason,
his travel agent had given him an aisle seat, so when he arrived in
San Francisco he had been beaten black and blue. He got knocked
about until he recognized his luggage and removed it from the
baggage-claim area. It took him a couple of hours to get into Oakland. Traffic had been tied up and bottlenecked bumper-to-bumper
ever since the 7.2.

Troy was slouched on the couch. Jo Hara, her friend, was asleep.
Troy kept looking at the tube, ignoring his entrance. He put down
his luggage. On the TV, Glenn Close was acting in some kind of
costume drama. Troy was a child of Berkeley. Lightskinned, freckle
faced and cornrowed. She was dressed in hip hop sneakers, pants
and jacket.

"There's a list of your phone messages on the table," she finally said without looking up. Her friend awoke, looked at him and scowled. He removed his coat and flopped down on the couch.

"Boy, am I exhausted. Fourteen-hour flight." They didn't say anything. "But did I have a ball. Switzerland, Germany, England. They treated me like a king." They glanced at each other as though they were about to burst out laughing. Jo Hara took the remote and began to rewind the film. Troy went to the closet and got their coats. Troy was slim and attractive. Her friend Jo Hara, well, she was of the sort whose depression was attributable to a poor body image as the newspapers would say. Her grandparents had robust genes, or as the Yoruba would say, "Òrìṣà bí ọ̀fun kò sí; ojoojúmọ́ ní í gb' ẹbọ lọ́wọ́ ẹni." "Her favorite deity is her throat. She sacrifices to it daily."

"Well, thanks for everything. I'll see you next week when you come to look after the yard."

"What do you mean, thanks?" Troy said in a dry voice, sticking out her hand. "You owe me three hundred dollars."

"What for?"

"For watching the house, that's what for," she said mimicking him. She was sarcastic and she eyed Jo Hara for her approval as she said the words.

"But you asked me to let you stay here. You said you needed a break from the dorms. Get away from all those silly white girls. Those were your exact words."

"Get your money from him, Troy. I told you he was a fema-phobe."

"What's that got to do with it?"

"You'd pay a man," they said in unison. He could tell by Jo Hara's look that she'd put Troy up to it. She was a bad influence on Troy. A real bad influence.

"Sure will be glad when April comes out here. Fire your sorry ass," Jo Hara said.

"That man next door came over here and pruned your trees. He said that they were blocking his driveway," Troy said. "I told you that I would prune them, but you were so cheap you wouldn't give me the job."

He thought of the lecture, "Tropes in the Poetry of Nathan Brown" and the intense attention that they gave him at the Italian University, built in the twelfth century, and now he was home and he had to deal with these spoiled women and with his neighbor who was becoming a nuisance. They left, and soon he heard their '79 Jeep rev up and jerk away. He was home. Back to work. Back to the controversy.

chapter thirteen

Dear Mr. Termite Control:

Enclosed you will find a check for a thousand dollars, a small contribution to your crusade to take things back to the way they used to be. I agree with you that this is a Western Christian civilization and those who don't like it can hit the road, Jack. We were all heartened that you came in second for Congress, which shows that a lot of our people in Southern California are sick of blacks, homos, and immigrants. Not to mention these black bucks who spend all of their time making babies and depending upon the taxpayers to provide them with milk. I was intrigued by your praise for Rudolf Hess, and plan to read up on this fine American's life.

There are a lot of people on Jack London College campus who agree with you, but are too pansy to come out with it. I was very happy that 56 percent of the white people in New Jersey voted in a poll that you were their candidate for president. Maybe during the upcoming Easter break I will be able to travel to your Massachusetts presidential headquarters and help out with your campaign. Of course, I will have to use an anonymous name, because if the people find out that a college president is . . .

President Stool's secretary advised him that Whitherspoon was there to see him. He hurriedly put the letter he was composing away. He picked up the newspaper lying on his desk. He pretended to be reading it. Shortly afterward, Vice President Whitherspoon was standing in front of his desk.

"I didn't know you were here. Did you see the papers this morning? Seems that some of the money that UC Berkeley received recently was traced to that Jap mob. The Yakuza. God, isn't it awful. I'm dreaming about Japs a lot since they just bought Rockefeller Center and Radio City Music Hall. Charlie Brown's. What's next? The fucking Liberty Bell? To think that my dad did the Long March at Bataan, and now the yellow monkeys are taking over the place. They came swarming on us in Korea, too. Human waves." The president spoke in the low trembling tones of an alligator in heat.

"Those were the Chinese, sir," Vice President Whitherspoon said. Being of the humanist tradition Vice President Whitherspoon was a splitter, not a lumper. He tried to hold his nose as he was accosted by the fumes of the president's garlic breath. There was a half-eaten submarine sandwich on his desk and a half-empty cup of java. A habit left over from his trading days when people on the floor ate anything that was shoved in their direction. The president was a refugee from the crash of '87 (Wild Friday), a CIO (Career Is Over) who had seen better days and had been recruited in hopes that he could sell the university as well as he could sell stocks. But there were complaints about his lavish dining habits, his unpaid bills, and his expense accounts.

"Next thing you know they'll be buying the Statue of Liberty. Mark my words, before it's over we're going to have to fight them again. This damned college is beginning to look like the University of Beijing, or someplace. It's going to look like that scum haven across town, Berserkley. They even hired a Chink to run the damned place. I guess they couldn't find a white man. It'll probably take them as long to hire another white man as it will take for another white Miss America to emerge. One has to look hard to find a white face on the campus at all." He was dressed like a 1920s Rumanian pickpocket. His fingernails were dirty and he had a habit of spitting on the floor. All of the lies of his life had materialized on his face. He was over fifty years old and still had acne. "And now you got that beatnik dean of yours, this Hurt cunt talking about suspending Bass's kid." Another reason that the board of directors at Jack London had hired President Stool was because he vowed to put an end to capricious demands for a global university. The board believed that Jack London should be dedicated to the values of the West. Jack London's values. Whitherspoon started to explain.

"Yes, but . . ."

"Yes, but my ass. Do you know what you're dealing with. Bass keeps those old farts pouring cash into this school and this dean is talking about putting his kid out of school, all because of some . . . some black. These blacks had their chance. There's nothing that white people are obligated to do for them anymore. Why, Puttbutt said as much in the *New York Exegesis*. You saw that piece he did on the dangers of affirmative action." A shady stock deal had jeopardized Stool's career and he had been investigated by the Securities and Exchange Commission, but because of his contributions to the administration in power at the time, the probe was called off. "He's right about them. They have to prove themselves in order to gain the respect of white people. A disloyal bunch. When the Japs invade California, these blacks will defect to their side."

"Invade California?" The silver-haired, portly Vice President Whitherspoon tried to restrain a look of incredulity.

"It's always a possibility. They're rearming. Even though it violates their constitution. They just bought a sharp new fighter plane.

And they're making the best rocket engines. Hell, if they sold semiconductor chips to our enemies instead of to the US, the balance of power would be tipped. Capable of boosting sophisticated satellites. There's even talk of nuclear weapons. Germany is reunited. We're going to have to fight them all over again. Hopefully, you agree." The look that Stool gave Whitherspoon was insisting upon agreement.

"You have a good point, President Stool." The vice president was chafed at the president's speech. He didn't like the president, a contempt shared by his colleagues in the Humanity department, and the president thought that people in the Humanity were a bunch of soft hands. He saw the world in terms of losers and gainers. Humanity people were losers. Hopefully. The vice president hated people who said "hopefully" for "with hope." He could hardly conceal his rage. He agreed with John Simon that there should be a law. That people who used the adverb "hopefully" should be arrested.

"Now you talk to that Hurt. I got his file." The president stared down at the manila envelope on his desk and began to rifle its contents. He took a bite from his submarine sandwich, leaving a smear of mayonnaise on his mustache. Whitherspoon couldn't stand it. "Son of a bitch likes to align himself with people who put his nose in a lot of shit. When the blacks kicked the whites out of the Black Power movement he was the last to leave. Now he's some kind of feminist, even though they've told all of the men to get lost. Talk to this guy." Whitherspoon pointed to the spot of mayonnaise on the president's mustache. Stool wiped it with the sleeve of his suit jacket. Whitherspoon thought that he was going to be sick. And to think, the governor was thinking about bringing him into the Elysian Club, which was like putting a diamond bracelet on a rat.

"What is he taking the side of this black professor over Bass's kid for anyway. I saw the professor's statement. He's not mad. So why is Hurt mad?"

"He's a very idealistic young man."

"I don't know anybody of his generation who can't be bought. Look, you tell him to drop this suspension idea. We've asked Putt-butt to do the same. Now there's a guy who should get tenure. Fine young black. His mother and father are doing this country proud. Hardworking. Disciplined. What's taking your department so long? That's the best affirmative action baby on campus. Didn't have a damned thing in print when we hired him. Now this masterpiece. *Blacks, America's Misfortune.* A brave work."

"There's some resistance to the idea of awarding him tenure, President. Dr. Crabtree and some of the traditionalists are unhappy with an article he wrote."

"Resistance, huh? Dr. Crabtree and his friends have the lowest enrollment of the Department of Humanity. The students are always complaining about them. They haven't published in years."

"But they are a small but vocal minority. They're very influential—"

"Influential my butthole. Look, if you guys don't award Puttbutt tenure then I'll go over your head and give him SOE myself."

"Yes sir."

"And Whitherspoon . . ."

"Yes, President Stool?"

"Get me a list of those troublemakers who are behind this diversity movement. We'll chill them during the summer. Send them letters warning them not to come back. I need the names of some of their faculty supporters. Matata has sent me a list from inside his department. He's a team player. There's a nigger who can be trusted." The vice president started to leave when his ears were offended by a large clap. The president had farted. Whitherspoon turned to see the president's lurid smile.

chapter fourteen

Puttbutt got up in the afternoon and was still jet lagging. It was cool and sunny outside. The neighbors were seated in Adirondack chairs. They presented quite a contrast. He was dark, but his wife was an ample blonde. One of America's clandestine interracial unions. She spent hours in the sun attempting to improve her skin color, once in a while achieving a biscuit color. Most of the time she looked like a three-week-old fryer. Maybe Matata's melanin group had a point, he thought. But then, it sounded like the same old superrace rubbish to Puttbutt. I mean, if black people, according to the Afrocentrics, were so humanistic and so compassionate, why would they expel their albino offspring from Africa? He'd seen albino members of black families being treated as well as their black brothers and sisters. Also, what explained the presence of white-skinned people in Africa who had no European ancestry? The Ọmọ Púpà.

He was in his kitchen, washing the dishes and looking out at them as they relaxed in the backyard. She spoke, but her husband seemed to have a lot of pent-up anger. He would never say hello. What was he upset with him about? About a half hour after the 7.2 he had gone next door to see if they needed some water or batteries, you know, trying to be a good neighbor. The guy said no and just about slammed the door.

Puttbutt had to go to Japanese class. In the class in Japanese he had taken at Colorado Springs, he'd gotten as far as the fifteenth lesson in the textbook. Now he was starting all over again. He was tired and he wanted to stay home. But given the choice between staying home and facing the anger of his tutor, Dr. Yamato, he decided to leave his Rockridge home for downtown Oakland where Yamato's office was located. The man was very businesslike. A very firm and effective teacher. Always serious. He remembered when they were doing their direct objects and Puttbutt said that the way the Japanese pronounced pati, as in pati o shimasu, was similar to the enthusiasm that blacks brought to the word "pati," when they were really enthusiastic about participating in a festive occasion; we're going to paarr-tiii. Yamato stared at him as though he had emitted a foul odor. No doubt about it, Puttbutt wasn't in the mood for tangling with Japanese direct objects while trying to recover from jet lag. (Little did he know that lesson nineteen he would have to battle with the notorious te and nai verbs. And that soon he would study how to ask directions in Japanese. The language lesson from hell.)

The lesson that he took before leaving for Europe had been grueling. Yamato from time to time would fiendishly spring a surprise test on him. Puttbutt messed up on the simplest things. He knew that when he couldn't remember his social security number that sticky blood was passing to the walls of his vessels. There had been strokes and heart attacks in the Puttbutt family and so family members were extra cautious about diet and sedentary habits. They had a genetic bent toward ATHS, or atherosclerosis susceptibility. Maybe that was the origin of their gung-ho-ness. Their desire to keep active. Distinguishing themselves in every war since the Civil War. Every war, that is, but World War II. He should have taken an aspirin because his synapses weren't functioning. His hippocampus was not revving up. He forgot the names of stores: Sakana ya for fish store, niku ya for meat store. Yao ya for vegetable store? He forgot taksun, for many. Forgot the names for colors, aka, kuro, chairo. Left out the Dare in Dare Mo Imasen. Forgot post positions. Numbers. Even forgot Japanese for man: Otoko no hito. And woman: Onna no hito. And for seasons, Haru, Natsu, Aki, Fuyu. Kyo wa, Nihon-go no Benkyo O Shimasen. He just wanted to sleep.

He was driving funny. The way people drive in California prior to an earthquake.

It was the 7.2 that hit Oakland on October 17, 1989 that got him to start thinking about survival, even more than usual. A real Ishmaelite. Survival. Lifetime security. Insurance. I don't mean having enough insurance, or that kind of thing (during a time when even John Hancock and Travelers were failing because of bad real estate investments during the eighties), but being able to get through the twentieth century and beyond. He asked a Yurok friend what the Indian interpretation of the earthquake was, because he could tell that it was some kind of trickster. Interrupting the baseball game. And most telling of all was the videotape that one of the television stations played. A student was making a presentation about earthquakes when all at once the earthquake became her respondent. She and her fellow students ran from the classroom.

But Chappie Puttbutt was from a long line of survivors. A tradition that was begun, according to legend, by an ancestor who was an aide to General George Washington. Even the women did their duty. Nurses. WACs. And his mother, constantly away from home on secret missions. During the Civil War one of his ancestors was General Grant's mistress. Mr. Grant would refuse to eat dinner unless she was there dining with him. But his father would never speak of his father. The other Puttbutt. There didn't seem to be all that much fondness between the two. They were not a very nurturing family, and once in an interview a reporter asked his father why Chappie hadn't shown up for his swearing-in ceremony that was held at the White House. He said that Chappie was his Patti Davis, a member of one of America's most recent top fractured families to hold office. He'd tuned in though. And after the president had pinned a medal on his father, his father insisted upon singing "You'll Never Walk Alone," to the dismay of the marine band that had to fumble from key to key in order to keep up with General Puttbutt.

The general always felt that his son's career as an English instructor was a strange choice for a Puttbutt, so willing to show the flag at the slightest provocation. His father always kidded him about it. The last time he'd seen his father was when he announced to him that he'd received a lectureship in literature at Jack London College. His father started to signify with his eyes. "Literature, huh," he said with a suggestive grin. He thought his father would be proud when he started to organize a Black Panther chapter on campus during his Air Force Academy days. Instead, the then Major Puttbutt flew in and disrupted the thing and threatened the other black cadets whom he'd recruited as members. He even had him tailed by military intelligence. In fact, one of the reasons that his relationship with his father was strained was because he had requested his files under the Freedom of Information Act and discovered that his father had put him under surveillance.

Puttbutt figured that with Japanese under his belt he would adjust to the new realities of the coming postsettler era, a time when the domination of the United States by people of the same background would come to an end. The Back to Basics folks saw it differently. They said that he was paranoid. They said that English would always be the official language of the United States. But language was always outside of the law. About as predictable as a fox. Besides, the English Only movement that stretched from Orange County to Queens College in New York and included New England liberal professors as well as Pacific Northwest nazis had been wrong before. They said that the Chinese communists were going to invade from Mexico, but it never happened. They said that everybody was going to return to the gold standard. They said that rock and roll was the music of the devil. They said that Dwight David Eisenhower was a paid Soviet agent. They said that postmodernist literature was just a passing fad and that people were returning to the ordinary. Their leader once told them that the world was going to come to an end and so all of the English Only people sold all of their belongings and gathered at Pikes Peak in Fort Collins, Colorado for the ascendance. It never happened. The end of the cold war caught them by surprise. Sartre's admission that he only became interested in existentialism as a way of picking up young girls caught the left wing of the English Only movement by surprise. For the official American intelligentsia there was one big surprise after another. And the shaky alliance between the left and right monoculturalists and English Only advocates could collapse at any moment. The feud between the Paleolithic Right and the Neoconservative Right was expanding. (What's going to happen when Jesse Helms learns that the Plato of *From Plato to NATO* was gay? Besides, they would have been surprised to learn that the official language of heaven was probably the tongue that Jesus spoke. Aramaic. If they'd ever gotten to heaven they would have to learn a dead language. A language spoken by dark-skinned people. Even dead, they would be wrong.)

And so, even though his Rockridge house was nearly destroyed by the earthquake, he was still alive and surviving. Had a job at Oakland's Jack London College. But the big thing in his life was the Japanese lessons. Each night he had cartoon nightmares in which he was trying to place particles. De, ga, ni, wa, no, ya, o, etc. are on his bedpost and chattering at him in Japanese, daring him to place them in their correct places in a sentence. They sound like the voices of bugs in one of those anti-bug commercials. The whiny, grating mechanical voices. And the textbook, *Japanese by Spring*, is enjoying it all. Standing on stick legs at the top of the bed, and rubbing its binding with stick hands, finding the whole thing to be hilarious. But he knew that if he could grasp Japanese, the future belonged to him.

When the Black Power thing was in, Puttbutt was into that. When the backlash on Black Power settled in, with its code words like reverse discrimination, he joined that. He'd been a feminist when they were in power. But now they were on the decline, unable to expand beyond their middle-class constituency and so for now he was a neoconservative, but since a split had developed among the financial backers of the neoconservative and between the new conservatives and the old conservatives, that might be over too. While op-ed writers and academics inveighed against multiculturalism which, for George Will, was a greater threat than Saddam Hussein, the business people were endorsing it. They didn't give a damn whether the people they traded with had a subscription to the Great Books Club.

If the Asian thing was going to fly he wanted to at least be in coach. Europe was combining forces to create a white market and Asia was forming a yellow market and the Japanese were asking to be the leaders. He'd heard that the coming nineties recession would happen because of a shortage in world capital. Japan was going to spend its money in Asia. The third-largest power, Germany, was going to spend its in Eastern Europe where all of those formerly socialistic enterprises were up for sale to the highest bidders. Studying Japanese would put him where the yen was. He would have gone into business had it not been for his math deficiency. Now that the writer was considered as obsolete as a 1960s computer, he could share in some of the profits of the growth industry of the eighties and nineties. Criticism. All you had to do was string together some quotes from Benjamin, Barthes, Foucault, and Lacan and you were in business. Even a New Critic like himself could make some cash.

chapter fifteen

D r. Yamato's office was located in downtown Oakland next to the Broadway Building. It had been built in 1907. There were the familiar yellow caution ribbons traveling around the building. Yellow ribbons, besides being a symbol for victory, stood for earthquakes. One had the feeling that, post 7.2, Oakland was so fragile that if you were to sneeze a dozen or so buildings would collapse. He'd go to Dr. Yamato's office each Friday and get what he told his friends was a good old-fashioned head whipping. When his brain was young and fresh he learned languages rapidly. He still remembered his German prepositions, an auf hinter in neben über vor zwischen. But with Japanese you had to learn post positions and an old forty-two-year-old brain is like an old mule. You had to kick it in the ass in order for it to get up.

Dr. Yamato had all of the charm of the head of a POW camp. But Chappie knew that if he couldn't learn Spanish and Japanese he'd be obsolete in the 1990s United States. Unless they expand and absorb, languages die, and already English was hungry for new adjectives, verbs and nouns. It could use some more rhythm from a language like Japanese, which sounded as though it were invented for bebop. Atatakakatta, past tense for the word warm. Doesn't that sound like a Max Roach attack? Even the word for ticket office sounded like the title of a song that Bird wrote, or a line from a Bob Kaufman poem: Kippu Yoriba. Or the word for boy: Otoko no ko. It could use some Yoruba drum talk. The black and Hispanic writers were doing their part, helping the patient walk around the room.

The English Only people and the monoculturalists were like the religious fanatics who didn't believe in blood transfusions.

Dr. Yamato was patient with him. He was a deliberate and cautious man. His movements reminded Puttbutt of the tempo of Leopoldine Konstantin's arm reaching for the cigarette case in Hitchcock's *Notorious*. Dr. Yamato looked at him with a blank expression, which meant that he was pleased, because usually he was frowning. During those moments he looked like Toshiro Mifune about to behead an adversary. He didn't know where Yamato lived or whether he had a family. He wore the same black suit to every session and carried an umbrella even when the sky was clear. His office was barely furnished. Two office chairs and an office table from the Officer's Club, an office furniture outlet near Oakland's Jack London Square. A map of the Japanese islands and Katakana and Hiragana charts decorated the wall. Yamato fired questions and asked him to translate English into Japanese. Puttbutt stuttered back his responses.

Puttbutt had gotten through his past tenses for i adjectives, which was bloody murder, and was walking downtown from the institute, which was located on Webster Street off Broadway. In front of the Clorox Building, two mounted Oakland police were driving a homeless person from the sidewalk. A spokesperson for the developers said that he wanted to rid a nearby park of winos. They looked as if they hadn't anything to do, the spokesperson had said. People who visited downtown Oakland had to seem busy. Isogashii desu. And so Chappie, whenever he traveled to downtown, always wore a tie.

During the lesson, Dr. Yamato kept congratulating him. Hai! Hai! as he put Puttbutt through his tenses. Chappie's mind was on his lessons. He almost stumbled over a man who looked as though he'd shriveled up. He was Japanese and dressed in dirty, tattered clothes. He was playing a Japanese instrument. Though the divide and conquer TV would have you believe that all of the Asian Americans were living on Easy Street, Glide Church of San Francisco 1989 had reported that some of them had walked miles from Chinatown and Japantown to join Glide's annual Thanksgiving feast. The number of homeless in Oakland had grown since the earthquake. In this cold, the man must have been freezing. What the hell, it was the first few days of the New Year, and Chappie was feeling pretty good, so he slipped a twenty-dollar bill into the beggar's cap, which lay in front of his legs that were sprawled out on the pavement. One leg. The other artificial leg had been detached from his knee. Its whiteness was a grotesque contrast to the beggar's yellow knee. His head was facing down. The man slowly lifted it to acknowledge Puttbutt's gift. It gave Puttbutt a start. Many teeth were missing. Sores were present. His mouth was open and his eyes bulging. His face became a fearsome o-tobide mask. He gave Puttbutt a dark smile. "Domo," he said, nodding his head rapidly. "Domo."

He had decided to pick up some Chicago Pizza on College Avenue before heading home. He was going to treat himself for doing so well on the i adjectives. Rewarding oneself was part of the New Age California style. If you weaned yourself from some habit like overeating, or if you overcame some challenge, in his case the i adjectives, you rewarded yourself.

chapter sixteen

He came home to find cars with strange-looking men inside at each end of the block. In front of his house was a black limousine. One man sat inside. He was dressed in a business suit like the men in the other cars. His neighbors were standing behind their curtains peering out. He had to show his driver's license in order to enter the block. The machine gun toting men waved him ahead. When he got to his house he discovered men in the front yard and on the sides of the house. God forbid that the crack plague that was devastating East Oakland had reached his neighborhood, at the bottom of paradise, at the bottom of the beautiful Oakland Hills. Two men were standing guard in front of his door.

"What's the matter?" he asked. They didn't say anything, just checked his papers. Opened the pizza box, looked underneath the slices, permitted him to enter. Puttbutt had written a piece for the newspapers that Americans had to give up some liberties in order to fight the drug plague, but when he wrote that, he meant other people's liberties, not his. He entered the house. His father was sitting in a chair, a cigarette in one hand, a glass of Tanqueray, his hero General Daniel "Chappie" James's favorite drink, in the other. He had adopted James's favorite quote as his own. "Yea though I fly through the valley of death I shall fear no evil for I am the meanest muthah in the valley." He was watching himself address a cheering audience of the Veterans of Foreign Wars. On television he was wearing a uniform, but sitting in his chair he was wearing a business suit like the other men. "Dad, must your visits be so dramatic?"

"Wasn't my idea, Son," he said without turning away from one of his usual jingoistic speeches. "Everywhere I go they follow me. When your mother used to go into a store, it was like a mobilization for war. It's because of our top-security assignments. Why didn't you come to the swearing-in ceremony at the White House when I received my star. We missed you." He was concluding his speech, tears in his eyes, as he congratulated "the brave men and women of the Gulf War for their tremendous accomplishment," and said, "As for our men from the Vietnam War, we say, welcome home buddy, we love you." That brought the crowd to its feet.

"We've not exactly been a nurturing family, Dad. Why put up a front."

"You're our Patti Davis, all right." He said that with both scorn and humor. He had a picture up in the den of his ranch-style home in Maryland of him and Ronald Reagan. Mr. Reagan was pinning a medal to his chest.

"Look, Dad, I got a lot of poems to examine. What's up?"

"You still got your flowers I see." He pointed his head to the garden in back.

"Still cultivating."

"You were always a strange one. Cultivating flowers. Violin lessons. Reading books."

"Dad, we've been through this a hundred times."

"We couldn't spend that much time with you. And your mother. Your poor mother. Captured by these sand niggers. No telling what heinous tortures they're putting her through. You stopped talking to her after you found out that she helped North plan that bombing raid on Libya."

"You know I grew out of my Qaddafi phase a long time ago. Those were the old days. When I blamed everything on the United States of America instead of on communism and the third world's lack of a work ethic. It's the fact that she worked with a man who spent government funds on a security fence and shredded govern-ment property, that bothered me. To think. My mother, working with somebody who would do that."

"Boy, did she put you through the ringer. Remember the time she threw you into the pool?"

"I nearly drowned. Her idea of teaching me how to swim. I haven't been able to go near a beach since then. I was really trauma-tized."

"And then she stopped speaking to you when they threw you out of the Air Force Academy."

He didn't answer. He wondered whether he knew about the faculty wife. His affair.

"Son, I have news about your crazy grandfather. We think that he might be heading in this direction. The Pentagon shrink department said that he might contact you. Something about grandparental instinct. We know that he's left the place where he was staying."

"I don't know what you're talking about." His father squinted. "I don't even remember my grandfather. Besides, if I were in touch with my grandfather you'd know about it. I'm sure that you're still having my phone tapped." His father was unfazed by that comment.

"I'm sorry, Son. But they do it to the relatives of all people in my position. I'm heading a top-secret mission." He leaned forward and clasped his hands. He resembled the actor Frederick O'Neal.

"I don't care. I insist upon my privacy."

"Don't worry. You're clean."

"But still . . ."

"Look, Son, your grandfather is getting old. I want to make up with him before I die." Another lie. He could tell.

"You sure that's the reason?"

"It doesn't matter anymore."

"What doesn't matter?"

"Skip it."

His father the general rose. Put on his hat and with a sharp turn, hands at his sides, started toward the door. His pictures never did him justice. Like the one in the newspapers that showed him knocking together the heads of two black dignity soldiers in Panama. He was stunned by his father's visit.

"Anyway, we'll find him. With or without your help."

"I'm sure you will, Father." And he would. His father always got his man. Rumor was that General Noriega surrendered to the Vatican because he didn't want his father, who had been nicknamed the Black Puma, chasing his ass through the jungle.

chapter seventeen

Robert Hurt, dean of Humanity, was in his office preparing to leave for the day when his secretary informed him that Whitherspoon wanted to see him. He knew why. The "tension thing." The vice president and the dean stood across from each other. Whitherspoon hated the famous psychedelic poster of Bob Dylan that Hurt had placed on his office wall. It hurt his eyes.

"Look, I won't waste any words. You know why I'm here." Hurt nodded. "They want me to talk to you about the Bass boy."

"So, what do you want me to do about it?"

"I want you to do what you think is best, Bob. You know that I wouldn't interfere, I only wish that you would reconsider. These kids, you know the hot weather, and the beer. The results were predictable. So they got themselves involved in a little prank." He shrugged his shoulders.

"A little prank. They sent death threats to his home, hanged his dog, and wrote KKK on his car. And if that wasn't enough they put this vicious cartoon in the campus magazine." The body was that of a naked black man with his penis buried in an ostrich. Making it look as though Puttbutt was into paraphilia. The ostrich had a pained, shocked look on its face. The head on the body belonged to Professor Puttbutt. Hurt was about to hand him the magazine that carried the offending cartoon, but the vice president pushed it away.

"I saw it. I can understand your passion, but look at it our way. Old man Bass is the bankroll behind this school."

"I haven't made up my mind whether to suspend Bass Jr., but I'm leaning in that direction if you must know."

"Can't change your mind?"

"No."

"Hurt, you have a great career ahead of you. But that old expression of going along to get along applies here too."

"I said, no deal. I don't care if he's the most powerful man in Oakland."

"Suit yourself. The alumni can cause a lot of trouble. They can put a lot of pressure on this institution. They can put a lot of pressure on me." Hurt didn't answer. The vice president turned around and started for the door. Just as he reached the door he turned to Hurt. Hurt looked up. His white hair was shoulder length. He wore denims and a blue worker's shirt. He still smoked marijuana.

"Tell me one thing, Hurt." Hurt didn't respond. Vice President Whitherspoon sighed. "Why is your attitude so different from Professor Puttbutt's? If anyone had a right to be offended by the cartoon, the threats, it would be him. Yet he's taken all of this very calmly."

"You'll have to ask him," Hurt said.

chapter eighteen

Puttbutt went over to the Women's Studies department to find out whether it was true that his position as part-time lecturer in the African-American Studies was going to go to April Jokujoku, who had one article to her name. Something having to do with Clitoridectomy Imagery in the Works of Black Male Novelists. He entered her office. Marsha Marx was at her desk. Above her head hung an Alice Walker calendar photo. She had written about a visit to Ms. Walker's house in one of the local newspapers. She wrote about it as though she were visiting some holy shrine. Marsha was dressed in a black pin-striped suit and a Victorian blouse. Her blond hair was set in an upsweep. A Gibson.

"Chappie, come in."

"Thanks, Marsha."

"Loved that piece you did on how black men originated the slave trade and how, during the slavery period, they treated their women worse than the slave master treated the slaves. It was brilliant." She was referring to an article he'd published when the feminist movement on campus was at its zenith. Now President Stool was talking about cutting into their budget. They'd have to cancel some classes. Let go some of their faculty.

"Glad you liked it, Marsha. I think that the brothers ought to get off this victimization kick. Face up to the fact that their problems are caused by themselves. Stop blaming the system and be held accountable for their abusive behavior."

"Must be lonely for you. Taking such a brave stand. You're sort of a father figure to these wanton black men." Puttbutt sighed.

"I don't mind. It's a thankless task, but somebody has to do it."

"So what can I do for you, Chappie?"

"Well, you know there's a rumor going around about April Joku-joku. They're saying that she's being brought out here by African and Women's studies to take my job. Is it true?"

"It's only talk, Chappie. Besides, I don't think you have anything to worry about. Your devotion to the feminist cause is irreproachable. Too bad some of your brothers aren't as enlightened."

"They used to make fun of me when I studied the violin, ridiculed me because I was bad at basketball."

"You poor boy. Is there anything else, Chappie?"

"That's about all, Marsha. How's Shirley doing?"

"We're still fervently and deliciously in love. We're thinking about buying a house together and adopting some children. To think that I went through two marriages with men. I had to be their housekeeper, chauffeur, as well as study for my third Ph.D. Listen, somebody told me that you're studying Japanese. Why would you be doing that? Japanese men treat their women something awful. They have geishas on the side, and are drunk all the time."

"I'm studying Japanese so that I can translate the poetry of some medieval women court poets," Puttbutt lied.

"Good for you, Chappie. You had me worried there for a minute."

"No need to worry, Marsha. Sometimes I wonder how I got along without feminist theory. All of those years of male chauvinist activity. Of exploiting women's bodies. Seducing them. Sometimes I don't even get to sleep until 3 A.M. I feel so guilty. I guess you might call me a recovering misogynist."

"I wish that there were more men like you. Black men who would realize that all of us have to unite to fight the common enemy. The white male patriarch who presides over the capitalistic system that oppresses us all. You're a role model for your brothers who often behave like savages."

"Thank you, Marsha. That really makes me feel better. A lot better. Thank you, Marsha. Hai, Arigato Gozaimasu, as we say in Japanese." She looked at him quizzically. "I'm sorry, Marsha but sometimes I get into a J.B. Spring mode. These lessons are always on my mind."

"You're welcome, Chappie. And Chappie," she said, as she escorted him out of her office, "don't worry about your job. Even if we brought April out here it wouldn't interfere with your position. It would only be a short-term appointment."

"Thank you, Marsha. That's reassuring."

"Maybe you can give Shirley and me some advice. We're thinking about starting a garden."

"Anytime, Marsha." He left the Women's Studies department thinking that at least he had a few friends on campus. Marsha also had influence in the English department. His tenure was so close that he could taste it.

chapter nineteen

One day he was coming out of the BART Rockridge Station, and was on his way to his car, a 1986 BMW, when two men sidled up to him. They grabbed him and shoved him into a car. He was blindfolded. The car drove for about an hour until it came to a stop. Soon they were in a forest and a great rushing sound indicated that a turbulent water was located somewhere nearby. He was led into the house. They opened the door. After they removed his blindfold he discovered that one of his escorts was black, the other Japanese. A tall black man dressed in a kimono greeted them. He had a Genghis Khan mustache and wore pigtails. He looked to be about sixty and seemed to have taken good care of himself. He bowed. "Irasshaimase," he said. The old man had manners.

"Domo," Chappie said, showing discourtesy.

"Dozo Osakini," he said, bowing and extending his hand for Chappie to follow him. Chappie followed him into a room. The room was decorated in a conservative Japanese style. They sat on the floor across from each other. A low black table separated them. There was a shoji screen separating them from the other rooms.

"Look, if it's money you're looking for, forget it. My dad's policy is never yield to terrorists. So you might as well kill me."

"I'm not looking for money, Son," the old man said.

"Well, what do you want?"

"Is there any crime in a man wanting to spend some time with his grandson?" Grandson? Chappie stared at the man.

"But, my grandfather is eighty-three years old, you couldn't be . . ."

"Been taking care of myself, Grandson."

"Why did you have to go to such extremes to bring me to your house, Grandfather. I would have come voluntarily."

"I'm hiding, Grandson. Your father. If he knew where I was, there'd be trouble. He wants me to stay in Hawaii. He's ashamed of me. Doesn't want me around. Otōsan wa baka desu ka."

"Demanding, but not stupid, Grandfather. You couldn't have come up through the military ranks in this country and be stupid." He blurted the words so fast that he had to do a take on the implications of what he was saying. He wondered what inside of him made him say that?

"Nani Mo Arimasen," he said, slicing the air with his left hand.

"Grandfather, if all you want to do is run down my father, then why don't you have your men take me back to Oakland."

"I won't bother you with our feud. Look, as much as I despise. my son, at least he's a fighter. But you, I read about you in the newspapers. Let this Bass boy screw all over you. I read about it. Let these Haku-jin use you. Subject you to their trickeration."

"I know what I'm doing. Besides, that's my business. I mean, I've never seen you before, and all at once you're trying to run my business. I've always wondered."

"Wondered what, Grandson?"

"Why did you leave the States? No Puttbutt has ever done that before."

"I don't go by that name anymore. That's my slave name. My name now is Sakanouye Tammamura Maro." The two men who had brought Puttbutt into the house bowed when he said that.

"I'm sorry."

"Do itashimashite. I was just ahead of my time. The black people are going to start to leave this country. I left because I saw the handwriting on the wall."

"What do you mean, Grandfather?"

"Back there in Detroit. Me and my friends didn't think like the rest of the blacks in those days. Bowing and scraping to the white man and worshiping Jesus. We were ahead of our time. Proud. All the rest of these niggers were spellbound by the trickeration of the white people. Now they have all of their ideas on the radio. These young people be rapping our ideas. Why hell, I'm the grand old man of Rap. We were saying these things long before Malcolm X and the rest of them. Son, you can't trust these devils. They got you thinking the way they think. They tried to take over Asia, but the Japanese people stopped them. Japan was the only country that wasn't colonized by them. That's what World War II was all about. Pearl Harbor. Hell, ain't nobody told the white man to come to Hawaii. Had no business having his ships there. All these other niggers was sorry when the Japanese hit those ships, those fools. Me and my friends was glad and we said so. Look, Grandson. The Japanese were standing up for the concept of Pan-Asia, just as the blacks were fighting for Pan-Africa. There ain't no difference. But some of the yellows were slow. China. Allowing itself to be taken over by these Anglo haints and imps. The Japanese stood up to them. Stopped them dead, defeating the Russians in nineteen-five. Then the Vietnamese finished them off. And since then they've been in retreat.

"They murdered millions of people in Asia, Africa and South America, now they're doing their crusades number in the Middle East. They will eventually lose there. The Japanese were intimidated by Admiral Perry because they didn't have a navy. The devil used a little liquor on the boys, too. Then they got one. Got a navy. Hussein lost because he didn't have an air force. But somebody in Syria or Iran or one of those countries will come up with a generation of weapons better than theirs. Now that the Russians are joining NATO, white folks gettin together, there are going to be a lot of unemployed scientists looking for jobs. Then where is Amerika-jin going to be. Calling on these young ghetto niggers to save them. And they got plenty of niggers, dying to rise to the occasion. 'Choose me, boss. Choose me.' " Relying on the enemy class to save one's ass wasn't new in history. There was an element of truth in what the grandfather said. Both politicians and scholars on the right were equating the multiculturalists, and the "rebels" and "rioters" who took to the streets after the Simi Valley jurors acquitted the four policemen who brutalized Rodney King, with barbarians. Visigoths was the name that one presidential candidate used. It was the Visigoths, the barbarians, who continued the values of Rome. Would today's "underclass" be tomorrow's rescuers of Western civilization? Appearing on the Arsenio Hall Show, shortly after the LA riots, gang members from the Crips and the Bloods spoke of their reconciliation and their devotion to the values of market enterprise.

"The Japanese lost the war, Grandfather."

"Lost the war! Lost the war! Nihon Ginko is the biggest bank in the world now. The Japanese are buying Amerika. Hell, they just bought the Sheraton Palace across the bridge in San Francisco. They're not acting like somebody who lost the war. Hell, if they started selling. If they stopped buying Amerikan bonds, they'd cause an inflation that would lead to a depression worse than the one in the thirties. What are you casting your lot with these beasts for?" As he finished that sentence, Puttbutt was sure that he heard some Do yells, and some clashing of sticks, both associated with Japanese martial arts. Coming from some distant room.

"It just ain't going to work. Even if all of the black people became prosperous tomorrow, there's no reason why they won't take it away from them. Marcus Garvey said that. How come you don't think they'll take it away from us." His grandfather seemed to have a tendency to overstate things. If they were pianists, he would be Billy Taylor, a competent survivor, his grandfather, Erroll Garner, given to flourishes and exaggerations, and his father—his father would be an accompanist for the Mills Brothers. "They took it away from the Cherokee, our ancestors, when they became middle class, they even took it away from the Nikkei-jin who were trying to be so goodygoody. Kissing up to the white man. Even fought in the war on the American side against their own people. Assisted in the American Occupation of Japan. Now, what makes you think that they won't take it away from us. Shit. They be writing in their newspapers about how black people are genetically inferior. What do you think it's all going to lead up to. You see them getting together with those Russkies who, although they have Asian ancestry, are nothing but white men like them. Admiral Heihachiro Togo kicked their asses back there in the battle of Port Arthur. Those little yellow men shocked Europe by beating one of their own." The two men bowed at the mention of the admiral's name. "Don't you think that when Africa gets itself together, the blacks will leave this country in droves. Some of those regimes are already marching. Moving up. Gettin what these folks are gettin. Gettin rid of these CIA gofers. These Bakamono. Nigeria got a satellite going up in the nineties. And don't think that these liberals are going to come to your aid. Even Roosevelt was a racist. At the end of the war, he considered crossbreeding the Japanese with the Pacific Islanders. Compulsory eugenics. Shows you how much he knew about the Japanese. The Japanese would have committed collective suicide had they been ordered to interbreed with the Pacific Islanders whom the whites disrespect and consider docile. Besides, the Japanese can't be all bad. You wouldn't be studying Japanese if they were so bad, now would you? Just like a Puttbutt, trying to develop some winning strategy." He paused from what was beginning to be a tirade. He distinctly heard what sounded like body slams.

As is always the case when two Puttbutts got together, they argued and argued. He was disappointed with his grandfather. He thought that there were a chance that he'd be different. But he was no different from the rest of the family. Chappie believed that negotiation was always the best remedy for revenge. As they talked Chappie was marveled by the fact that his grandfather shared his interest in Japanese. But for what reason Chappie did not know. Of course, it was nothing unusual these days. Courses were proliferating throughout the country. All of the smart money was on Japan. His grandfather's aides kept bringing them delicious dishes as they sat on the cushions in the tatami-matted room. By the early hours in the morning they'd become chummy from the refills of sake. At one

point Chappie said, "Gochiso-sama deshita." His grandfather nodded and said, "O-somatsu sama deshita." He was drunk, too. Finally
they bade each other sayonara. The two men who brought him
blindfolded him politely. At one point he had the sensation that
they were traveling across the Golden Gate Bridge. That remark his
grandfather made about the Sheraton Hotel across the bridge gave
him a clue as to his whereabouts. Chappie decided that he liked the
old man.

chapter twenty

The dispute between Hurt and the Bass family was the talk of Jack
London campus and of Oakland. Some of the faculty and the students said that it was a free speech issue and that Bass should have
the right to print a collage of Chappie Puttbutt having intercourse
with an ostrich, and that black people called each other "nigger" so
why shouldn't Bass Jr. be able to do so. That this was just another
example of PC demands on the part of minorities, women and
homosexuals. That if someone wanted to print a poster, Club Fag-
gots Not Seals, or a cartoon of a black professor having intercourse
with an ostrich, or if a white fraternity wanted to celebrate Hitler's
birthday and pass out copies of Mein Kampf at Yom Kippur services,
then they had every right to do so. If they wanted to take out a
full-page ad in Koons and Kikes, arguing that the holocaust never
happened, they were exercising their First Amendment rights. Puttbutt agreed. They said that Hurt was full of self-hatred against his
own people. They said that the politically correct movement was
bringing a new campus McCarthyism.

A lot of the black faculty and students avoided Chappie even more
so than before. They thought that he should have been on the side

of those who wanted to discipline Bass Jr., no matter what influence
his father had over the alumni. It came up in his class, and the
student from Long Beach said that black people were just too sensitive, and that as a woman she had suffered as much as they. Probably
more. She looked up at Puttbutt with an idiotic smirk on her face.
The warrior in his genes wanted to smash her face in. One day she
came to visit him during his office hours. She had showered herself
with some kind of cheap perfume. He opened the window. She was
smoking a cigarette and traces of red could be seen on the filter.
She crossed her legs so that her dress fell back up to her crotch.

She had runs in her stockings. On that particular day the purpose
of her visit was to ask him whether he could do something about
the black men who were always coming on to her whenever she
walked down Telegraph Avenue in Berkeley. His Puttbutt warrior
genes started to ask her what she thought any black man would see
in such an ugly bitch as she. Or, with a little more style, he could
have said that if she wouldn't dress so provocatively maybe men
wouldn't notice her. He didn't want any trouble and so he told her
that he'd look into it. Muzukashii said that he thought that the
cartoon was an ingenious work of art and that Puttbutt should be
flattered at the fine representation of him in the cartoon. The
class laughed. Muzukashii looked around, thrilled that he'd made a
remark that gave such delight to the white students whom he wanted
to impress.

chapter twenty-one

How do they look?"
"They're coming," Troy said, sullenly. She was pruning the

cherry trees. In the spring they would blossom in a daze of whites and reds.

He went into the house and upstairs to his study. From his window he looked down on the garden. Nature was stirring. His was fallow. He couldn't recall the last time he'd had sex. With the AIDS epidemic one had to just about dress up like a scuba diver and dip oneself into hydrogen peroxide before having sex these days. He didn't spend a lot of time thinking about sex, and nowadays a man didn't know what to say to a woman, the words that began the series of movement that would end up in bed. He always felt himself doing and saying trite things during courtship. He had missed out on a lot of sex in his life because he hated cliches. He never thought all that much about needing a woman, or a wife. He once thought of going to a therapist to find out why he didn't make commitments, but after hearing all of the horror stories about modern relationships and having experienced the unhappiness in the lives of those who were married, he decided that he was perfectly fine as he was. He listened to KPFA every morning and from what he heard on that station, relationships were sounding as dangerous as living in California. For black men, relationships with women, the society and with other black men had been especially dangerous during the previous decades. Many had been wiped out in the eighties. It was a period fraught with Abuni as the Nihon-jin would say. Though he disdained his family's inclination toward solving all issues with the use of force, he sometimes could appreciate their analysis of life and society. Life as war. The use of tactics and strategies in everyday life. The daily inspections during which his father would bounce a quarter on his bed to determine whether it had been made up in military fashion. Lining up for his mother as she examined his shoes, and his grooming. He was still devoted to spit and polish. Knew how to fold his trousers and shirts. Still walked with his spine straight and his chest out. Could cook, clean, launder and sew. He had about as much need for a wife as a cadaver for bifocals. But he was not a warrior like the others. His father, a general. His grandfather surrounded by strange men all of whom were respectful toward him and eager to do his bidding. What was his grandfather into? Dope. And his anti-American ravings and pro-Nihon sentiments? Who were those men and what was he in the States for?

"I want to plant those azaleas next week."

"Fine, Troy."

"I made up a list of fertilizers that you need to buy."

"OK, Troy. Troy, what are people on campus saying about the . . . well, you know . . ."

"About how that Bass boy is fucking all over you? They're saying that you ought to kick his ass." Her father was a psychiatrist, her mother the state assemblywoman. She'd gone to boarding schools in Switzerland.

"But what good would that do?"

"I was just telling you what they were saying. I was just telling you." She pouted and rolled her eyes to the ceiling.

"Thanks, Troy." He heard the horn honk. She got her wraps and was about to leave the house. He looked through the curtain. Jo Hara was outside in the Jeep. "And Troy?"

"Yes?" He could tell from the way she said it that she was annoyed.

"Look, you know I'm sure that I'll be receiving tenure very soon and I was thinking about buying a house in the Oakland Hills. The university has this low-interest program for tenured faculty. I could buy a house—how do you like living up there?"

"It's like living in a matchbox, if you want to know my opinion. They planted eucalyptus and Monterey Pine up there adding that to the dry wooden slate roofs—it's an inferno waiting to happen. I keep trying to tell my folks this, but they love the view, and think that if they live down here they'll be mugged or murdered."

"Thanks."

"Is that all, now."

"Yes. Mata Raishu."

"What?"

"That's next week in Japanese. Just practicing my Japanese." She rolled her eyes about in annoyance and left.

He watched as the car left the neighborhood. He went into the kitchen. He looked into the window of the house across the way. Somebody was peering out of the curtains at him. He pretended he wasn't noticing. Living in the exclusive Oakland Hills would bring him neighbors who were refined. People with art collections and jewelry. They'd be artists and writers and professors. With tenure, he'd be eligible for that university loan.

He heard the familiar klunk. The mail had arrived. He went to the box and removed it. One letter was from the Office of the English Chair. It was marked confidential. Here at last was the good news. Here at last was his ticket out of the African-American Studies department. He'd said on a panel about Afrocentricity that the idea of blacks discovering America before Columbus amounted to little more than elevated feelgoodism. He chuckled to himself as he thought of his fellow black panel members fuming as some members of the white audience rose to their feet and gave him an ovation. He opened the envelope eagerly and a smile began, and his heart began to thump with pride and joy. He'd said that American education was being threatened by the triple-headed dragon of mediocrity, heterogeneity, diversity and—halfway down the letter his smile disappeared. What? He had been denied tenure! They said that they hoped he would continue on the year-to-year basis and that they felt him to be an asset to the department. He thought of the Japanese word for every morning, that sounded similar to an American cussword. His legs almost gave way from under him. He thought about how he'd kept his nose clean, how he was a team player. He thought about how he had been a sort of intellectual houseboy, like the one in the novel of the same name by Ferdinand Oyono. Free to comment upon the behavior of his fellow housepersons, but fearful of describing the illicit activities among his employer's class. Denouncing affirmative action, criticizing blacks for exploiting white guilt. He had been patient and had tried to negotiate. He had developed a power smile and wore blue blazers and white shoes. He had written an op-ed against divestment in South Africa. He had taken the platform and said that racism was an illusion and that if the campus were 95 percent white male, it was because white men were more qualified than the others. That there seemed to be an almost divine mandate for them to rule. He thought about the time that he debated those who wanted to make Ethnic Studies courses mandatory, his voice dripping with sarcasm as he hit them. Praised Greece, Rome. He thought about how he had said that the idea of blacks originating Egyptian civilization was the looniest thing he ever heard. He thought about how he had denounced Miles Davis. Said that Miles should have remained at Juilliard. Studied the classics. Purcell. He thought about how he had once referred to jazz as noise. He thought about his demand, printed in a right-wing literary magazine, that black writers imitate the Victorians. He thought of all of the butt he had kissed, the boots he had licked, all for tenure. All for SOE. Images arose in his mind. The dressing-down his mother gave him when he was thrown out of the Air Force Academy. His father laughing until tears came to his eyes when he told him that he wanted to pursue a career in Humanity. That he was more interested in a soaring intellect than spending the rest of his days in the cockpit of a fighter plane. It was his father's business to destroy humanity. Son of a bitch, he kept thinking to himself. Son of a bitch.

There was a smaller envelope. It was engraved. Maybe somebody was inviting him to a party. A party would cheer him up. The invitation said: Marsha Marx and Charles Obi of the African-American and Women's Studies Department invite you to a reception in honor of April Jokujoku, newly appointed full professor in Women's Studies and African-American Studies at $150,000 per semester.

He felt like having a drink. He went and got himself a bottle of sake that he kept around for special occasions. He heated some and poured himself a cup full. And then two. Then three.

What a double cross. All the while telling him that he had nothing to fear from the appointment of her, they had made a deal. Just like these devious Californians. Give you that serene surfer smile while stabbing you in the back. He gulped down the sake and poured himself another. He flung the cup into the fireplace. He started turning over chairs and tables. It was the sake that Jingo had introduced him to that night. He felt like hearing some rough angry charging music. Blue Trane. Coltrane's sax began to move out of the station. Maybe his grandfather was right. He said these suckers are never going to change. He took down the portrait of his hero, Thomas Sowell, and started to take down the one of Booker T. Washington. He decided against it. Booker T. was complex. He brought out the framed photo of Malcolm X from a desk drawer where it had lain for many years. He dusted it off. He nailed it into the wall with a vengeance. He stayed up all night. Hurt. Disappointed. Betrayed. At about five in the morning he heard the paper being thrown on the porch. He went out and picked it up. It was dark outside, and Mars was so bright and close that he thought that it was a plane. But it wasn't a plane. It didn't move.

PART

Two

•

chapter twenty-two

Another beautiful California day. Sunny. A temperature that was just right. A fall breeze that lightly massaged your skin. The birds were doing a jam session. He threw a bran muffin into the toaster and cut up some fruit. He began his bath. He poured himself a cup of the dark French roast mix. The drink had mitigated some of his anger. He had a big headache, but he felt better. John Coltrane had put some fight into his craw. Would he leave? Hell no. Being denied tenure usually meant that the institution to which you were attached wanted you to shove off. But he liked the weather. The Thai, Haitian and Gumbo restaurants. DeLauer's Newsstand. Lake Merritt.

He hadn't felt angry in twenty years. It felt good. During the long night he had gotten his old Black Panther beret out of the trunk. It still fit. The first paper that he always read was the *Tribune*. JACK LONDON BAILOUT DENIED. Just as he had warned, Robert Bass of Caesar Synthetics had pulled his money out over the threatened suspension of his son, and his friends had followed suit. No relief could be expected from the state, either. They owned the governor, whose name in Armenian meant "the servant" (the servant to corporate interests). The governor's every speech indicated that he hated education. But a new buyer had stepped in. He couldn't believe what he read. A one-hundred-million endowment. A mysterious Japanese group had put up the money? When he arrived at school to find out whether he'd been rehired by African-American Studies, he found little groups gathered, discussing the deal. Charles Obi was coming toward him like one of those fast walkers, hips moving.

"Dr. Obi," he said, "you still haven't said whether I'll be teaching this semester. The semester opens in two weeks." He was almost pleading.

"Can't talk now, Puttbutt. Got to go to a meeting." Obi buzzed on by and disappeared into President Stool's house. Puttbutt went to the African-American Studies department. The secretary, Effie Singleton, was at the Xerox machine. He never noticed before, but she was very attractive. He wasn't supposed to notice, but he couldn't help his eyes. They were straying over her hefty bosom and down to those hips that spread out. The weather was warm for fall and he could tell that she didn't have much on underneath her light cotton dress. For a moment a sweet sensation swelled up within him.

"What's up?"

"They're worried about their jobs. Matata has been switching up and down the hall all morning and Ms. Giddy went into her office. I peeped into her room and she had her head on the table and was crying."

"I don't understand." She pressed the stop button on the Xerox machine. She whispered.

"Rumor has it that the Japanese went to make some changes around here. You know what they think of black people. Everybody knows how they treat their minorities, the Koreans and the Pakistanis. The Okinawans." Then, changing the subject, she said, "How was your annual trip to Europe?"

"Lovely. Wined and dined in Rome. Standing room only in Geneva." He went into the mailroom. Some secretaries were standing there, drinking coffee. When he entered they got real quiet. Then they broke into laughter. He figured that he knew what they were laughing at. Him. He ignored them.

He looked at his mail. Protest Japanese Invasion. The flyer said that a meeting would be held at the Sea Wolf Lounge that evening. It was signed by—by Robert Hurt! The academic post-hippie. One of these radicals with tenure!

chapter twenty-three

He went to Hurt's office. Hurt was listening to the FM radio. Some composer was talking. ". . . The piece might be called minimal because it's simple, repetitive, yet aggressive." Sounded like somebody pushing a new type of wine cooler.

"Hi, Bob."

"Yeah, hi," he said, looking up only fleetingly. Puttbutt wasn't his type of Negro. Hurt liked his blacks raw and ungenteel.

"This letter signed by you. I just wanted to see if it were true. I mean, you're one of the few humanists around here. I never expected to see your name on this blatantly racist document. You're always putting me down for my reactionary stances. And here you are. Signing this chauvinist document."

"When it's war, it's all hands on deck."

"What do you mean?

"It's just going too fast. A few months ago we were debating

about whether our admissions policy was unfair to Asians. Now the
Japanese have bought the school. If they want white men to be fair,
then they have to give us a little time to catch our breath. What's
going to happen to white men? And not only that, they're buying
think tanks, politicians. I mean, in a few years people in this country
will be speaking Japanese." I'm way ahead of you, Puttbutt thought.
"There won't be a place for us. They're already the biggest investors
in California. California is going to become a suburb of Tokyo.
What are they going to do with us. First they buy Radio City Music
Hall, the Empire State Building. Next thing you know, they'll be
leasing the White House to the president. When is it going to
end. Hell, this is nothing about multiculturalism versus high art or
Afrocentricity versus Eurocentricity. This is about civilization
against barbarism."

"But I thought that you were against Eurocentrism. You were the
one who helped the students get through their global requirement
courses. I was opposed to it."

"This is different."

"But what about your suspension of the Bass kid. That's what
caused the financial crisis in the first place. The university lost
Robert Bass, Sr., and the alumni's support.

"A mistake. Look, the kids and I have our differences, but the
things that join us are far stronger than those that separate us. I
mean, you didn't get mad. Why should I get mad. Why should I
stick out my neck for you. In fact, his group is going to serve as
bodyguards at the meeting tonight. You know, I had them all wrong.
Those SS uniforms and swastikas they parade around in? Kid's stuff.
Just a style. They call it nazi chic. Besides, what are you worrying
about this innocuous nazi paraphernalia. Haven't you heard? Nazism
is dead. Germany is reunified now. Anyway, the Nazis killed the
Jews. Not the blacks." That wasn't exactly true. Allied troops found
blacks imprisoned at Buchenwald. "I'm beginning to doubt whether
the holocaust took place. I never voiced such opinions before, but
now that I'm reunited with my brothers, I can say what I please."

"But, but you were the one who wrote that piece in the *Berkeley Espresso* saying that the left was riddled by anti-Semitism. Now you're sounding like that Frenchman, what's his name."

"La Pen. He has some good points. Besides, how do we know that the Jews haven't encouraged the Japanese to buy this school. To my way of thinking, the international Zionist bankers and the Japs have gotten together. They want to split up the West's institutions among them. Jack London goes to the Japs, the way I see it."

"I don't get it. You were going to suspend Bass Jr. on the basis of principles, now you're talking about joining those people."

"Are you coming tonight? We have a place for a black man like you. You know I attacked you in the campus paper about your book, *Blacks, America's Misfortune*. But now I think that you've raised some issues worthy of discussion. Like all of these single black women on welfare, for example. Fucking anything with pants on. Look, our group is color-blind. We could use somebody like you. An individual."

"I don't think so," Puttbutt said. He started out but then wheeled around. "I know that you're not like the rest of these fellows. Keeping everything in secret. Why was I turned down for tenure?"

"You'll get it eventually. I can tell you that the majority of those voting were on your side, but one of the speakers opposed your receiving the honor. Something you wrote," he said without looking up.

"Something I wrote?"

"Yeah. The old guard, the Miltonians, led by Professor Crabtree were bitterly opposed to it."

"Racists."

"Racists. Don't be paranoid. Professor Forrest died last year, leaving the department with one less Miltonian, and they want a Miltonian to take his place. You know that they're in a war with the deconstructionists, the feminists and the New Historicists." Did Puttbutt know. As a lone New Critic in the department he felt about as secure as a Gypsy in Czechoslovakia. The Miltonian bias against French theory and multiculturalism had been shaped by Milton. The prescient Milton warned about the seduction of the American critical fraternity by French theorists when he said, "Nor shall we then need the monsieurs of Paris to take our hopeful youth into their slight and prodigal custodies, and send them over back again transformed into mimics, apes, and kickshaws." Their feud with the multiculturalists was also Miltonic. For Milton, the leader of multiculturalism was Satan. "Besides, you're the one who wrote in the *New York Exegesis* that race was of declining significance, and that we were now in a color-blind society. Make up your mind, Puttbutt."

"Paranoid, huh. Well what about Marsha Marx. She told me that they weren't going to bring April Jokujoku out here, and I get an invitation to a party for April Jokujoku." Hurt sighed and leaned back in his chair.

"You black guys are always obsessing behind black feminists. Paranoid misogynists. April Jokujoku is just a better writer than you and all of those other black writers trying to threaten white males. Now if you'll excuse me, I have to make some calls. We have to get the press out tonight. Tell the word to the country. The invasion has begun."

"The Japanese couldn't be any worse than the people who are running things now," Chappie muttered.

"What did you say, Chappie?"

"Nothing." He had to keep his opinions to himself. It was a humiliation, but it was better than nothing. Hurt might tell the other racists on campus what he said. That after being double-crossed by white racists who played him like a violin, using him to front their side of the argument concerning affirmative action, minority enrollment, etc. that he was willing to try some new kind of racism, yellow racism.

Chappie went home and slept for the rest of the afternoon. He always handled stress like that. When the 7.2 struck, he slept for three days. The earthquake had left many Californians stressed out. One thing good had happened though. Dr. Yamato had canceled the Japanese lessons until further notice. Totemo Yokatta Desu, Puttbutt thought. He felt great. He wanted to continue the lessons but he needed a rest. They were in the middle of te verbs and nai verbs and you had to memorize the ones ending in consonants and vowels in order to know which endings they would take. He had been thinking about giving up. He never thought he'd appreciate English so much.

chapter twenty-four

For a week before the beginning of the fall semester, rumors flew across the campus. Everybody was talking about the quiet Japanese scholar who had moved into the president's home and who was running things until a permanent president could be found. The Japanese were minding their business, running the university, their public appearances as rare as those of Bigfoot. Even Effie, who knew everything, didn't know who he was. The African-American Studies department hadn't advised him as to whether he would be teaching. What would he do? This was the agony of the year-to-year appointment. Both departments pretended that his appointment was automatic, but he'd always have to go through the old runaround before getting his year-to-year papers signed. If he spoke to one of the good old boys and the GOB didn't answer, or answered him curtly, he took this as a sign that he'd been fired. If Obi or Ms. Marsha Marx didn't give him so much as a smile, he would worry for days. Obi was torturing him by holding up his contract. He couldn't report him to the union for fear of being against the brothers and sisters. Besides, the union was more interested in international left-wing issues than in the rights of the employees it was supposed to be representing. Hell, he'd heard that Daniel Ortega lived in one of the most expensive houses in Managua and owned a three-thousand-dollar watch. He couldn't understand why the Berserkley left were always supporting these Marxists who were doing better than they.

The English department and the African-American department were similar. They had a habit of weeding out dissidents. You just weren't rehired. They were both paralyzed by theory, too. A famous black feminist reflected the thinking in her remark that she was more interested in representations than in reality. (While thousands of black families were living out in the streets, the black intelligentsia at the *New York Exegesis* were obsessed with the questions of identity.) But nobody complained about these attitudes for fear of playing into the hands of the enemy (white people). Before his tenure denial he would have opposed such thinking. But now, he wasn't sure. He was beginning to see himself caught between the struggle between black and white nationalists, though the white ones didn't see themselves as such. Though black nationalism was seen as the only nationalism around, bitterly excoriated in the mass media, whites bonded with whites all the time. When a white was murdered or raped the story was played up by the victim's fellow whites in the press. Whites looked out for each other in business, politics and culture. Whites were even praised by white critics for "evolving" forms that blacks invented like the blues, rock and roll and jazz. The white government that begrudged every dime that was seen to go for the aid of blacks readily supported their fellow whites in Europe with a multibillion-dollar Marshall Plan. They sent relief to the Kurds after they had "won" the war against Saddam Hussein. Many blacks thought it was because, in the words of Lesley Stahl, some of the Kurds had blond hair and blue eyes. They were even considering sending billions of dollars to the whites in Russia, who had been their enemies for many years, even threatening them with annihilation. Blacks weren't the only ones who saw the new Russian–United States cooperation as an example of two Caucasian countries getting it together. Shintaro Ishihara said the same thing in *The Japan That Can Say NO.*

                        •   •   •

When Chappie wrote articles denouncing black nationalism the white nationalists who controlled the publications he wrote for happily published them. He could write about the humiliating experience he had working in a department dominated by black nationalists, Afrocentrics, and accuse them of thought control and the like. Before his tenure denial he wouldn't have hesitated. But now he didn't want to be seen as favoring one group of nationalists over the other. He thought that any kind of nationalism was for the birds, and usually led to struggles with groups different from the favored group and led to anti-Semitism since the Jews, being considered cosmopolitan and rootless, were seen as a threat to nationalists.

It was usually the whites and the blacks who were seeking separation from each other, though any examination of American culture would show that they couldn't do without each other and that the blacks had become a sort of Schmoo of American culture, Al Capp's creature, who was an all-purpose thing. You could hate it, love it, exploit it, despise it, enjoy it, eat it, wear it, wash with it, kick it around, feel it up, pat it down, and it would still be there for your use. Chappie wasn't for any group. He was for Chappie, which is what he meant when he was always referring to himself as an existentialist, the hip philosophy for the individualist. One day, after he became tired of waiting for Charles Obi to come to his office so that he could find out whether he'd be teaching, he decided to check out his mail in the Department of Humanity. There was a note instructing him to report to the president's house as soon as possible. Why would anybody be inviting him, a thirty-thousand-dollar-a-year lecturer, to the president's house? Maybe they were going to fire him. With trepidation and apprehension he started

toward the end of the campus where the president's two-million-
dollar house stood on a slope. In the distance he could see the
Golden Gate Bridge. Behind the house one could see the beautiful
Oakland Hills, where mansions stood and lavish homes of the cream
of Oakland society.

He had heard about the art collection that was on exhibit at the
president's office. Van Goghs, Gauguins, Monets and Renoirs, but
when he entered the house he discovered that all of this had been
removed. Japanese paintings hung where these modern paintings
used to hang. Dominating the wall was a painting divided by five
lines. It was done in dark and light greens, reds and oranges. Hundreds of soldiers, adorned in the armament that feudal Japan dressed
in for war, some of it so beautiful that it wasn't meant to be used in
battle (the Edo style), are engaged in battle. They fight in between
trees and in the foreground of mountains. He read the name of the
painting. "The Battle of Sekigahara, 1600." He gave the reception-
ist, a Japanese woman, his note. She picked up a phone and the
man on the other end said that he would see him. He went inside
of the office that he was directed to enter and saw the man sitting
behind the desk. He rose. It was Dr. Yamato! His Japanese teacher!
    "Puttbutt-san, O-genki desu ka," the doctor said, bowing. The
president's desk had been replaced and what appeared to be an
ancient hand-carved Japanese desk was in its place. Some paintings
from the Kano and the Tosa school hung on the wall. One was by
the great flower painter, Hanabusa. Hana was the Japanese name
for flower.
    "Genki, desu," Puttbutt said, surprised. Staggering from surprise.
I'm sorry, he said. Dr. Yamato looked at him and said, "Hai." Dr.
Yamato smiled. He couldn't believe it. He'd never seen Dr. Yamato
smile. It was like seeing the Ayatollah Khomeini smile.
    "Where is the president?"
    "He's retired to the Ozarks," Dr. Yamato said. In that halting
but steady manner of his.

"What? The president went without a fight?"

"He's like these other greedy American executives. He wanted us to give him a golden parachute. But there was a matter of this two-million-dollar home, and the unauthorized purchase of cars for some of the big wheels in the administration. Seems that he brought his ugly arbitraging methods into the university." Dr. Yamato, wearing that same old black woolen suit, walked to the window.

"You Amerikans pay your executives too much money, that's part of the problem here. Waste. You're over your heads in credit. Each American should be limited to two credit cards, and you should take rapid transit and stop consuming so much energy. BART de Ikimasu. The school is suffering from budget cuts and this man was being chauffeured around in a limousine. Needless to say, he went quietly. Your vice president, Whitherspoon, has been forced into retirement too. Allowed these various factions of ruffians to run this school. The FF and the skinheads. They've taken control of the place. We're going to take this campus back. There are going to be many changes around here." Dr. Yamato had a glint in his eye. "I'm going to need your help."

"My help? But I'm just a lowly lecturer. Why would you need my help?"

"I need somebody with whom I can communicate. Somebody that I can trust." When he said that, Puttbutt knew that the $245.00 he paid to learn Japanese by Spring had been worth it.

PART

Three

●

chapter twenty-five

Yes. The reason that the Americans are so backward is because of what they call their core curriculum. Changes are in order. We will help them. Try to civilize them. Show them that there are some things that all educated people must know in order to be culturally literate. Get them to realize that there's more to life than Captain Video. Your president, how do you suppose he was spending his time. Chotto Matte Kudasai." Dr. Yamato rose and went into an adjoining room. Puttbutt wondered would Yamato ever change those frumpy clothes of his. The black suit. The hat. The beat-up briefcase. He'd probably abandon the limousine that had been made available to him. Yamato would probably still take BART and remain in his office during lunch hours, eating bowl after bowl of noodles.

On the wall was a print of a sushi by Yoshitoshi. Blood was pouring from the sushi's wounds but he stoically ate his rice cake. Just before Dr. Yamato reentered the room carrying a box, Chappie glanced at a newspaper clipping that lay on his desk. It showed a photo of Kazumi Tajiri, who was identified as a subchief of a small right-wing political group. He was a suspect in the shooting of the mayor of Nagasaki, Hitoshi Motoshima. The mayor had criticized Emperor Hirohito for being responsible for World War II. Yamato opened some of the boxes. Racing magazines. Playgirl centerfolds. It was full of whiskey bottles. Jack Daniel's. There was another huge stack of *National Enquirers* and *Star*. A newspaper bore the headlines about an ailing JFK, from the secret place he had been kept since he was wounded in Dallas, commenting about the direction the family's morality was taking and denying his liaison with Marilyn Monroe. Dr. Yamato shook his head in disgust.

"He was little more than a cash cow for the Bass group, hired to lure funds to the school. We also discovered that he was using funds from government research grants to buy first-class theater tickets, flowers for his women and for entertainment."

"What kind of changes are you going to make, Doctor."

"Many of your colleagues will not be coming back."

"I don't follow, Dr. Yamato."

"We're going to close down the Department of Humanity and move it into Ethnic Studies. You have African Studies, Chicano Studies, Asian-American Studies, Native-American Studies and African-American Studies. We will have a new department, European Studies, with the same size budget and faculty as the rest. My backers would like to eliminate all of these courses which allow for so much foolishness, but they also want to show to the faculty and students how conciliatory we are. We will allow for these frills. Are they really necessary? All they accomplish for these people is to glorify some mythic past and to promote such dubious claims that Europe is the birthplace of science, religion, technology and philosophy. I've been reading this so-called philosopher, Plato. All about such foolishness as to whether the soul has immortality. What nonsense. Hegel and the rest are full of such nonsense also. This ignorant man maintained that the Chinese had no philosophy. What rubbish.

No wonder the Americans can't make a decent automobile. Their intellectuals spend all of their time on these fuzzy and useless Greeks and German idealists. If one were to apply the empirical razor to all of these so-called theories, the entire history of Western philosophy could be covered in one week. Also, I am considering dropping the inordinate number of courses devoted to the work of John Milton. My staff has checked his character's background. He spent some time in jail, you know. We do not think it appropriate to include courses about an ex-convict in our catalog. That also goes for pederasts. We found out that his nickname at Cambridge was The Lady."

"I'll have to think about it, Dr. Yamato."

"Now, I want you to see your new office."

"My what?"

"Your new office." The Japanese woman showed him to a spacious office. There were other Japanese moving about the building; files were being taken out in boxes. He could see all the way down to San Mateo. He just sat there for a while. He picked up the right-wing student newspaper. Dean Hurt's picture was on the cover. He was speaking to a rally of faculty and students, mostly white, who were complaining about the undue pressure on the university that this mysterious Japanese money, as they called it, would pose. Hurt was shaking his fist in the manner of Lenin in a picture he'd once seen. He went over to the literature division of the Department of Humanity to start packing the office that he shared with three other lecturers. On the way, he saw Professor Crabtree who tried to manage a weak smile. He smiled back. Professor Crabtree had always ignored him and now he was trying to be friends? What was that all about, Puttbutt thought.

chapter twenty-six

The Department of Humanity had gotten the word to clear out, though they didn't know where they were going to go. Dr. Yamato had recommended that they hold classes in some of the coffee shops located near the campus until some space could be found. The atmosphere was gloomy. He noticed among their boxes one entitled CONFIDENTIAL FILES. He went over and picked it up. One of the secretaries saw, and protested.

"Mr. Puttbutt, you can't touch those boxes." It was the Latino woman who worked in the office. She came on to the white men, affecting a Billy Burke type musicality in her voice when relating to them, cozying all up to them. She treated Puttbutt and even some of the Latino males on the staff shabbily. He picked it up anyway.

"But . . ." She tried to block him from leaving the department.

"It's all right," the chairperson said, sighing. "He's working in the president's house with Dr. Yamato." The chairperson, Dr. Milch, could hardly conceal his annoyance but tried to be pleasant.

"Thank you," Puttbutt said.

"Chappie, may I talk with you for a moment?" He put the box down and followed him into his former office. He glanced at the boxes full of books and papers. A family photo was sticking out of a box. Some back issues of the *New York Review of Books* were lying on his desk. Keys. A memo pad.

"I'm disappointed in you, Chappie. Consorting with this Yamato character, this creature. Besides, you're the second most powerful person on this campus. The first time that a black has achieved such status. The job should have gone to a black woman." He was raising his voice. Puttbutt hated for people to raise their voices. Perhaps it was because during his early years people were constantly barking at him. Shouting into his face like the character played by Lou Gossett, Jr., in *An Officer and a Gentleman.*

"What?" Puttbutt was surprised at Milch's fury. Milch began moving toward him from behind his desk. The guy was breathing heavily and stammering.

"You black guys had your chance. Wright and Baldwin were once the canon, but Zora overthrew them. Sent them hurling from the literary firmament. Cast them down. The fact that they would choose you, a black man, instead of a black woman shows how backward these Japanese are."

"Mr. Milch if you and your colleagues don't like Mr. Yamato then I'm sure that some other universities would be interested in your candidacy. Besides, the black and Chicano men are always complaining about your favoritism."

"I don't follow."

"They say that you encourage them to enter the master's program while you're always setting aside positions for the women in the Ph.D. program."

"Women have been held back. They need more encouragement. You black fellows are the worst offenders. Black women writers say that black men mistreat their wives and the wives throw them out."

"That's what I thought it was about. Well, if you're a feminist, then why can't I be a masculinist? Do you need for me to send some more boxes over or may I offer you some assistance in packing your things?" His pale face lit up like a fire. He left him that way. Glaring at him, angrily. He never thought he'd hear himself say those words. What was coming over him. His grandfather could be right. That you couldn't expect a fair deal with whites. As soon as Puttbutt got to his old office, a crummy ill-lit room which he shared with other lecturers, including two TAs, who received more respect than he, he opened the files. He removed his. He read the confidential report on his tenure. Apparently he had some support, but the Miltonians had been rallied by Crabtree who had fought against Puttbutt's candidacy citing the article he had written many years ago in which he said that Shakespeare's *Othello* was racist. He'd forgotten all about it. It was his master's thesis. Written when he was in his Black Power period. Nobody discussed racism anymore. Racism was something that blacks had made up in order to make whites feel guilty, so the line went. Puttbutt had learned the argument well. He used it. Published articles about how blacks couldn't seem to get it together. The *New York Exegesis* even considered him for a seat on its editorial board. All sorts of foundations offered him fellowships for using this line. He'd hoped nobody would ever find it, but apparently it had been shown to the members of the tenure committee. He didn't have anything to lose now. Dr. Yamato had sent them packing.

chapter twenty-seven

His picture was on the cover of the *Sun Reporter*. Puttbutt named special assistant to the acting president of Jack London College, the story announced. People were lined up outside his office door. Matata Musomi, who said on some resumes that he had attended Oxford, and others that he'd attended Cambridge, was there; he looked up from the European newspaper at Puttbutt with sarcasm in his eyes. Charles Obi brought his greasy smile. He took Crabtree first. Crabtree gave him a watermelon grin.

If Crabtree had been a hat wearer, he would have been holding his hat gingerly in hand. The corners of his mouth pushed back into a huge smile, revealing some very expensive dental work. He looked around the office. He must have been impressed. The sleek Japanese furniture. Paintings on the wall. The view of the Pacific. The grand light shafting in.

"What can I do for you, Professor Crabtree?" Puttbutt said, leaning back in his chair, his hands supporting his head. He tried not to rub it in, considering the reversal of fates. Professor Crabtree paused for a moment before speaking. Finally, with a good deal of effort:

"I know you must be surprised that I came in today. After the rude way I've always treated you."

"You have been rude, Professor."

"I . . . I'm not the most pleasant person in the world, but once you get to know me I, I play a good game of poker. You play poker?"

"Come to the point, Professor. Dr. Yamato has a great deal of work for me to do. He wants all of us to husband our time. He feels that Americans waste too much time."

"You heard about what happened over in the Department of Humanity. Seems to have been a big shake-up. I understand that the English and poetics departments have been moved to Ethnic Studies. Anglo-Saxon Studies. From Chaucer to the Beatles."

"That's right."

"A lot of my colleagues, including myself, are, well, you know, concerned about our status."

"I did hear something to that effect, Professor. What do you want me to do about it?"

"I . . . well, it seems that you have some pull with that Japanese chap."

"Dr. Yamato."

"Yes, that's his name."

"Dr. Yamato and I decided that it would be wasting money to keep people on the staff whose courses were drawing only a few students. Your Sir John Suckling seminar and the course in Old Norse. There are only three students attending. The Japanese don't like to waste money." The professor didn't say anything. "And, you haven't published a book or an article in fifteen years, and the articles that you have published show considerable borrowing."

"I . . . just haven't had the time. I . . ."

"I know. Going to these Humanity conventions which provide you with an opportunity to meet women other than your wife, and to sample exotic cuisine. Why your professional organization's program included more information on the restaurants in Chinatown than on the topics when it met last year in San Francisco. I also found out, Professor, that it was you who was instrumental in getting my tenure denied."

"Who told you that? That's supposed to be a secret."

"I took the liberty of looking at my confidential files."

"But you're not supposed to look at those files! They're off-limits." He began to rise from his chair until it apparently occurred to him that he didn't have the clout he once had. "Your article on *Othello*, I felt, wasn't first-rate. Your thesis that race relations in this country haven't changed since Shakespeare's time. The play was written in sixteen-three. That's preposterous. And to call Shakespeare a racist is really overdoing it, don't you think? What claptrap!" Crabtree squirmed in his chair as he said "claptrap."

"I wrote it during my Black Power days."

"Cockamamie detritus."

"Oh, is it now?" Puttbutt didn't feel like defending a paper he had written years before, but he was irritated by the imperious tone now creeping into Crabtree's voice. He stood and leaned on the desk, staring right into Crabtree's eyes. Crabtree recoiled.

"The only thing that has changed is that thick lips are in now. All of these white women desiring lip enhancement operations," Puttbutt said. Even saying that gave him relief.

"Come now, Professor Puttbutt." Crabtree smiled wryly.

"Shakespeare makes Othello into a primitive. He's warlike. His moods change rapidly. His anger is always on the surface, ready to burst. It arises from a 'hollow' hell. And the character, Othello, is always down on himself. He says in act 2, scene 3, 'I am black/And have not those soft parts of conversation/That chamberers have.' Why would a general, a man of war, especially an African, be so down on himself. African warriors see themselves as the cock of the walk. They have these griots who follow them around like Bundini Brown, telling them how great they are. Shakespeare also promotes a common belief among white men that they can have any woman of any background, but when a black man and a woman of another race get together the motive has to be perverse. You white men can have all of the women you want, while anytime a black man and a white woman fall in love it's because, according to Shakespeare, she's enchanted by him. The black has put some kind of spell on her, or she is fascinated by his oppression. What incredible ego. Shakespeare believed that the only uncorrupted interracial relationship can be that between a white man and a colored woman."

"William Shakespeare didn't have a racist bone in his body. Surely you're projecting." Puttbutt rose and went to the window. He looked down. A white fraternity had set up a platform. Some of the pledges had painted their faces black. One large white boy had put on the mammy attire. Head rag. Red and white polka-dot dress. Huge pillows for breasts. The "slaves" were being auctioned off to the older brothers. This was the fraternity's Annual Slave Day. Despite Dr. Yamato's memo to all of the departments and to the students that racism would be punished severely, the overt racist acts were continuing with broad support from the media, who were insisting that these young bigots be allowed to "express themselves." It was the target of their abuse, the media and the corporate-financed think tanks were saying, who were the real oppressors. They were accused of insisting that everyone be politically correct.

"You blacks are always complaining about racism. Racism this and racism that. You use racism to explain away your failure. All of this talk about racism on the campus of Jack London. I've been teaching here for thirty years and have never found a single instance. Do you hear? A single instance. And now you have to reach back and drag Shakespeare into it. Is there no end to you people's paranoia? Now you have some sort of code that makes it an offense to call someone a nigger. Why that word doesn't bother me at all." While Crabtree was speaking, Puttbutt was thumbing through a copy of *Othello* that had been left behind in Whitherspoon's hurried attempt to clear his former office.

"Scene 3, Othello's speech, 'She loved me for the dangers I had pass'd, And I loved her that she did pity them.' "

"Doesn't prove a thing."

"He paints Othello as a noble savage."

"Where? Where did you find evidence of that?"

" 'The Moor is of a free and open nature,/That thinks men honest that but seem to be so,/And will as tenderly be led by the nose/As asses are.' When's the last time you read the play, Professor?"

"I . . . I—"

"And if you don't think that Shakespeare's play can be applied to contemporary situations, what about the character of Emilia, a racist feminist?"

"Feminism in Shakespeare's time. You are stretching things, Puttbutt."

"Act 3, scene 4, Emilia says, speaking of men: 'Tis not a year on two shows us a man;/They are all but stomachs, and we all but food;/They eat us hungerly, and when they are full/ They belch us.' Certainly some misandry reflected in that speech, Professor Crabtree. As for racism, in act 5 she calls Othello a 'black devil.' There are many feminists on Jack London's campus who could be Emilia."

"But I thought you were on their side."

"I'm on my side, Mr. Crabtree. My side." He studied Crabtree's face. He couldn't believe what he said. He was sounding like his father. Accepting his father's vision of the world. As a battleground between the strong and the weak. His countenance flagged for a moment before reassuming his supercilious demeanor. Like many Eurocentric professors, as they were being called in the newspapers, he regarded Shakespeare as little more than a cultural hammer to be used to intimidate the infidels. So busy counting iambic pentameter, they'd never taken Shakespeare at his word. They could read *The*

Merchant of Venice and *Othello* without taking into account what some of the characters and the language meant to Jews and to blacks.

"You've been here thirty years, Crabtree. That counts for something. Maybe we can work something out. It's not like the old days when you only needed to know Greek, Latin, English and French. Dr. Yamato is requiring that every faculty member study Japanese." Crabtree turned from his usual chalk white to red. He wished that he could read his thoughts. He threw one of the copies of *Japanese by Spring* that lay in a stack on his desk at Crabtree. Crabtree caught it, examined it and then threw it to the floor.

"How about teaching a course in freshman composition."

"Composition. That's preposterous, a man of my rank."

"Suit yourself."

"You'd better respect your betters, young man. I was teaching the Milton seminar when you were in high school. Don't you forget." Puttbutt glanced at a sheet of paper on his desk. "Two students."

"What?"

"You had exactly two students enrolled in that course on Middle English. Dr. Yamato believes that such courses constitute Anglo-Saxon ethnic cheerleading and feelgoodism. It has to be freshman composition or nothing." Crabtree rose. He stood there staring at Puttbutt for a moment. The anger contorted his face. He finally spun around and left the room in a huff. Puttbutt shrugged his shoulders.

chapter twenty-eight

The dark European was rubbernecking. This was a quiet California street, but he could imagine the local primitives staring out from behind their blinds like the invisible savages in a Hollywood movie, spying upon a caravan whose inhabitants were unaware of their presence. Herman Melville said that the true savages were not located in West Africa, but in the suburbs of upstate New York. That was becoming true of the American suburbs. Though Puttbutt pushed the media line that the inner cities were the Paradise Lost part of the American Dream, and that blacks needed to change, to become self-reliant, and to be more responsible, he knew from talking to his white students that drugs, alcoholism, incest, spousal abuse, child abuse, violence, fractured families were widespread in American society, extended beyond the city limits into Paradise Regained. One of the jobs of the media was to protect white America, its customers, from their devils. They must be seen as selfless stewards presiding over a society overrun by blacks, Latins and yellows, engaged in "a tangle of pathologies." Though 12 percent of those arrested for looting—including Santa Monica yuppies—during the Great Los Angeles Uprising of 1992 were white, the pictures of whites were associated with cleaning the streets after the chaos.

The object of his neighbor's gaze was a white stretch limousine easing up in front of his house. Robert Bass got out, a middle-aged man, well tanned and fit. He was with his son, Robert Bass, Jr. Bass Jr. had gotten rid of his neonazi uniform and was wearing a blue blazer and white slacks and black hosiery. His hair was beginning to grow back. It was combed and neatly parted. They came up the steps. Knocked on his door. He could imagine the shocked neighbors. He opened the door.

"Yes." He pretended that he didn't know who Bass Sr. was, but he'd often seen his photo on the society page.

"Mr. Puttbutt?"

"That's right?"

"My name is Robert Bass." Puttbutt shook his hand warmly. "Of course, you know this asshole. My son." Robert Bass, Jr., stared at his shoes, shined to a black gloss. Then he looked up at Puttbutt.

He was really hurting. Puttbutt could tell that the old man was sore with Bass Jr.

"I'm glad to meet you. Won't you come in." They followed him into the living room. His Japanese texts were lying on the table. He offered them tea in Japanese. He made some kocha (black tea) and poured it all around. The young Bass was very silent. Whenever Puttbutt would look his way, the young Bass's eyes would retreat.

"What can I do for you, Mr. Bass?"

"I just want to apologize for my son. He was mixed up with the wrong crowd, but we're hoping that it's a passing thing. Hell, I hadn't been following the little bastard. Found all kinds of nazi paraphernalia in his room. I gave him a beating he'll never forget. Just to think, we licked those bastards back in forty-five, and my own son, a kraut lover. As for his complaints about affirmative action, his high school grades were so low that it was only my influence that got the rascal into London anyway. He's been kicked out of every boarding school in the West. Thought he'd be an upstanding college man like me. Why I was captain of the Berkeley rowing team in '39. Used to participate in the races at Lake Merritt."

"I'm sorry, Mr. Puttbutt. How can I ever make it up to you?" the Bass boy said. Puttbutt almost fell out of his chair.

"I told him that we'll cut him out of his inheritance if he doesn't find some way to make amends." It was rumored that Bass Sr. was worth about ten million. "And I hope you don't have any hard feelings about my role in this matter, Mr. Puttbutt. If I had any idea of the racist hell that my son and his friends were putting you through, I would have sent his ass to military school. You know, we're not a very close family. I'm always in the Lear. Trying to bring the free-market ideas to the underprivileged areas of the world, I haven't had a chance to attend to my responsibilities as a parent. But I think we've come upon a solution."

"What is that, Mr. Bass?"

"We want him to wait on you hand and foot. Sort of like doing community service."

"I'm at your beck and call, Mr. Puttbutt. I'll do whatever it takes to make it up to you."

"We want to install a phone direct to your house and the little son of a bitch will have to be your servant. Now let's talk business. I know that you're in touch with some powerful Japanese people. What ya say you introduce me to some of them. Come over to the club." Robert Bass, Sr., was leaning toward Puttbutt now. Sort of man-to-man. This club had been in the news for years for not admitting blacks.

"That may be a good idea, Mr. Bass."

"Hell, I have to go with the flow in order to remain in business."

"That's the way it looks, huh Mr. Bass?"

"This Yamato chap. How do you know him?"

"He's my teacher."

"You study Japanese, Mr. Puttbutt?"

"Yes. It's like mental push-ups. In fact, I have a little reading material for you." Puttbutt reached into a box and handed Bass Sr. a copy of JBS. Bass Sr. accepted the book with a smile.

"Mind if I have one, Professor Puttbutt?" Puttbutt handed one to Junior.

"I'll have my secretary call you next week, maybe your Japanese friends can meet us over to the club. I've reserved a private room there. They have a tennis court. Maybe your friend likes to play tennis. Sauna. Anything. You tell Dr. Yamato that Bass and Co. is at his service. My son is at your service." He frowned at his son.

"Professor Puttbutt . . ."

"Yes, Robert?" The three stood. Robert Bass Jr.'s voice was trembling. He broke down and began to cry. He put his arms around Puttbutt's neck and cried on his shoulder. Puttbutt kept his hands at his side as he'd been taught by his parents. Sort of at a parade rest position. He had been taught to be undemonstrative. Puttbutt was embarrassed. He tried to put himself in the kid's place. If he were about to lose on ten million dollars, he'd crying too. The kid stepped back.

"I have a gift," he said. He placed a fancy package on the table.

The company parted. The old nosey neighbor next door couldn't stand it. The sucker had moved outside and was pretending to trim the bushes. The Basses got into their white stretch limousine and eased on down the street. The neighbor's blond, blue-eyed wife was staring at Puttbutt. She was wearing her gardening shorts. She was, as the Nihon-jin would say, so-so. Her husband looked at her and then to Puttbutt; he began snapping at twigs angrily. Puttbutt went inside and opened the package. The gift from Bass Jr.; the very individual who had been making his life so hard. It was a beautiful sweater. Made in Bologna.

chapter twenty-nine

The changes on Jack London campus were occurring quickly. He'd become adjusted to his new position as assistant to the acting president and was kept busy in his new office. A lot of people came to ask him for requests and advice. People who had formerly treated him like shit. He felt like Pirate Jenny in Kurt Weill's *Threepenny Opera*. He gave them all a copy of the text *Japanese by Spring*. Dr. Yamato permitted some of them to retire without problems, others protested. He was walking up the hill toward work when he saw some commotion going on in front of the campus entrance. It was Robert Hurt. He was haranguing some of the students. His listeners were mostly white, but there was also a sprinkling of some yellows, browns and blacks. Led by Hurt they had presented Dr. Yamato with their demands. He was in Dr. Y's office when he received them. Dr. Y had smiled contemptuously, balled the paper on which the list was written in his fist, and flung it into the wastepaper basket.

Hurt looked as though he hadn't slept in days and had taken a lot of drugs. His speech was incoherent and rambling. He was attacking the Japanese character and made other scurrilous remarks about Japanese culture and values. He spotted Puttbutt.

"And there he is now. Chappie Puttbutt. Not only is he a traitor to white people, but to blacks as well. Let's get him." Puttbutt began to trot toward his office at the end of the campus. Some of the students who were passing on their way to and from class paused to watch this strange sight. The third world nationalists were calling him a banana. Robert Bass Jr.'s former friends, who were providing some sort of protection for Hurt, were also in pursuit as well as some of Hurt's listeners. Just as one of them began to catch up with him, as he ran near the Student Union, which was built along the architectural lines of London's Klondike Cabin, he noticed a line of men dressed in black and assuming a martial arts position. Hurt and his followers halted. Assessed the situation, and retreated. Bass's ex-allies, however, stood their ground. They were daring the men who were dressed in quiet suits, ties and shoes. The leather-jacketed Amerikaners moved toward the men. Suddenly there were some swift movements. Legs flying. Hands chopping. A knife flashed. After a fierce and murderous melee that lasted less than sixty seconds, Bass's former allies were lying on the ground moaning. Wounded. Those who weren't began hightailing it from the campus. The arrogant yellow-haired youth who'd assisted Bass Jr. in making Puttbutt's life miserable was spitting out some teeth. His mouth was bloodied and he was bawling and screaming. These ruffians finally received their comeuppance, Puttbutt thought. He walked past the men, who were brushing off their clothes and straightening their ties. Some of them were Japanese, a few were black. They behaved as though nothing happened. Domo Arigato, he said. The men bowed. Two of them followed him to his office and stationed themselves outside his door. Were these the extra measures that Yamato had in mind when he said that he would bring order and stability to the campus? The phone rang. Effie Singleton told him that April was at the airport and there was nobody there to greet her. African-American Studies were undergoing a transition and considering

Marsha Marx's new status, nobody had advised April that her services were no longer needed. Ms. Jokujoku was demanding a chauffeur-driven limousine and police escort to bring her to the university, after which she wanted Indian food and a massage. He told the secretary to tell Ms. Jokujoku to take the next plane back to New York. That there had been changes on campus and that he would have somebody write her a letter that would tell her what's what.

"Marsha Marx is out here in the lobby," Effie Singleton said. Marsha came into the office. He could tell that she was angry.

"What can I do for you?" he said.

"This is what you can do for me." She handed him the letter informing the Women's Studies department that they had to move their things into the new Ethnic Studies department, the Department of European Studies. She was leaning on his desk and stamping her feet.

"You're moving us over there with those patriarchal pigs?"

"I'll be frank about it, Marsha. The new owners of the university have decided to cut back on the budget. The Women's Studies department is merely a front for European Studies. You said so yourself." Puttbutt picked up a sheet of paper that was lying on his desk. "Europe is the source of our law, our values, and our culture, yet little had been done to recognize the role of women, the establishment of this great civilization," he quoted from an MLA speech she'd made. "The way we see it, there's no significant difference between your aims and those of your patriarchal allies. You just wanted in. What we've decided to do in European Studies is to hire fifty percent men and fifty percent women. That should satisfy you."

"What?"

"Look, European Studies is just one of the many departments on this campus. Things have changed." Puttbutt was becoming impatient with his colleagues.

"The members of my department insist upon working in a male-free department," she said. She was furious.

"If you feel that way why don't you move your people to Mills? As long as this is a coed college we will not tolerate any separation between the sexes."

"But Chappie, I thought you were different from the rest. Sympathetic to the goals of women."

"I am. But my mother raised me not to take any flak from anybody, man or woman. She is an expert on the choke hold. I've always disagreed with her and my father. They told me that the world was a scumbag. They told me that every day would be war. But I didn't believe them. I always supported you but then I discovered from the confidential files that you assisted the Miltonians in getting my tenure denied. You wanted to bring April out here to get the tenure that I was denied, while all along assuring me that this wasn't your aim."

"But you understand, don't you? We just wanted one of our own. Besides . . ."

"Besides, what?"

"Our study group discovered that you once rented a porno movie."

"What?" He'd forgotten all about it. He had rented some combo films in connection with a study on fascism and pornography after reading that white male neonazis were fascinated by porno films that featured black and interracial sex. Really got off from these films. According to *Spy* magazine, David Duke owns one of the prime collections. Wouldn't you know.

"You checked out my movie rentals. But you're the ones who are always insisting on the right to privacy."

"The private is the political. You men do all of your oppression in the dark. It is our right to shine a light upon your black deeds."

"Well what about women and pornography. Half the people who rent porno movies are women. *Playgirl* has six hundred thousand subscribers. What are you going to do with them?"

"Look, Chappie." Softer now, pleading. "We should be on the same side. United in our fight against white male patriarchy and its control and manipulation of modes of production. Both sexism and racism are equal contradictions."

"Oh yeah, then explain to me why black and brown women are worse off than white women. Why there are few women of color in the main feminist organizations and why the black and brown women are always accusing you of racism. One of the reasons you wanted to bring April in was to stifle the criticism that your department includes few women of color. Besides, you're looking out for yourself. I'm going to look out for me. And I'll tell you what. A lot of black men and white men are getting sick of your double-dealing opportunistic feminist bullshit. I'm also sick and tired of you comparing your situation with that of blacks. I'm sick of gays and the rest of them doing it too. Gays have more money and jobs as a group than black people ever will, yet all we hear about are these middle-class women and their eating disorders, when millions of women and children have nothing to eat. You don't jump on men of your background as much as you do the fellas. You lynched Clarence Thomas. You white gender-first feminists in the media and on the campuses have gone Clarence Thomas crazy. What do you want from the man?" He thought that he knew. "The only difference between you and the women in the Klan is that the women in the Klan dress better."

"Chappie. What happened to you? It was only last year that Women's Studies ranked you as among the ten male instructors on campus who were sensitive to women's needs. It must be the Japanese. How can you work for those men. The way they treat their women. They used the women in Korea as comfort girls during the war. And why aren't they among the other Ethnic Studies departments?"

"The Japanese feel that they've been at the civilizing business longer than the rest. They feel that all culture and knowledge emanates from their islands. And that's why they've created a new Department of Universal Studies. They feel that Japanese culture should be emulated by the world."

"But that's the most Asianocentric garbage. Married men with geishas. They're so homogeneous."

Homogeneous. Homogeneous. Puttbutt was having a humongous pain from this word. This word was making a real nuisance of itself. Showing up in studies and magazine articles. He hated the word as much as he hated hegemony. Paradigm. Discourse.

"You white people make me sick with your homogeneity. You're the ones who are into some kind of narrow-assed homogeneity. The Japanese language includes thirty-five thousand characters of Chinese language. Kanji. They have Korean components in their culture. They absorbed English during the occupation. They have a special Katakana set aside for English. They read books by Western writers. They trade with the world. And you call them homogeneous. You're the ones who are homogeneous. No matter how high a white may rise in this society's intellectual circles, with few exceptions they're still monolingual and culturally restricted crackers. You are the ones who want everybody to be like you, through your enforced assimilation. You—"

"Chappie, what's wrong with you? I've never heard you talk this way. Your white friends are beginning to worry about you these days. You sound so, so bitter. So angry. These windy incoherent diatribes. These Japanese chauvinists must be getting to you." He tossed her a copy of *Japanese by Spring*. She caught it. She had a surprised look.

Marsha's mouth ruled her face. Sometimes, it seemed as though it ruled her. It was like the hand in *The Beast with Five Fingers*. Like the maniac killer's limb in *Body Parts*, her mouth seemed as though it were independent of the face. It had a life of its own. Thought processes of its own. It was like the act he'd seen on the Ed Sullivan show. A Spanish ventriloquist shaped his hand into a mouth. The mouth was like a little human with its own eyes. Her twisting, flat red mouth slashed and burned men. Pale gates through which dry cutting words flew. He'd seen the mouth in action. Spewing language in rapid-fire bursts. Mowing down whatever man found himself unlucky enough to be in its way.

But jobs were hard to find these days. So dire was the job market that whites, some of whom had criticized multiculturalism formerly, were boning up on Native American literature and Latino literature and becoming experts on these disciplines so that they might find teaching jobs. Though Richard Bernstein, a *New York Times* critic, was writing yet another book—a book that was supported by a fellowship from the Freedom Forum—arguing that multiculturalism benefited African Americans, Asian Americans, Hispanics and Native Americans, only whites were the ones who were making the big dollars from this burgeoning industry. Though some were sincere and qualified, others were merely out to improve their incomes, during the era of George Herbert Hoover. The American Cultures program at Berkeley was inaugurated after student demands that the university become more multicultural. With the American Cultures program, the university was requiring that each student take at least one course in ethnic culture before graduating. This program was being ridiculed as a black giveaway program by D'Gun ga Dinza and other anti-diversity personalities in Eastern think tanks. Ishmael Reed attended a meeting of American Cultures Fellows at the University of California at Berkeley. After reading the Bernstein proposal, he thought that he'd find a room full of brothers and sisters. He and one other black man were the only "people of color" present. Those who were benefiting the most from multiculturalism, in this room, were white women. One white woman asked another, who was addressing the group, her advice about what to do if a "third world" student challenged her authority to teach a multicultural course without her having experienced oppression in her background. She was advised to tell her students that multicultural people weren't the only people who were oppressed. She said that an unwanted sibling had it just as bad as a "person of color." Hmmmmmmm, Ishmael Reed thought. Gerald

Ford was an unwanted sibling and he became president of the United States.

The millions of dollars that were going to multiculturalism were being exploited by some whites in another way. He was told by a person in Berkeley's American Cultures office that some departments were taking the funds earmarked for multicultural courses and transferring these funds to the traditional-courses budget. This is the irony. While neoconservative Eastern intellectuals, fearful that re-ethnicity would reveal their having undergone an identity transplant (many of those who were writing angry op-eds about black culture had changed their names), were pushing back-to-basics and denouncing multiculturalism as an infidel movement, millions of multicultural dollars were being spent on traditional courses. How did Don King put it? Only in America.

Marsha Marx was mad. Her mouth looked as though it would leap from her face and give him a good mouth-smacking. His skin began to crawl. But the mouth held its place. Marsha wanted to keep her job and Chappie Puttbutt was doing the hiring and the firing. He remembered the expression that Colin Powell used during the Gulf War. About bringing all of the tools to the party. That's what he, Puttbutt, was doing. His parents were right. Life was war. And on this campus, he was second in command.

"If you're going to remain on this campus you'd better start to get down with some of these Japanese verbs."

Marsha was silent for a moment. "Chappie, do you know what you are, you're a reactionary asshole."

Puttbutt leaned back in his chair. "Ms. Marx, without the asshole, human life would cease to exist."

She left, slamming the door.

chapter thirty

The next day he walked into his outer office to see Dr. Crabtree sitting. "Ohayogozaimasu, Effie."

"Ohayogozaimasu, Chappie-san Ikaga Desuka." Effie was practicing her Japanese. He pretended as though Dr. Crabtree wasn't even there. As Puttbutt began to enter his office, Dr. Crabtree cleared his throat.

"Professor Puttbutt . . ." Puttbutt turned.

"Oh, yes Dr. Crabtree, what can I do for you?"

"About that composition course." Effie paused and looked up from her computer.

"Maybe I was a little too hasty, but it's been a long time since I taught freshman English."

"Who said anything about freshman English. We want to teach freshman Yoruba."

"Freshman Yoruba?"

"Of course. We've decided that we're going to take advantage of your knowledge of this West African language." Puttbutt lifted a copy of a local magazine that had carried an article by Crabtree denouncing Afrocentricity and multiculturalism. It was full of the usual neoconservative cusswords. Balkanization this. Quotas that. Two neoconservative hitmen had been accused of lifting, word-for-word, an article written by other neoconservatives. There was so much duplication in these articles, Puttbutt wondered how they could tell. It was almost a formula. He knew the formula well. Say that the blacks were lowering the standards of American education. Jimmy some facts about test scores. Argue that the blacks desired multicultural education because they couldn't cut it with the tough

Eurocentric curriculum. Justify the Eurocore curriculum by arguing that American liberal values arise from the West. Wind it up with a plea for a common culture (white) and suggest that any deviation from this would lead to balkanization. The neoconservative and conservative media were shooting at what they called the threat to Western civilization, taking the most extreme positions as an excuse to denounce the whole thing. The "MacNeil-Lehrer Newshour," which was a sort of war room against multiculturalism, feeding verbatim propaganda from right-wing think tanks and calling it news, reached what was a how-low-can-you-get moment when they ran a report that included two Oakland children denouncing those adults who had opposed the textbooks from Houghton Mifflin that were considered racist. Stereotyping and cartooning the opposition. Tom Brokaw always had a good smirk about ethnic cultures requirements at Berkeley, or Berkeley's change of Columbus Day to Indigenous People's Day. He and another newsman, Keith Morrison, had a good back-slapping good-old-fraternity-boy time as they promoted some sarcasm about the UC Berkeley students demanding American cultures programs during the spring of 1991. They dismissed it as a rite of spring. The media's favorite target was a foolish slogan that had appeared on the walls at Stanford. Ho, Ho, Ho, Western Civilization must go. D'Gun ga Dinza, who was traveling all over the country spreading lies about "diversity," used that slogan to death in order to make his case. The monoculturalists were reduced to recruiting foreign mercenaries like D'Gun ga Dinza and a children's army to fight a losing war. A seventeen-year-old kid named Reich had written a letter to the *New York Times* complaining about there being too many questions about Maya Angelou on the SAT tests. Crabtree had written in one of those articles that if Yoruba would produce a Turgenev he would be glad to read him. Puttbutt quoted from the article.

"In order to have made such a statement you would have required some knowledge of the language."

"But, I—" He was sweating by now.

"Being the scholar that you are, you wouldn't comment about a language of which you had no knowledge, would you?" The stuffed shirt was visibly becoming hot under the collar. Before Crabtree could say anything, Puttbutt pressed the intercom button.

"Effie, give Mr. Crabtree that package I left for you." Crabtree left the office, he slammed the door like the rest. Shortly, Effie entered his office. She was laughing.

"You should have seen him. He put his hands on the package like it contained a bomb." They both laughed.

chapter thirty-one

Puttbutt made Charlie Obi wait three days before deciding to grant him an interview. He was paying him back for the times Charlie had made Puttbutt wait.

Momentarily Charles Obi walked in. He could tell by his demeanor that Obi hated to have to come and ask Puttbutt, whose Ph.D. was from a small Utah college, about his future. He rose and shook Charlie's hand. The handshake revealed that there was no love lost between them. As usual Obi was overdressed. Leather pants, leather overcoat, fancy shirt, and he carried what looked like a handbag.

"Professor Obi, I'll come to the point. Dr. Yamato has asked me to request that you take early retirement." Puttbutt looked down at his desk. He didn't want Obi to see how much he was relishing this moment.

"What? But I have a Ph.D. from Harvard."

"Dr. Yamato regards Harvard as an overgrown high school. He talks of a Japanese educational tradition that's thousands of years old. Harvard is only a few hundred years old. You can't impress Dr.

Yamato with your 'background' and your 'credentials.' I'll see to it that your retirement won't mean the end of African-American Studies, but there are going to be some changes made." Obi started from his chair. He looked as though someone had slapped his face. His mouth was open in shock. He stood in front of Puttbutt's desk. His anger raised the room's temperature.

"I've watched you as you've squandered the opportunities for Black Studies on this campus. Everybody knows that you made a deal. That Black Studies exists so that these football players, whom Harry Edwards calls meat on hooves, could get easy grades."

"Who told you that?"

"I have this memo from you to the corrupt president Bright Stool, who used to run this school. We've looked into his files. You were his front man in Ethnic Studies, assuring that they would never rise above mediocrity. The Eurocentrics were afraid that the high enrollments in Ethnic Studies, when they were first inaugurated in the late sixties, would threaten the existence of their departments. So they fired all of the rebels and brought you in to front what amounted to a neocolonial regime. If this were war you'd be hanged for treason." He didn't say anything. His eyes shot pellets at Puttbutt.

"From now on, there will be a solid curriculum with an emphasis on African-American culture. African-American art, music and culture in the United States. For the African section we will emphasize Yoruba, which after all was the language of our ancestors. Not Swahili, the language of slave traders. I'm giving all of the members of your department notice. The club will be retired and fresh blood will be brought in." He thought Charles was going to hit him. He stood for a moment, shaking from rage.

"You son of a bitch. If it wasn't for me there'd be no Black Studies. Yeah, I made a deal. Sports are what draw the revenue to my department, but look at all of the other people who benefited from what we did. I'm proud that we were able to make it easier for the black students to find something on this racist campus that they could feel at home with. Courses that had backbone and were of substantial intellectual worth. And if I had to give those pathetic football and basketball chumps Bs and Cs to get what programs that we had . . . the way I look at it, it was all worth it. It was our club that made all of this possible, making shit wages and having to go and beg the president for money to keep the department going. I had to turn the crack of my ass up to the white man and get fucked in order to keep some of these kids going on fellowships and financial aid. I had to take shit from these feminists who might be militant against me and you but who are still the white boy's concubinage. And now you're working for this chop suey fucking Jap. They're the most racist people in Asia. Do you think it's going to be any better for you? You're going around with a chip on your shoulder because they didn't give you tenure. I know. That drunken bastard Stool told me the whole thing before he left town. Now that you've whored for them you want to get even by giving them the clap. The whites used you and now the yellows are going to use you. This newly found aggression on your part is only a cover. You're still a pacifist. A coward."

If Puttbutt thought that he was going to savor this moment he was in for a surprise. He thought for a moment.

"Look, why don't you take partial retirement and then I'll find you a teaching job that will only require a few hours per week of your time. You can teach one semester part-time and the alternate semester you'll take a pension." He pushed some forms toward Obi. Obi picked up the forms, tore them into pieces and flung the pieces into Puttbutt's face. By the age of ten, under his mother's instructions, Puttbutt had a black belt in karate. He knew blows that were capable of paralyzing Obi from the chest down. But as a pacifist he exercised restraint.

"I don't have to take charity from you. I'm a black Ph.D. About as rare as the whooping crane. All I have to do is send out the word that I need a job and I'll be able to write my own ticket." He was right. The black Ph.D.'s, especially the women, who were considered less contentious than the men, were in demand. Black Ph.D.'s were in so much demand that they played a game on potential employers whereby they would pretend that they were favorably inclined toward being hired at a particular institution, be wined and dined, only to back out at the last moment. This would demonstrate to their home institution that they were in demand and the home institution would raise their salaries. It was an academic version of the old Murphy game that the blacks played but didn't invent. Even a Ph.D. from a minor college would seem to have placed Chappie in a position for getting his share of the money that came with being black and Ph.D.'d. Little did he know that every time an institution considered him for advancement they'd receive a call from General Puttbutt threatening to cut off their government funds if they did so. In fact, Bright Stool was about to overrule the Miltonians and award Chappie tenure, only to receive a phone call from General Puttbutt warning him of a reopening of a Securities Exchange Commission investigation about his financial dealings. You see, Chappie's dad still held on to a faint hope that Chappie, in the tradition of the other Puttbutts, would abandon the academic career and enter government service. Obi gave him another hostile glare and stalked out of the room. As he left, Matata crept in. Puttbutt didn't even look up.

"What's on your mind?" he asked Matata. In a phony British accent, Matata wanted to know where he stood. Puttbutt gave him the signal. Thumbs-down.

"What do you mean?" he said in a clear pronunciation.

"I've looked at your record. Most of your classes are taught by teaching assistants, while you go gallivanting around the world to these percussion conferences. Last semester you missed fifteen classes. Dr. Yamato has decided that all of the professors will have to earn their way. Teach. That's what we hired you for, to teach. Not the TAs. Graduate students. But you."

"But I have commitments."

"Not anymore. You're fired."

"But . . . but . . . they'll deport me. I'll have to return to Nairobi. They'll have me jailed. The men who run my country don't appreciate the finer things of life. Art. Percussion. You can't do this to me." He was pleading. He had left a trail of bad checks all over Kenya. Yamato's staff had checked.

"I'm sorry, but we'll make a cash settlement. Would you like to have the money in pounds?" He was angry. Puttbutt enjoyed this.

"You . . . you slave. Albino lover. Why my ancestors were kings in the great empire of the Mwanamutapa when your people were swinging in trees with monkeys. You'll hear from my patrons."

"If you're referring to those tired old businessmen's wives who run the Oakland arts scene, those volunteers who invite you to their parties, where you entertain them with fake African drumming, your smile as wide as a refrigerator's, then they don't have any influence here. Their husbands have filled Dr. Yamato's calendar for the next three months. Fighting each other for a chance to get to know him. To have lunch with him." He exited. Slamming the door behind him.

Himmlar Poop walked in. Puttbutt extended his hand. Himmlar refused to accept it. His shoulders were stooped. His mustache and goatee were white. His nose was turned up in a permanent sneer. Puttbutt handed him a sheet of paper. Himmlar Poop read the paper, his hands trembling.

"What is the meaning of this?"

"Isn't it clear? You've been dismissed."

"You can't dismiss me."

"Oh yes we can."

"On what grounds?" He paused. His face lit up. "Oh, I get it. My lectures about blacks. That's what you're against. You're using your influence with this Japanese fellow to get even with me. For telling the truth."

"Not at all."

"Then why?"

"Well, if you believe that there is a correlation between brain size and intellectual capacity, then what are we do to with your small brain?"

"I don't follow." Puttbutt handed him a paper. Poop examined it. He began to read. ". . . Sandra F. Witselson of MacMaster University in Hamilton, Ontario, says that her autopsies of sixty-two brains found that as men age, the size of their corpus callosum . . ." Poop gasped before continuing, ". . . gets smaller." Poop straightened up. He looked as though somebody had thrown some cold water into his face.

"You maintain that blacks have a smaller brain size than whites, so elderly whites such as you have smaller brains than young blacks or whites. One could say that young blacks are brighter than you are using your own theory, right? It's on account of your own theory that you're out of a job."

"I . . . I . . ."

"That's not all." Puttbutt was having so much fun that he couldn't stand it. "I've also looked into your biography and there's one period that's not accounted for."

"Which period was that?"

"Nineteen forty-one to nineteen forty-four."

"I . . ."

"I've brought someone who may freshen your memory." Puttbutt called into an adjoining room. A black man came out. He was neatly dressed in a plain black suit. Only his tie bore some snappy colors. His hair had been cut short and neatly. He looked to be about sixty years old.

"Hey Poopovich, remember me?" Puttbutt thought that Poop would faint dead away right there.

"This is Harvey Jameson. He's the new dean of students. We're not going to have any more of these LSD parties and druggies disrupting classrooms. He'll see to it that those students who violate the drug laws are treated no differently from the way the poor crack addicts are treated in the ghetto. He says that he knows you."

"That's right," Jameson said. Poop was sweating. "You remember, we got you out of the concentration camp. Saved your life, Poop." Turning to Puttbutt, he said, "Poop followed us all the way into Berlin. Shined our shoes, did odd jobs. We used to feed him. Take care of him. Gave him candy bars and some clothes to wear."

"Yes, well," Poop muttered.

"You were so glad to see us that you said that you'd lick us all over for fifty cents and a piece of a bread crumb, don't you remember? We had to rescue him from the other prisoners. They accused him of finking to the Jerries and giving them lists of troublemakers. He was only a kid. We took mercy on him. Why did you change your name, Poopovich?"

"Poopovich." Puttbutt feigned surprise. He knew about Poopovich's background because Yamato's Japanese staff had checked out his background as well. "He's up here preaching the small brain size of black people. Says that they are inferior to white people," Puttbutt said.

"What?"

"Their test scores just don't measure up," Poopovich said.

"Why, you—" Harvey Jameson pretended to threaten Poopovich and Puttbutt pretended to intervene.

"Don't hit me. Don't hit me. This is a complete debasement of discourse. You blacks are volatile and emotional. You can't debate things reasonably—"

"Debate things reasonably, huh. If it wasn't for the black soldiers who liberated Buchenwald, your Hungarian ass would have been goulash."

"Keep your temper, Harvey. There are a lot of people who think the way that he does. He's just up front with his, that's all. Now they can be over there in European Studies together."

"I'm not going anywhere. I quit," Poopovich said.

Poopovich was halfway out of the door. Harvey had sat down. He was shaking his head while winking at Puttbutt.

"We should have turned him over to that mob. We took pity on

the kid. He was only about fifteen years old." Poopovich backed
into the door, turned around and rushed out. Harvey and Chappie
had a big laugh.

chapter thirty-two

As he delved into the study of Yoruba he found that some of his
views were no different from those of that first generation of Africans
who disembarked from the dreaded slave ships onto Atlantic beaches.
They were individuals but they also believed in sharing. (Alienation
was a taboo.) They were devoted to the work ethic (Iṣẹ́ l'òògùn ìṣẹ́,
"work is the medicine for poverty") and had strong views about crime.
The Yoruba word for thief (olè) was similar to that for idler (ọ̀lẹ)
because it was assumed that an idle person would steal.

He liked the etiquette that the Yoruba had established between
older and young people because he'd had modern children call him
by his first name (the United States could use some of the polite
levels that existed in both Yoruba and Japanese). A youngster whom
Ishmael Reed told not to pick his peaches without asking permission,
said: Fuck you. The highest insult that a child in Yoruba culture
could receive would be to be told to "go home." Which meant that
one had not been properly trained.

The more Ishmael Reed studied Yoruba, the more he appreciated
his West African ancestors, who must have been geniuses to be able
to communicate in a language which was not only of great charm,
beauty and poetry, but whose qualifiers were frustrating to someone
who'd been raised on a simple language like English. The qualifiers
picked at you like ticks. Another thing. Not only did one have

to remember words, but their tones. Though one monoculturalist referred to Yoruba as a dialect, millions of people in West Africa, Brazil, Cuba and Puerto Rico still spoke Yoruba. Yoruba had influenced the lengthening and gliding of words practiced by the great oral poets, the preachers of the Black Church; it influenced the vocal styles of Anita Baker and Sarah Vaughan. Americans could learn much, not only from Yoruba social values, but from its ecology. For the Yoruba there were certain animals and birds which, being sacred, one didn't touch. He wondered whether the kids who threw rocks at birds at Lake Merritt would do so if they had attended Yoruba school, just as Chinese kids attend Chinese school, and Hebrew kids attend Hebrew school.

He wondered whether American blacks and whites could use some instruction in the Yoruba prohibitions. Má puró mợ mi (do not lie against me), Má kànjú (do not be impatient), Má mu ợtí o (do not drink alcohol) Má k'ẹ́gbẹ́kẹ́gbẹ́ o (do not cultivate the friendship of nonentities), Má ṣè' ṣekúṣe o (do not have illicit sex), Má jẹ' jekújẹ o (do not eat indiscriminately), Má b' ólè rìn o (do not associate with thieves or burglars) and one of the cardinal rules of the family-centered Yoruba, Má gbàgbé ilé o (do not forget your homestead). (John Milton would add: avoid spicy drugs.) Ishmael Reed frequently gave cash to beggars because he didn't know whether one might be a god. Yoruba had influenced him on that score also. (Ishmael Reed was a skeptic, but one who never took chances.) In Yoruba, gods dwelled among the living (Leslie Silko knows this too). In the Yoruba religion the gods are always testing, demanding sacrifices which, if ignored, got one into trouble with Èṣù, the spirit of efficiency, punctuality, discipline and revenge.

There was the story in *Ifa*, the epic of the Yoruba, in which Ọ̀rúnmìlà was visited by Èṣù, Death and Disease. Though disguised, Ọ̀rúnmìlà knew their identities. Ọ̀rúnmìlà, though broke, sold all of his belongings in order to provide food and drink to his visitors. Was the idea that West Africa would eventually become a global leader the only thing that attracted Ishmael Reed to Yoruba? Or his need to cultivate a conservatism based upon the spirit of Yoruba so as to distance himself from Puttbutt conservatives, who could only practice their conservatism on blacks. But maybe there were other reasons why he was attracted to Yoruba. Perhaps it was Peter Nazareth's catching Ishmael Reed red-handed anglicizing Yoruba (Yoruban). Maybe it was because of Derrida's 1968 message about the age of the death of the author. There was no perceivable role for the critic in Yoruba art.

The formal critic was nonexistent or at least difficult to detect. Ògún Sànyà, his teacher, said that the British were always wary of the Yoruba who lived in Ileṣa. They were considered too cryptic. When he spoke of Matata he always said of him that he was a loudmouth East African. One of the best detective works he'd read was Bob Ferris Thompson's account of how he had tried to discover organized criticism among the Yoruba, only to discern a wink or a nod as perhaps representing approval, a frown indicating disapproval.

"Ishmael, where are your lessons?" Ògún Sànyà was giving Ishmael Reed a class at his bookstore. The lessons were usually interrupted by shoppers. Reed didn't mind because sometimes the exchanges between Sànyà and his visitors and customers were as interesting as the lessons. Sànyà had the eyes of an ologbo, and dark skin. He wore a fila and a buba today, but sometimes he dressed in the Western style, gray cap, gray coat and a black scarf. He had just completed a conversation with a white man. Apparently a teacher. The teacher was saying that he wished that his African-American students were as disciplined as the Africans he'd met. He saw Ishmael Reed sitting at a table toward the rear and turned red. Sànyà once told Reed that a white professor under whom he was studying was commenting upon the innate inferiority of blacks. When Sànyà objected, the professor apologized and said, "I didn't mean Africans, I meant blacks." The man paid for his purchases and left.

* * *

Sànyà was on a mission. He would straighten out the gulf between the Africans and the diaspora. He wanted to repair the triangle, which was how he described the tensions between Africans, West Indians and Afro-Americans. He planned to build a university in Oakland that would accomplish this dream. As a Yoruba, Sànyà followed his dreams.

"Ishmael, your mind is not on the lesson." Reed had been daydreaming. While Sànyà attended to his customers, Ishmael Reed recited his lesson.

"Tal' ó ńta ẹja, Tal' ó ńta kòkǒ, Tal' ó ńta mọ́tò, Tal' ó ńta kẹ̀kẹ́, Tal' ó ńta iwě. (Who is selling the fish, who is selling the cocoa, who is selling the car, who is selling the bicycle, who is selling the book.)" If a language book told you as much about the values of the culture, then Yoruba people were devoted to the family, to honor and respect. However, many of the lessons were about buying and selling. The Yoruba people had been operating a market economy for two thousand years. Their devotion to the market had created one of the most complex numerical systems known to man. They even had a god of business. Òòṣàálá.

Sànyà said that African socialism was a fraud. That Nkrumah invented this concept in order to attract trade credits from China and the Soviet Union.

"You still must work on your tones." Sànyà illustrated in such a way that Reed doubted whether he'd ever get them right. This was the language that one spoke and read as though one were reading from a song sheet. The foundation of jazz. The language that was the only real jazz poetry. Maybe that's why Reed studied Yoruba. To end the jazz poetry hype. The situation was so out of hand that even Vachel Lindsay, the Edgar Rice Burroughs of American poetry, was considered a jazz poet. Very few poets writing in English— Redmond, Rahman, Toure, Baraka, Joans, Waldman, Bremser, Cortez, Troupe, Cannon, Hughes, Kaufman, John Gould Fletcher, Lawson Inada—had accomplished the jazz poetry. Yoruba played like a drum. Reed had written two songs in Yoruba. They just about played themselves.

"That's all for today." Ishmael Reed got his books together and was about to bid Sanya 'O dàbọ̀ when Sànyà said:

" 'Nj' óo gbọ́?"

"Hear what?"

"Chappie Puttbutt has become assistant to the Japanese man who has taken over Jack London. He's hired me to teach Yoruba."

"He what?" Ishmael Reed had shared a panel with Puttbutt and Puttbutt drew boos and hisses as he ridiculed a recent Ashanti enstoolment ceremony that had been staged by the Afrocentrics at the Ramada Inn. He said that he was an American and that he'd never give up his Brooks Brothers suit for a grass skirt and never give up his cottage in Lower Rockridge for a mud hut.

"What's come over him?"

"That's not all. He has assigned Professor Crabtree to teach an elementary course in the language."

"What?" He'd seen Crabtree on MacNeil-Lehrer, where spokespersons from Mr. Only's think tanks denounced multiculturalism in no uncertain terms. Crabtree had said that the Europeans had invented democracy and freedom and that he didn't need some naked cow-manure-headed Zulu jigaboo lecturing him about the failures of the West.

"Are you sure?"

"He's the one. Crabtree's been studying intensively. Pays me extra for classes on Saturdays and Sundays. The man has become fanatical. Has almost bought up the store." Sànyà sold Malcolm X's speeches, Nigerian clothing, talking drums, wood sculpture, records, and books by Adekanmi Oyedele, D. O. Fagunwa, Afolabi Olabimtan, Duro Ladipo and Oluremi Onasanya, volumes of poetry and fiction written in Yoruba, a language that had been converted from orature into a written language by Samiel Adjai Crowther.

Reed had quite a file that included the numerous ignorant and sneering remarks about diversity. Though Asian Americans, Latinos and women were all demanding a change in the curriculum, the Eurocentrics and their powerful allies in the media were singling out the blacks as ringleaders. Critic David Littlejohn said that he knew Mozart was better than Rap. Not that Mozart was better than maharaja music or Cantonese opera. But better than Rap, a black form. There was hostile, hysterical denouncement of any claim that major figures in Egyptian history or mythology were black, but very little criticism of the other members of the multicultural coalition, Latinos, Asian Americans and feminists. The fact that Irish Americans, Jewish Americans and Italian Americans were also members of the diversity movement was conveniently ignored so that the opponents of the movement could dismiss it as racist. Hundreds of thousands of dollars had been awarded to Mr. Only's subsidized intellectuals for the purpose of pressing the attack on multiculturalism. Whittle Direct Books had published two books by antidiversity critics. In James Atlas's *The Book Wars*, Mr. Atlas describes Yoruba as a "dialect," advancing the notion that the antidiversity movement is an anti-intellectual movement which criticizes things without investigating them. In Arthur Schlesinger's *The Disuniting of America* there appears an ad for Federal Express written in Japanese characters, subverting the book's message: warning America about its contamination by cultural diversity. The anti-Glossos' main contention was that Eurocentrism should be at the core of the American curriculum because the ideas of democracy and freedom arose in Europe, which means, one supposes, that a study of Shakespeare's monarchies, the Napoleon Era, the Hapsburgs, the Romanovs, the Age of Cromwell, Charles the First's reign, Mussolini's Italy, and Hitler's Germany— all absolute monarchies and dictatorships—should be expunged from the curriculum, not to mention the fact that Rome and Greece were slavocracies.

The antidiversity movement's main war rooms were the history departments, those who had covered up the most, distorted the most and had the most to be defensive about. The Cherokee are mentioned only once in Arthur Schlesinger Jr.'s *Age of Jackson*. Ishmael Reed's grandmother, on his father's side, a full-blooded Cherokee woman, was spared the trip to Oklahoma by marrying his grandfather, an African American, near Knoxville. When Reed gazed at the Smoky Mountains from the fourteenth floor of the Knoxville Hilton on that April afternoon in 1992, his bones were telling him that he'd been there before. So for Ishmael Reed, Mr. Schlesinger omitting the Cherokee removal from his book about the American pharaoh Andrew Jackson is like a European historian omitting any reference to Exodus in one of your standard Western history tomes.

James Mooney describes how the Cherokee were rounded up for their removal from their traditional homelands: "Squads of troops were sent to search out with rifle and bayonet every small cabin hidden away in the covers or by the sides of mountain streams, to seize and bring in as prisoners all the occupants, however or wherever they might be found. Families at dinner were startled by the sudden gleam of bayonets in the doorway and rose up to be driven with blows and oaths along the weary miles of trail that led to the stockade. Men were seized in their fields or going along the road, women were taken from their wheels and children from their play. In many cases, on turning for one last look as they crossed the ridge, they saw their homes in flames, fired by the lawless rabble that followed on the heels of the soldiers to loot and pillage." By ignoring the history of the Cherokee, of African Americans, of Latinos, of Asian Americans and of European ethnics, American historians were contributing to the United States' racial nightmare. It was appropriate that the leader of the antidiversity movement, the Scots-American David Duke, had received a degree in history.

The views of artists were not solicited by the media, who were creating sensational tabloid TV, featuring mostly right-wing proponents of antidiversity on panels and talk shows, members of Jack

Only's think tank and the Washington-based Woodwork Foundation. D'Gun ga Dinza's high-pitched and high-strung profile was on a lot. Those who appeared in the mass media magazines defending diversity had been there a few years before, studying Victorian literature. When Ishmael Reed asked the mass media–created leader of multiculturalism, in the Battle of the Books, his opinion of a book by Gerald Vizenor, he said he'd never heard of Gerald Vizenor.

Glossos United, an organization of artists, were using the term "multicultural" in the middle seventies, a few years before the right brought Dinza from India, and before its cooptation by the academic jargon planting machine. Look at it this way, using the central antidiversity argument that freedom and democracy are Western inventions. Suppose that André Derain, Maurice de Vlaminck, Henri Matisse, Pablo Picasso, Juan Gris, Georges Braque, Constantin Brancusi, Ernst Ludwig Kirchner, Max Pechstein, Erich Heckel, Emil Nolde, Karl Schmidt-Rottluff and Franz Marc had denied themselves the opportunity to borrow from the art of Africa, because the countries which contributed the African sculpture which influenced their art had no history of democracy. Or suppose Bud Powell, considering a concert of Bach music, said, "I can't play this music because the Germans have had little experience with democracy." Or Maurice Ravel: "I can't borrow from the rhythms of North Africa or from Le Jazz Hot, because these are marginal cultures." Or Charlie Parker: "I can't record Fiesta because the Latins have never experimented with a democratic form of government." Or Alvin Ailey: "I can't borrow from the ballet of the Russians because they were ruled by czars and communists." If artists had paid attention to the central antidiversity argument, the tanka and the haiku would never have been introduced into American poetry, and so on.

The diversity movement would win the Battle of the Books because it included artists. The other side was made up of education bureaucrats, critics and historians. Their rhetoric was so similar that when two of its advocates were accused of plagiarism, Ishmael Reed was wondering, how could they tell? The language of warfare was being used by both the monoculturalists and multiculturalists. David Kirp described this war as the Battle of the Books, and Henry Louis Gates, Jr., mused, "How did we come to appraise works of cultural criticism in terms appropriate to combat," and George Will, who in 1990 received more space to write about black literature than any black writer, critic or scholar, said that while Secretary of Defense Cheney was a general of the Gulf War, his wife Lynne Cheney was a general in the war against diversity.

chapter thirty-three

Ishmael Reed was seated in the Faculty Club of Jack London College when Puttbutt strode in. Strode is not the word. Puttbutt always seemed to be marching as though life were some kind of parade ground. Reed had been invited by a writer to talk to his class about his books and, of course, the topic merely provided a theme on which his mind could improvise, sort of like a jazz musician stating a song and then dancing around it elliptically. Somehow the discussion had gotten around to the Gulf War, and being one of those who believes that history's leftovers are just as fascinating as its main course, he talked about a remark that George Bush had made before Operation Desert Shield, that he was going to kick Saddam Hussein's ass. During the 1984 presidential race he'd bragged about kicking Geraldine Ferraro's ass. Kicking ass was on a lot of American lips these days and so he tried to make a connection between America's fascination with the lower digestive tract, the other side of the alimentary canal, and the fact that the name of the chairman of the

Joint Chiefs of Staff was Colin. He put what he was reading into his pocket and watched the scene. A brass band seemed to follow Puttbutt as he walked through the cafeteria. People were fighting each other for the privilege to assist him. One of them ran and got him a lunch tray, and those standing in line moved so that he could select his food. When he reached the cash register, another faculty member volunteered to buy his lunch. Reed tried to finish his coffee before Puttbutt spotted him. He'd written a book review of one of Reed's apocalyptic series—*The Terribles*—and has said "For those looking for plot, character development and logic, skip this one." No success. Puttbutt and his entourage headed for his table. Reed had met him on a couple of occasions and was still trying to get through his book *Blacks, America's Misfortune* that was so full of the critical jargon and Victorian diction of which some nineties black critics were so fond. Puttbutt knew how to wow his colleagues. All about binary this and that. Liberal quotes from Walter Benjamin, Lacan, Foucault, Barthes (but his reviews fell back on Freud and Tate). He'd read from the book at one of the local bookstores who called him brilliant for his "original" theses that blacks had become hooked on victimization and that affirmative action had "spoiled" them. Uh-oh. Puttbutt spotted Reed and headed toward his table, his hangers-on following closely behind. Puttbutt was well built. He still exercised at the gym. He was of a sort of maple color. Though forty-four, he still had all of his black hair.

"Ishmael Reed, how are you?" he said. Grins everywhere. "This is Ishmael Reed everybody. What brings you here, Reed?" But they were not interested in him, they were interested in Puttbutt. Remember, the author was dead in the age of theory. Reed remembered going to a writer's conference in Finland and the deconstructionist critics asking why the newspapers were interested in covering authors. Puttbutt finally had to tell all of those people who were surrounding him to leave so that he could eat in peace.

"This is the last time I'm going to eat in the Faculty Club. Guess I'll have them bring my lunch into my office. See those people who were just here? Used to spit out my name. Wouldn't even talk to me. Called me a white dog. But now they're embracing me. Fighting each other over who's table at which I'm going to sit. 'Let me buy you a drink, Puttbutt.' 'Please join our club, Puttbutt.' " Reed could tell that Puttbutt took a great deal of pleasure in the fawning manner with which his former colleagues now regarded him.

"It's disgusting what these intellectuals will do when they see somebody who can do them some good. Gained some weight, huh? What brings you to Jack London?"

"I was invited to a class. One of your teachers is using one of my books," Reed said.

"Come more often. You know, I'm the second most powerful man on campus."

"I read."

"Lot of these people who were kissing my ass, they want to keep their jobs."

"You still living over on Ocean View and Broadway?" Reed said, trying to change the subject.

"Yeah. But when I get my raise I'm heading straight for the Oakland Hills. I gaze up there every day. I'm looking around for a realtor." He gave Puttbutt the name of his agent from Red Oak Realty. Peter Campbell.

"Thanks, Reed." He put it into his pocket. Reed got another cup of coffee and headed back to the table. Puttbutt was off into his steak and salad.

"How are things over at Berkeley," Puttbutt asked.

"Lot of media coming out telling lies about diversity. You know how they are. They do a quick tour of the campus and decide that it's undergoing a black takeover."

"That so." Reed thought that this would start an argument. Puttbutt had written a op-ed in one of the local newspapers arguing that it was more important that students know about the restoration of King Charles II in 1658 than the Akwamu's attack on the Danish fort of Christiansborg in Accra in 1693.

"Conditions at Jack London are much better. Dr. Yamato, the

acting president, says that he wants each group to have equal status,"
Puttbutt said.

"What? But you've been one of the most vocal against diversity."

"I'm not taking sides anymore. From now on my policy is one of
enlightened self-interest," he said, poking his thumb into his chest.
He ate another piece of steak. He had sliced the steak into small
pieces and ate one by one slowly. Reed could tell that he had been
trained to use kitchen utensils skillfully, a craft that most Americans
don't know. While small particles of food surrounded his plate there
was not a "dollop" on his plate as one of the neovictorian black
writers would say. He ate his salad last.

"I hired Sanya to replace the Swahili group in African-American
studies. If we're going to study our ancestry then we ought to do it
right. Listen, I have something for you." He reached into his bag
and brought out a copy of a book, *Japanese by Spring*, and handed it
to Reed. Reed glanced at it.

"This is the book that got me to where I am now. You'd better
get with it brother. The twenty-first century is going to be a yellow
century."

"That's what you think," Reed began to say.

"You'd better get on the yellow Shinkansen before it leaves the
station and maybe you can get up to where I am. Shinkansen, for
your information, Reed, means bullet train."

"Yeah, sure." Reed said good-bye in a sort of a daze. Reed left
him at his table eating away cheerfully. His Black Panther beret
lying next to his plate. He was endorsing the study of African
ancestry, saying that each ethnic culture would receive equal status.
What had come over Puttbutt? Was he merely getting even with
those whom he felt had denied him tenture, or was there a deeper
reason. What had happened to change his mind. This man who was
a one-man black public relations department on behalf of Western
civilization was now a big Asia booster. A man who had denounced
African Studies was now bringing Sanya into the college. Puttbutt
was what the Yoruba would call an Olójumeji.

chapter thirty-four

Chappie was so happy that he was beside himself. He had sent a letter to the campus deconstructionists, informing them of their termination. The letters said you're fired. Those who believed that the words "you're fired" meant exactly that could finish the semester. Those who felt that the words only referred to themselves would have to leave immediately. He left the president's house, whistling to himself when he bumped into Jo Hara and Troy.

"Troy, Jo Hara, how are you?"

"We were on our way to see you," Troy said. That was the first time that she had addressed him directly and in a complete sentence. "We want to invite you to lunch." He couldn't believe what he had heard.

"You want to invite me to lunch?"

"Yes," Jo Hara said.

"We can understand why you wouldn't want to go with us. The way we've behaved," Troy said.

"Forget it," Puttbutt found himself saying. He was taken aback by their courtesy, after all of the ridicule and the sarcasm, the smart-aleck way that today's youth referred to people of Puttbutt's age. They were taking him to lunch.

The three of them walked in silence down the hill toward the Korean restaurant which was located in a plaza just below the college. Passing the campus parking lot, he noticed that the sign standing before a spot marked RESERVED bearing Dr. Obi's name had been taken down and his familiar gray Mercedes was missing. Matata's bright red TD was also missing. There were other names missing from privileged reserved lots. Instead of American cars there were Hondas, Hyundais and Toyotas parked in the parking lot. The Korean restaurant was located between a nail establishment and a burger joint. Inside, there were a number of Korean Americans eating lunch. They stood for a long time, waiting for the waiter to show them to a table. He ignored them, until Puttbutt finally asked if they could have a seat. He showed them to a table that was dirty from having been occupied previously. He wiped off the table and disappeared into the back. They sat there for a long time, not talking. The girls seemed to be beaming at him. It made him nervous. Puttbutt noticed that the waiter was taking the orders of people who'd entered the restaurant after they had. He called him over. Only then did he take their order, grumpily. A few months before Puttbutt had come into the store to buy his customary thirty pieces of sushi for $10.30, but since that time a new Rap record had been released, which denounced Korean Americans and a Korean grocer who had shot and killed a black teenager in Los Angeles and had been given a light sentence by a white woman judge. The young women ordered some rice and pork and Puttbutt ordered the tofu soup. It was hot and spicy.

"Do you mind if I take your picture?" Jo Hara asked.

"What?"

"We want to take your picture," Jo Hara said. She took out a camera, aimed it at him and shot. What was going on?

"Tell him, Jo Hara."

"No, you Troy."

"What is it?"

"We want you to address the Ethnic Studies department graduation." Puttbutt nearly fell out of his chair.

"What? Aren't they still calling me Uncle Ben over there?"

"Not anymore."

"They're calling you the black fang." Jo Hara said. She sighed when she said black fang.

"Black fang?"

"The way you're handling these racist dogs. You and that Jap."

"Japanese, Troy. Japanese."

"Japanese. You should have been there for Professor Poop's farewell lecture," Jo Hara said. "We were cracking up."

"He said something about the forces of political correctness driving him from the campus." Puttbutt had giggled to himself when he learned that Poop had taken a job at Stanford's McKinley Institute and that his boss was a black man.

"I'm glad that drunken faggot Matata is gone, too."

"Troy, I will not tolerate homophobic remarks."

"I'm sorry, Professor Puttbutt."

"They're saying that you're the head nigger on campus, Professor Puttbutt. That these racists have to take their orders from you. You should see them over there in the Ethnic Studies department. Lining up with Indians, blacks and Latinos in front of the copy machine. They hate to have to do that, they hate to have to wait their turn," Jo Hara said. The girls laughed. He smiled.

A few weeks before they were calling him white dog. Now they were calling him black fang. He was the one making an incision into the skin of their oppressors. He thought of what Obi had said. The whites had used him, the yellows were using him and the blacks were now championing his every move. He was becoming everybody's attack dog. Pit bull. Their instrument of revenge. Was he a pacifist or was he like old Milton, lusting for revenge. The Milton of the sonnet "On the Late Massacre in Piedmont," holding the pope responsible for the murder of Protestants in Italy. If he were Milton, was Yamata Cromwell?

chapter thirty-five

With the doors to *Koons and Kikes* closed, and the Amerikaner branch of the Boer Order disbanded, the Jack London campus was now peaceful. The student lounge, which had been a rowdy playpen for the most privileged youth in the world, was now an additional reading room. The students who were causing so much trouble on campus had been expelled. Gone was the television set with the fifty-inch screen which was on all day playing soap operas. The bars and restaurants had been closed down, cutting down on alcoholism, which was a big problem on American campuses. Rape was a big problem too. White males whose average age was nineteen had committed twenty-five thousand assaults and five thousand rapes in 1989. They were responsible for a crime rate that was 15 percent higher than that of the communities surrounding their colleges and universities. Another piece of white pathology that had been covered up by college public relations departments and the American media. Where once the students would mill about a noisy courtyard, there was silence and decorum. Sororities and fraternities were closed. In their place were friendship clubs where students would meet under the supervision of chaperons and discuss Nihonno art and culture. Robert Hurt and his followers had been moved ten blocks from the campus and occasionally you could hear their protests. Nobody paid much attention to them. Robert Hurt had appeared on some of the television stations, those which hadn't been bought out by the Japanese, and after a while, through advertisers who represented Japanese firms, he was canceled on those. Once in a while you heard him on the community access stations in Berkeley and Oakland.

* * *

One day Puttbutt came to work and found no references to Jack
London College. The huge statue of Jack London had been removed
from the campus. In its place was the statue of a small bespectacled
man dressed in military uniform. He was wearing riding boots. Signs
posted about the campus referred to it as HIDEKI TOJO NO DAIGAKU.
Daigaku was Japanese for university. The Student Union was now
called Isoroku Yamamoto Hall. The campus, which had been lively
with much goofing off, was silent under Dr. Yamato's new regime.
There were, however, signs of dissent.

Puttbutt had finished his work for the day and was leaving the
campus when he noticed elderly men, some walking stiffly and with
the aid of others who also seemed fragile boned. Some were on
crutches or using walkers. Others rolled along in wheelchairs. Few
were there to witness this procession, not even the ever-present
news crews. Dr. Yamato wasn't in his office and his secretary told
Puttbutt that he wouldn't be in until the following Monday. Puttbutt wanted to ask him the reason for the sudden change. And
who on earth was Hideki Tojo? Isoroku Yamamoto? The men carried signs, WAR CRIMINAL. REMEMBER PEARL HARBOR. LEST WE FOR-
GET. He was stunned by what he saw next. The Japanese flags
were flying alongside the American flags and the yellow ribbons.
The students were subdued, which seemed to be their mood under
Dr. Yamato's administration. None of them had even heard of
World War II, and the Korean War must have meant as much to
them as Victory Bonds. They were at a loss to answer such trivia
questions as what were the slogans for the Charlie Barnet and
Sammy Kaye bands? (Answer: Swing and Sweat with Charles Barnet, Swing and Sway with Sammy Kaye.) One lad being inter-
viewed by a TV crew had an answer. Wasn't that the war Elvis
was in? he asked. But then those lines came to him. The ones
from John O'Killen's mighty novel, *And Then We Heard the Thun-
der*, the best novel about World War II written by an American.

In that novel, the name Tojo was synonymous with Japanese. Japanese soldiers were referred to as Tojo. The country was referred to as Tojo. Tojo was used as a synecdoche for Japan. He went home and sought the answer in some secondhand volumes he had bought on Japanese history after his grandfather's diatribe. Nihon no rekishi. Hideki Tojo was prime minister of Japan during World War II, he discovered. He had been hanged for war crimes, though some believed that he had taken the rap for Emperor Hirohito. It gets better. Isoroku Yamamoto was the mastermind behind the Japanese attack on Pearl Harbor.

chapter thirty-six

He was in Dr. Yamato's office the following Monday.

"But Doctor, don't you think it provocative to name the university after men whom Americans view as war criminals?"

"They're not war criminals. They were attempting to push the American and European devils out of Asia." That line exploded in Puttbutt's face. He didn't know that Dr. Yamato was political. He'd never talked about politics when he was teaching Puttbutt Nihongo.

"The Shiroi-jin started the war with their expansionism. Their growth fanaticism. The British, French and the Dutch wanted to divide up the Asian countries, convert their people into slaves and exploit their resources. They had no business in Asia. As for Pearl Harbor, this national obsession that you Americans have developed, our country was lured into bombing those aircraft. Your people knew in advance that a raid on the harbor had been planned. You did nothing to stop it. Pearl Harbor was merely another Gulf of Tonkin. A trap. In fact, it was the Americans who fired first on that day.

The US destroyer *Ward* fired on one of our submarines at 0651. The attack from our aircraft didn't occur until about two hours later at 0800. It was clearly retaliation." Dr. Yamato paused for a moment and lit a cigarette. "Pearl Harbor and all of the battles that preceded it and the ones that followed were mere battles in one war. The war that was begun when our glorious Japanese Navy defeated the Russian fleet in nineteen-four. The war that ended with the fall of Saigon. And now the gods have willed it that Clark Air Force Base in the Philippines be closed down. They exercised their will through the volcano. And as soon as the capitulationists in Tokyo have been dealt with, Japan will be restored to its ancient glory and the foreign devils will be banished forever." He pounded the table as he spoke and raised his voice, which was uncharacteristic of Dr. Yamato. He sounded like his grandfather.

"Dr. Yamato, I really don't want to argue politics. I just think that it's provocative to name the university and the Student Union after those men. Some people will remember that we lost three thousand men at Pearl Harbor."

"We? What we? You. Don't make me laugh. They were lynching black people all over America in those days." Dr. Yamato puffed on his cigarette and inhaled, slowly.

"I still think it's a mistake, sir."

"Nobody's complaining. Look, Puttbutt-san. You do your job. Leave the decision making to me. I'll decide what name to give this school. The men I represent are paying good money to invest in Tojo. Importing equipment all the way from Japan. Computer equipment. Laser technology. We plan to make Tojo the best school in this country. A center of science and the humanities. We've raised the salaries of the faculty and they've ended their protests. Oh, of course they were complaining about what they called the Nihon-chu-o curricula, but we all knew that they had car payments. Obligations. I know they don't want to work at the burger counters. They're all studying Japanese. Besides, I don't know why you're upset. I read your paper on *Othello*. You said that the racism of Shakespeare's time still exists. You called him a dead white male. So why are you so worried about how the Shiroi-jin fared during World War II, as your historians call it." Puttbutt didn't say anything. He was embarrassed by the paper, but he didn't have to defend it anymore. Dr. Yamato was smiling slyly at him. Dr. Yamato knew that he'd scored one. But Puttbutt didn't feel right. Yamato had revealed a side that he'd never seen. Yamato was tough. Something that he wasn't. And to think that he had humiliated Crabtree and Obi. Had sent Matata packing, while doing the bidding of a man who was far more chauvinistic in his values than they. Maybe the graffiti he'd seen on the wall of the faculty toilet was right. It read, "Yamato. The Yellow Satan." If Yamato was Satan then he was second in command, Beelzebub. Swayed by Satan's style and oratory. (Lines 272, 273, 274, *Paradise Lost.*)

Why couldn't he, Puttbutt, be like his father, General Puttbutt and General Colin Powell? Here he was feeling sympathy for his tormentors, for Crabtree, the man whose devotion to traditionalism had caused his tenure denial. General Powell said that Iraqi deaths were none of his business. He talked about killing the enemy's army. Why couldn't he be like that. Defeat his enemies without so much as a wince. Why didn't he have the gall of the kind that could bomb a baby food factory, or incinerate five hundred women and children, then have big tasteless gaudy parades to celebrate with Whitney Houston singing her heart out. His father had always talked of the necessity of degrading the enemy. The way the Americans had slaughtered Iraqi soldiers even though they were in retreat. On that highway, full of mutilated Iraqi corpses. Why was he so weak? Why couldn't he stomach the burial alive of all those Iraqi soldiers. Why couldn't he be like Schwarzkopf, whom feminist Ellen Goodman called a real hero even though he was responsible for the deaths of thousands of her women-of-color sisters and their children. Why couldn't he be coldhearted like the so-called American public. Indifferent to the fact that as a result of the Gulf War, three hundred thousand children would die of malnutrition, not to mention the deaths due to cholera, typhoid and dysentery. Why couldn't he get into a Desert Storm state of mind. A New World Order mode. He'd been a conservative and in a pinch the conservatives abandoned him. Now he wanted revenge and he was too yellow to even do revenge right.

chapter thirty-seven

Weeks passed and the renaming of the university was forgotten. He was working on his manuscript about the poet Nathan Brown when the doorbell rang. It was the woman next door. She'd made her face into a showcase. Cobalt blue mascara over the eyes, rouge. She had a greasy look. What have I done now, Chappie thought.

"I hope I'm not interrupting you," she said.

"No, not at all," he said. "Come in." She walked into his living room and looked around.

"Coffee, tea?" He asked. She shook her head. She was wearing a blouse and her breasts were, as an inferior writer would say, overripe. They were contributing to the war effort. Standing tall. Her thighs were huge and streaked with blue lines. She had painted her toenails red, and they were neatly trimmed. The sandals she wore exposed them. He pointed to one of his cane-seated Italian chairs for her to sit on. He sat down.

"Look, I know that we haven't been good neighbors." Chappie made no response. "My husband. He's from the old school. He was brought up in a strict Catholic home. His family came from Palermo." So that's why he's so dark, Chappie thought. "They lived in a very restricted environment in Brooklyn, and the children were brought up with all of the working-class prejudices." He knew what

she was talking about. He'd read Pete Hamill in *Esquire*. He'd read
Joe Flaherty's *Tin Wife*. Her blond hair was thinning.

"He is not as worldly as many other men, but he's a good husband. He has a temper which flares once in a while, but he's not a
mean-spirited man." Chappie didn't know what all of this was leading up to. "He's been working at Caesar Synthetics for fifteen years.
As you know, they've been bought by the Japanese."

"Yes, I do remember reading that somewhere." Dr. Yamato had
introduced Bass Sr. to some Japanese investors and as a result the
Japanese owned the majority of stock in the company.

"They've given him his thirty-days notice. We have bills, responsibilities." She began to cry. Chappie gave her some Kleenex. She
blew her nose.

"Thank you."

"Do itashimashite," he said, forgetting his native tongue tempo-
rarily.

"What?" She looked up.

"Don't mention it," Puttbutt said.

"We thought that since you . . . well, since you seem to get
along with them, that—"

"You want me to help your husband keep his job." She nodded
her head. Her face was red. There was a silence. He smiled.

"I'll do what I can."

"You will?" She leaped up from the couch and threw her arms
around him. He could feel her groin against his. She kissed him on
his cheek.

"You're so kind. What can I do to repay you?" Said with a tinge
of passion. Chappie thought for a moment.

"What are neighbors for?"

chapter thirty-eight

He could tell when he entered the campus that something was up. You could feel the tension. Students and faculty were talking in little groups, but would lapse into silence when he walked by. They didn't ridicule or lampoon him in their newspapers anymore. There was a padlock on the door of the *Koons and Kikes* office. He had their respect now. He walked past Effie whom he'd made into his administrative assistant.

"Dr. Yamato really did it this time," she said. She didn't raise her eyes from the computer.

"What do you mean?" he asked.

"You'll see."

He went into his office and found the letter. All faculty and students had been required to take an IQ test designed by a Japanese educational firm. The results were in. Most of the faculty and the students had flunked. Dr. Yamato called Chappie into his office.

"You read the results of the tests, Chappie?"

"Yes, Dr. Yamato."

"My backers are very disappointed."

"Disappointed, Dr. Yamato?"

"They're saying that the reason that Americans are slipping is becoming very obvious. Your lazy, illiterate workers, little more than coolies. And now you're asking for affirmative action and quotas, insisting that we buy your inferior automobiles and planning to send a delegation of corporation owners—overpaid welfare queens—to go to Tokyo and lecture us and make demands."

"Dr. Yamato, I'm really not interested in yet another anti-American speech." Yamato glared at him before continuing.

"Well, at first we all thought that it was just the Puerto Ricans and blacks who were holding the country back, but now it seems that the whole population is one big genetic cesspool."

"Isn't that sort of extreme, Dr. Yamato?"

"The questions were very simple. Information that any civilized person in the modern world should have a command of." Chappie picked up the test. He examined some of the questions. Who was the first novelist and name her book? Name the monk who introduced Zen Buddhism into Japan? What was the former name for Tokyo? For Kyoto? Name three Kabuki plays and their plots. So as to deflect the criticism that the test was Nihon-chu-o, they had included some questions about European thinkers. What famous philosopher said that Indian literature was more imaginative than Homeric literature?

"We included that question and others like it so that they wouldn't complain that the test wasn't multicultural, that awful word that you use. The whites are complaining because, let's face it, they want easy questions so as to mask their inferiority. They want questions that will allow them to continue to mythologize about the greatness of Europe. They like the SAT tests because they can afford to provide their idiot children with coaches. They're even claiming that the ancient Egyptians were white when everybody knows that they were members of an Asiatic race. Besides, if the ancient Egyptians were white, what happened to them, they all move to Cairo, Illinois?" Puttbutt stood frozen in his tracks, shocked. That was the first time he'd ever heard Dr. Yamato make an intentionally funny line. He seemed surprised himself and a delighted grin appeared.

"No wonder they're behind in every important field. Biotechnology. Superconductivity. Robotics. Microchips. That Hubble telescope. Sent it up without even checking it. No wonder you Americans are so dependent. The world's largest debtor nation.

Obsessed with a welfare mentality. Your products are shoddy. Twenty percent of your banks are owned by foreigners, meaning that your interest rates will be determined by outsiders. We Japanese are tired of keeping you afloat. Backing your treasury bills. And now you've gone into the gunslinging business again. Have gun will travel, like an old television rerun. Wild Bill Hickok." It was funny the way Yamata pronounced the gunslinger's name. Every syllable given emphasis. "It took your air force and twenty-eight nations, most of which had been bribed by your government, to subdue a third world country. You were always a generation or so ahead in weaponry of the groups that you practiced your imperialism on. If Japan had had a navy, Commodore Perry would never have black-mailed the shogun. If Iraq had any kind of air force, you would not have won your victory. And eventually you will receive a punish-ment worse than Vietnam. One day, you will engage a small nation with a generation of weapons superior to yours, and then your cities will be under attack. After all, in your Westerns, the gunslinger is always bested, ultimately, by an upstart."

"What are your backers proposing?" Puttbutt interjected, trying to steer the conversation into another direction.

"We've decided that the student body and the faculty will have to attend courses in order to remedy their intellectual deficiency. If that doesn't work, then we will bring in a Japanese faculty. Maybe Americans should be put to work at things that will not strain their capacities. Wrapping packages and opening doors for their betters, or ladling out ice cream, taking hotel reservations lest they become a permanent underclass among developing nations. The advanced nations can no longer carry their tremendous debt. They will have to do more to earn their way. To work for relief. Workfare. And another thing, Ethnic Studies will now be called Bangaku." Ban-gaku. Puttbutt wrote the word down. He looked it up when he got home. It meant "barbarian studies."

"I am still willing to indulge your fantasy about Africans, Europe-ans and Latinos having contributed something worthy of scholarly pursuit, even though their claims seem extravagant. My backers are saying that this Bangaku may be a luxury that this campus can't afford. Navajo blanket weaving and African drumming. English literature. Aristotle, he believed that nonwhites were natural slaves. What rubbish." He removed his glasses and began to wipe them. "I don't know, Chappie, but I'm beginning to think that some of our anthropologists are right."

"Right about what, sir?"

"American brains. They're beginning to say that Americans have smaller brains than those belonging to the people of other nations. Look at their test scores. I'm beginning to think that even this Bangaku should be abandoned."

"You sound as chauvinistic as the Afrocentrics and the Eurocentrics, Dr. Yamato."

"Well, that's not the most shocking intellectual shortcoming of this campus. We discovered that very few of the faculty or students were acquainted with Nihongi. The basic work of world literature." Puttbutt had attempted to read the Nihongi once. He got as far as page 3. In English!

Chappie got up to leave. He thought of Robert Bass's former skinhead friends. Sure, they were stupid and nasty idiots but did they deserve the broken noses. The teeth punched out. Nobody knew where the men who surrounded Dr. Yamato had taken them, none was showing up to their classes. He thought of how he had revenge on his soul so that he just stood there, not saying a word. Letting Dr. Yamato's security guards pummel these kids. Burn their nazi flags. Some of them were in the hospital. They wouldn't be burning crosses and defacing synagogues for a long time.

chapter thirty-nine

It was 11:30 P.M. when his doorbell rang. As he opened the door he noticed the lights in the neighbor's house flick on. The whole block was interested in what was going on in his house. It was Muzukashii, the Japanese-American student. He was all out of breath.

"Kombanwa Muzukashii-san," Puttbutt said. Muzukashii frowned. Quizzically. "Kom-what?"

"Come in, come in." He paced about nervously until Chappie directed him to a seat.

"Dozo okake kudasai," Chappie said. He pointed to the chair or else Muzukashii wouldn't have known what he meant. Chappie thought about all of the times that he wanted to take this little bastard and twist his head until it come off in a toilet. Bash his toylike body into pieces. He was shaking. Gone was the cocky self-assurance of his when he was surrounded by those Shiroi-jin whom he wanted to impress.

"Professor, you've heard about the expulsion?"

"What? I don't know what you mean."

"Dr. Yamato is expelling all American-born Chinese and Japanese students."

"But why?"

"He says that we can't be trusted. That we're agents for the foreign devils. He talks the way my grandfather and the Issa used to talk. Calling white people devils. Ghosts. Dogs and snakes. White people aren't devils. The guys in my fraternity treat me nice."

"When did this happen?"

"Each student received a notice in the mail. Chappie, I mean Professor, you know the man. He's crazy. I was part of a delegation that went to see him today. He said that . . . that the whites brainwashed us while we were in the internment camps. That Japanese Americans underwent behavior modification. And he said things about the Pacific Islanders. Said that all they were worth was diving for pearls for tourists and that the Philippines and Thailand were nothing but whorehouses for white men. That the AIDS that the white men have brought to Indochina will eventually do more damage than the barbarian Americans did with their diabolical air force. He said that we were collaborators and traitors that couldn't be trusted. He hates the Chinese Americans even more. Said that they were chickenshit. Called them pets for white people. Brought up World War II memories."

"What do you mean?"

"The Chinese wore *I am Chinese* badges during the war so as not to be confused with the Japanese, Professor, and the American Occupation used Japanese-American advisors. We're nothing but collaborators to them. Many of us are worried. Where will we go if we're expelled. I have only one more year. I had my eyes set on Harvard Business School."

Yamato had gone too far. Sure Muzukashii was an asshole and had joined his enemies in making life miserable for him, but maybe Hurt was right. It was time to join ranks. To restore Jack London to the American people. To rename the college after the author who admired Friedrich Nietzsche. Jack London.

"There's one more thing, Professor."

"Yes, what is that?"

"You know those guards he has around campus."

"What about them?"

"They . . . well they've been taking some of what they call troublemakers into the basement of the police headquarters and torturing them."

"Come now."

"They've taken some of the most attractive coeds and made them into concubinage. And those Tomodachi clubs. The students are forced to take allegiances to Japan and the coming emperor."

That did it. He told Muzukashii to go home and remain there. He hated to say it but his father was right. Before he left for his showdown with Dr. Yamato, he fastened an American flag tie clip to his neckwear and tied a yellow ribbon around the tree in his front yard. A neighbor who happened to be passing him at the time looked from the tree to Puttbutt and smiled. He lived on a real gung-ho block. One neighbor owned a red, white and blue mailbox.

chapter forty

When he went into Dr. Yamato's office, Yamato was examining a scale model of a scene that resembled the Port of Oakland. There seemed to be a battleship anchored at the port. On the battleship there were little men dressed in uniforms and formal wear.

"Dr. Yamato, I've tolerated every possible infringement you've made on the academic environment. The naming of the school for ignominious war criminals. IQ tests, your goons, the way you've humiliated the faculty, and now . . . now the expulsion of the Japanese and Chinese Americans from the campus. I'm handing in my resignation." It was the first week in October. Since their last meeting Dr. Yamato had begun to converse with Puttbutt on such low polite levels that he was becoming rude, using the verb shiyagaru instead of shimasu when he desired that Puttbutt perform a task for him. While Puttbutt, when addressing the doctor, still used the verbs of respect.

"Don't bother, Puttbutt-san. You've been fired, but before you go I want to share my plans for our December celebration with you."

"What celebration?"

"On December 8, Tojo no Daigaku will celebrate the fiftieth anniversary of the attack on Pearl Harbor. Many of the businessmen and leading citizens of Oakland will join. They will apologize for the invasion of the Pacific by American forces. The Soviets apologized to the people of Afghanistan for invading their country. The Japanese recently apologized to the Koreans. And now it's time for the United States to apologize. We're bringing the USS *Missouri* to the Port of Oakland for the occasion." He pointed to the scale model, and with a pointer identified some of the figures standing on the *Missouri*. Instead of Japanese diplomats dressed in formal clothes, it showed Dr. Yamato receiving an "apology" document from the mayor of the city of Oakland, who represented the United States. To add to the humiliation, at the end of the signing, the flag of Commodore Perry, whose black ships were the scourge of the Japanese, would be burned. Perry's flag had flown on the *Missouri* during the Japanese signing of the ignominious surrender document. The supposed signing ceremony was scheduled to take place during a three-day "apology" festival.

"You're insane. Kichiga, desu," Puttbutt said, slamming the door to Dr. Yamato's office behind him. The Japanese secretary was so taken aback by the rage that Puttbutt displayed that she ran into Dr. Yamato's office to see if he was all right.

chapter forty-one

When he returned home, Bass Jr. was vacuuming the rugs.

"The breakfast dishes are washed and I did the windows. After

I finish vacuuming I have to leave for school, unless there's something else that you want me to do, Professor."

"Look, you won't be coming here anymore. Dr. Yamato fired me. You can go back to drawing those cartoons about me and making watermelon jokes."

"Oh, I could never do that, sir."

"What do you mean?"

"I'm really ashamed. You see, I had received most of my information about black people from television, movies and the *New York Times*. But these past few months I have been able to observe you up close. Why . . . why, you're no different from any other American." Chappie just looked at the kid for a long time.

"Thanks, Robert. I think."

"Well Professor Puttbutt, if there isn't anything else you want me to do, I'll be going."

chapter forty-two

He sent out faxes and at the appointed time the recipients assembled in his office. Dr. Yamato had gone to Tokyo for a week and so the coast was clear.

Dr. Himmlar Poopovich, mudpeople theorist who was threatened with retirement on account of small brain size, after running into his old friend, had been persuaded to attend.

Matata, who believed that whites were icepeople afflicted by the N gene, was there too. Matata's theory, based on a theory of Dr. Milford Wolpogg, of the University of Michigan, was that instead of being wiped out, the genes of the Neanderthal survive in the genes of Europeans and their American cousins. Matata said that their incessant warfare and extermination of other people could be traced to the period during which they were nearly exterminated by a more advanced species that came into Europe and was able to adapt to the ice period. Matata had landed on his feet. To make ends meet Matata had opened a Thaw Out Clinic on Lakeshore Drive. Its clientele was made up of upwardly mobile and rich Oakland icepeople who wanted to pursue defrost therapy. Defrost therapy included something called Afrocentric aerobics. Every morning you'd see some of Oakland's cultural and business leaders swaying off-time to Matata's fake "African" drumming and dancing. Only Dr. Charlie Obi was missing. After attempting to contact him, Effie explained to Puttbutt that Obi had left town for a job interview at a well-known black college.

He called the meeting for the afternoon so that they could make their evening shifts. Robert Hurt, fifty-year-old sixties radical, was present. He looked as though he'd spent the night on the Greyhound Sacramento-to-Oakland run, in the backseat among the rowdy and inebriated. Puttbutt had set up about twenty chairs in front of his desk. He cleared his throat, a signal for the meeting to begin. Some were already seated. Others were taking in the gorgeous view from the window of the office. Some were standing off to the side, talking. Now those who were standing joined the seated faculty. He'd miss the office, which formerly belonged to Dean Whitherspoon. The office that Yamato was forcing him to abandon.

"Gentlemen, I know that you're wondering why I called you here," Puttbutt said. The murmurs that followed this remark indicated that they were indeed curious. Marsha Marx walked in and took a seat. She folded her arms and began glaring at Puttbutt.

"It was absolutely traitorous what you did. Joining that Japanese fellow against Americans. Against your own people," one of his colleagues said, feebly rising, shaking his fist at Puttbutt and then resuming his seat. Muttering followed, indicating that most of those assembled were in agreement.

"I realize that I've made a mistake. I'm on board now. I'm singing from the same song sheet." Puttbutt was repentant. Another white-haired professor whom Puttbutt recognized as a teacher in the "classics" department spoke.

"Nobody would hire me. I'm living in a trailer with ruffians and cutups. People are shouting obscenities all night. I think the other night I heard what sounded like a pistol shot. And it's all you and that Jap's fault."

"Me too," another Miltonian said. "My wife had to take a job in a San Francisco law office in order for us to have food on the table. It's humiliating for me. A man who believes in valor and honor." Himmlar Poop joined the complainers.

"I've had to take a job at the McKinley Institute at Stanford. My boss is a conservative black man. The ultimate letdown. I had to call in sick in order to make this meeting. He won't give me any time off. Made me read a book called *The Protestant Ethic and the Workplace* just because I was five minutes late one day."

"Serves you right," Dr. Matata Musomi said. "Shows that you Europeans don't run the world anymore."

"Shut up, you," Poop said. Matata Musomi started toward Poop.

"Motherfucker, who you tellin to shut up?" Matata lost his British cool. "You low-down nazi rat. You're talking about the small brains of women and blacks. Over in Germany, Hitler would have grinded your ass down to a bag full of borax."

"Oh yeah. What about your icepeople nonsense. Tracing the alleged European inclination toward aggression to some sort of glacial experience. The Swedes, Danes and Icelanders have little history of imperialism against Africans and the Romans come from a warm climate. If you'll look at the map, you'll see that Italy is a stone's throw from Africa. Anything below Naples is Africa, as the expression goes. You Afrocentrics are nuts."

"Oh, yeah. Well what other people have terrorized the whole world as much as the Europeans. Destabilizing and exterminating people on continents all over the world and even committing cannibalism on their own during World Wars I and II. Why is it that crazed serial murderers are usually white men?"

"Last I heard, Idi Amin wasn't a white man."

"Oh, yeah."

"Yeah."

"Oh yeah."

"Yeah." The two were staring each other down and up in each other's face like two boxers about to compete in a grudge match being given their instructions from the referee.

"Please, please. Let's not lose our tempers. Look, I just want to tell you that I'm sorry about what happened. I . . . I was angry because the Department of Humanity denied me tenure." Puttbutt said it as though he was offing a demon that had been smothering him. Matata Musomi laughed at him sarcastically. The others seemed startled.

"It wasn't because of your race, it was because of that paper on Shakespeare. Calling Shakespeare, the great bard, a racist. A DWM. We white men are sick of being demonized. Sick, do you hear?" The Miltonian who made this remark received a round of applause.

"Hear, hear," some of his other colleagues joined in, as though they were at a session of the English Parliament, which is where most of them aspired to be. Sitting in the House of Lords. That's what all the second- and third-generation Anglo wannabes wanted.

"That's not important anymore. What's important is that we get our college back. It's become nothing but an indoctrination center for Japanese propaganda."

"So, finally you see," one of the Miltonians said. Marsha Marx kept raising her hand. She wanted to say something. But every time she tried, the men would interrupt her. Just as it seemed that there was an interlude of silence during which she could express her views, Crabtree entered. Nobody said a word. He was dressed in a white skokoto, white ewu and was wearing a white fila. Some of those assembled snickered. Musomi stared at him until he took his seat. He paid them no mind.

"Yes, ah so. You'll all get your jobs back with back pay. I've broken with Dr. Yamato." More murmuring. A little more excited this time. "The expulsion of the Japanese and Chinese American students was the last straw. I should have ended my association with the man when he had his hoodlums beat up the Amerikaner students. I dismissed all of the rumors about their being tortured and about the coeds being used as comfort girls. I was so joyful about their receiving what was coming to them that I ignored the abuses. The intimidation. The censorship. And I'll tell you what. We should see to it that *Koons and Kikes* publishes again. The way I see it, those young people are entitled to air their views, no matter how offensive they may be to you and me." The Jewish Americans among the faculty began to whisper among themselves. They stared at Puttbutt stonily. "Why didn't I see the signs? Why was I so naive?" Some of the men began to smile and nod. Their eyes were following Puttbutt, who had risen from his seat and was now walking around the room, stressing points by using his hands. "The naming of the university after war criminals. The IQ tests, the planning of a ceremony to apologize to the government for the defeat of the Japanese. It became apparent to me finally that the man was a Japanese chauvinist."

"Now we can go back to teaching the universals," said one of the traditionalists. The classics. Spenser and Milton."

"The classics. You make me sick with your goddam classics." It was Crabtree. He rose to speak. The colleagues whom he once led were shocked. "I agree that Dr. Yamato's two-month reign of terror should be ended but I am of the opinion that we should be grateful to him. He was just giving us a dose of our own medicine. As for Spenser and Milton. One wrote anti-Irish tracts for the British government, and the other was a Cromwellian political hack. Speaking of propaganda."

"Now listen here, Crabtree, just because you broke ranks. Acquiescing to Puttbutt's little jokes here, that you teach Yoruba, an exercise in feelgoodism and ethnic cheerleading, doesn't give you the right to . . ." a Miltonian said. Crabtree approached the man and stared right down his throat. He towered over the man who was recoiling.

"You sit down and shut up. You don't know a damned thing about African civilization. Not a damned thing. You fucking ignorant bastard. You're nothing but a bunch of 'oní-ṣọ-kú-ṣọ intellectual yànmù-yánmú." Crabtree was speaking Yoruba. And unlike many non-native speakers, he was getting all of his tones right. His intensive sessions with Sanya were paying off. Musomi was shocked. The others were stunned. Crabtree took a deep breath and steadied his nerves.

"For years we've been saying that our tradition and our standards were universal, but Dr. Yamato has taught us that two can play that game. And Puttbutt, I want to thank you. Thank you for opening my head. I thought that it was dead. But you know, it wasn't dead. I was starving it. I was depriving it of intellectual nutrition. I needed a new head on. We can always learn something. We don't have to stop learning. And God gave us this . . . this precious organ, this wonderful machine that can take us to places beyond our wildest dreams. It was my stupid arrogance, my devotion to these standards that we're always talking about that almost prevented me from embarking on this wonderful adventure. Learning this new language. Learning a new language and a new world. Discovering Yoruba. I haven't had so much fun since I learned to play poker. I have learned a language that transports me to a culture that's two thousand years old. Have they ever produced a Tolstoy? They have produced Tolstoys. Have they produced a Homer. They have hundreds of Homers. We were just too lazy and arrogant to find out. We're always condemning rednecks, but do you know who the real rednecks are, gentlemen? We are. Not the people who drive the pickup trucks and listen to Hank Williams. We should be the ones to lead our students and our country to new intellectual frontiers. Instead, we're like the archaic Dixiecrats of the old South, but instead of yelling segregation forever, we're yelling Western culture forever."

"But Dr. Crabtree. I ordered you to teach Yoruba because I wanted to dress you down. Humiliate you."

"I know, Puttbutt. I realize that. But that'll teach me to watch my words from now on. To stop commenting about things I have little knowledge of, out of racial pride. It's our silly racial pride that's preventing us from living together in peace. I have it. You all have it. At its most ridiculous, it's Poop claiming that the blacks are inferior because they can't blush and it's Matata claiming that white people are icepeople. They represent the highest level of intellect that a racist society is capable of producing. The fact that they are on this campus is a disgrace."

"I'm not going to have you address me in that manner, sir. You owe me an apology," Matata said.

"You can't say that. Matata and I have as much right to teach here as anybody else," Poopovich joined in.

"You deserve each other. Ignorant Àjàní-oní-ràdàràdà."

There was silence after Crabtree spoke. He looked around the room in such a manner as to indicate that he found all of those assembled contemptible. The silence was broken by Puttbutt, who gave instructions to those assembled about the plan for the Monday morning of Dr. Yamato's return. They would all go to Yamato's office and sit in to draw attention to the chauvinism that Yamato and the Japanese had brought to Jack London. Only Crabtree refused to participate.

chapter forty-three

I hey met at the cafe across the street from the college as they planned. Had coffee and went over last-minute plans. The procession started through the campus, reminding one of those quiet dignified processions which the French intellectuals formed in the streets of Paris during France's war against Algeria. Himmlar Poopovich and Matata Musomi walking arm in arm, joined in what they regarded a common effort. They carried the banner, JACK LONDON FOR THE AMERICANS. Puttbutt had his overcoat draped over his shoulder, was wearing dark glasses and puffing on a Gauloises. He'd seen denizens of the Café Select on Rue Saint Michel dressed this way. He'd primped in front of the mirror for half an hour in order to affect this look. They hadn't gotten far when they noticed a group of soldiers and two civilians heading toward them. It was Dr. Yamato and his administrative assistant. Holding bayonets, the soldiers had them under guard. Puttbutt looked over his shoulder to the street, and sure enough there was his father sitting in a limousine. The windows were dark but he was sure that it was his father. It was the same car that had brought him to his house. The students were throwing paper cups at Dr. Yamato and jeering him like a bunch of Sacramento fight fans upset by an unpopular decision. He was in handcuffs.

They had Dr. Yamato under arrest. As the group walked toward them Dr. Yamato paused. Seeing Chappie, he bowed slightly and said quietly, "Sayonara, Chappie." Chappie looked at the pavement. A coke bottle aimed at Dr. Yamato landed at his feet. They were told that the school had been closed until further notice. They split up. Chappie headed back to his house. He was really exhausted. He felt like a hurricane that had been downgraded to a tropical storm. He was totally confused. Dr. Yamato arrested by soldiers. The school closed. As Dr. Yamato and the soldiers pulled away, the students began cheering.

That night they had a big bonfire and cars caroused through the streets carrying wild and drunken students. The story was on all the evening news and they showed the students in the school's auditorium, waving American flags and tearing down the Japanese flags. Some of them made speeches and Muzukashii was cheered enthusiastically when he said that the distance between him and his Japanese heritage was about the distance between the tortoise and the moon. That he was an American and that he was proud to be an American, and if there ever came a showdown between the United States and Japan there was no question as to whose side he'd be on. The students applauded him wildly and they began to sing that stupid song that was made popular during the Persian Gulf War, "Stand Tall." Holding each other's arms and swaying from side to side, against the rhythm. Some were bawling and hugging each other. It was disgusting. It was at that time that Puttbutt decided he wasn't the NWO type. He just wanted to go to bed and sleep. He hadn't felt this way since Colorado Springs. He was suffering from posttraumatic stress.

chapter forty-four

Lesson five of his textbook was driving him crazy. For some reason the form that Japanese counters take (Kazu) depends upon the object being counted. For example, Ko for apples (1, Ichi Ko, 2, Ni Ko, etc.), keys and glasses; Dai for cars, motorcycles, telephones and buses; Mai for stamps, shirts, pictures and sandwiches; hon for bottles, pants, trees, ties and pencils; nin for people; satsu for books; and hai for cups. He was working his brain double shifts over these matters. Professor Miller was always inviting students to come to his house. Miller reminded him of Mel Ferrer, who played the quiet doctor in the "passing" drama, *Lost Boundaries*. The skeletal face. High forehead. Large ears. Concentration-camp eyes. He looked depressed all the time. As though he lacked a healthy supply of opiate receptors. His skin was a squash yellow. His mother was a blue-eyed blonde, his father a black jazzman from Memphis. Maybe Miller's being grounded was what attracted Puttbutt to him. Chappie didn't want to fly. He enjoyed viewing the world from the ground up. He only entered the Air Force Academy to satisfy his parents. Military life had worked for them. They always said that the military was the most integratable institution in American life. Their hero was Harry Truman who, in 1948, ordered the integration of the armed forces and who ordered the dropping of the A-bomb on Hiroshima and Nagasaki. His father always talked about the time, in the forties, when a white restaurant refused to serve him. The restaurant was crowded with his men who were white. He announced that if he wasn't going to eat nobody was going to eat. The restaurant emptied to the shock of the owner who ran after the soldiers, begging them to finish their food. Chappie decided to take Miller up on his offer. One day he drove to the professor's house, which was located in the fashionable section of Colorado Springs. He found the professor home. He was wearing a sleeveless sweater and a red and black bow tie and neatly creased pants and moccasins. He followed him into the living room and sat down as he was directed. They had spent about a half hour on the Kazu chapter when he heard some music. It was coming from upstairs. It was Horace Silver. The relentless driven rumbling left hand. The hand that always kicked up a storm.

"Somebody in the family like Horace Silver?"

"Yes. My wife. Have you ever met her?"

"No. Can't say that I have."

"Dear?" Momentarily she came downstairs. She was wearing a loose black blouse and black shorts. Kanojobi wa kirei deshita. As beautiful as the cello solo in Prokofiev's Lieutenant Kije suite. Her silky black hair hid her face. It was a blunt, aggressive black. A Horace Pippin black with tints of ink blue. He'd heard that the professor had met her in Tokyo during the American Occupation.

Her name was Jingo. he couldn't take his eyes off her. She knew it. She smiled. The professor could tell that he had been unsettled. He cleared his throat.

"Kochira Wa Tsuma desu, Jingo Miller," he said by way of introduction. "Hajimemashite," Puttbutt finally said.

"Hajimemashite," she said. She brushed back her hair and walked into the kitchen. Soon he could hear some utensils being pushed about.

The professor kept reviewing the lesson, but Puttbutt wasn't listening. He thought of the professor's wife. He caught her eye as she returned to the living room and headed up the stairs. She responded by blushing. Soon, Horace Silver's restless and hyperkinetic left hand began to funk throughout the house. Noticing that Chappie wasn't concentrating, the professor finally told him that he was tired and that he would go over the chapters the following week. He was an Oni-şe-ku-sé in those days and he thought to himself that if he had something as fine upstairs as the professor had he would always be desiring to turn in. He would spend most of his life in bed.

chapter forty-five

Sake o mo ippai ikaga desu ka."

"Iie mo kekko desu." They had both drunk too much sake one night and were in a room where Miller kept his swords. He was showing them to Puttbutt. Before displaying them he had identified the Kabuki actors whose faces lined the walls. Masks that he had bought in Tokyo. They were making a lot of noise and staggering around the room. He was showing Puttbutt his prize. A golden lacquer-emblazoned sword that dated from the 1330s. There were other swords. A tsuba, a kozuka and a tachi. He also owned a dagger that dated from the fourteenth century. A tanto. Dave Brubeck's "Jazz Goes to College" was playing. Chunk after chunk of chaotic and brilliant Brubeck chords were hugging the room's walls. The door flew open. Jingo was mad. "Blubeck wa soon desu!" She was shouting to them to shut up. As she said that she plugged her ears with her fingers. This reaction caused her kimono to part. He caught a glimpse of her underwear. She was wearing a floral silk chemise design. It was hitting her at the top of her thighs. Puttbutt felt a red hot pepper growing between his legs.

chapter forty-six

He had on his air force shades, leather jacket and silk scarf. And he was sitting in an outdoor cafe. The Colorado air was sharp and pointed. The sun was clear, as though it had been scrubbed to a bright yellow. The mountains were visible on this day. It was a day like this that made him appreciate the West. There was still space here. A sky. He had a copy of *Manyoshu* sitting on the table, next to his coffee and newspaper, *The Rocky Mountain Times*.

"Yoku Kono resutoran ni kimasu ka." He turned around. It was she. Jingo Miller. "Mind if I join you," she said. He smiled and stood. She sat down. Heads turned, and then resumed their places. She was one of these postwar Japanese women. Liberated. Hip. Licentious was the word that Nagai Kafu used to describe these women.

"Amari Kimasen."

"You forgot the *Iie.*" He was always omitting Iie no and omitting ka in interrogative sentences in those days.

"What are you reading?" she asked.

"It's the *Manyoshu*, he said, one of the great Japanese classics."

"It's Korean."

"What? Surely you're wrong."

"And it's all about fucking."

"What?" He pretended as though he didn't hear.

"Chizu o kakimasho ka." He looked down.

"No, but your husband says it's Japanese."

"He knows very little about either," she muttered under her breath. He pretended as though he hadn't heard her.

"It's been very hard for us. When he's not teaching he is in his study preparing to teach. When he's not doing that, he's away consulting lawyers. For recreation he plays those blasted Dave Blubeck records all day. Blubeck. This man doesn't give the piano a break." She was smoking a cigarette. He looked down at her genkina futomomo. When she got up to refill her tea, his eyes caught a glance of her chiisai butt.

"He's so bitter. Angry." She leaned back and blew out some smoke rings as the kocha was brought to the table.

"Look, I don't want to pry into your business."

"He's at home right now meeting with lawyers." She was tapping a foot and began smoking nervously.

"Lawyers for what?"

"He's suing the air force. He's saying that they are depriving him of something that rightfully belongs to him. They gave him this teaching job so that he'd quiet down. He won't be appeased." They spent the rest of their encounter talking about piano jazz. She said that she had been turned on to the music during the occupation. Horace Silver, then Hampton Hawes and Randy Weston. She'd also read Ted Joans, Kerouac, Rexroth, Ginsberg, Bob Kaufman and Gary Snyder. She talked about going to San Francisco once and book shopping at City Lights. Attending a poetry reading at the Anxious Asp and listening to jazz at the Black Hawk and The Place. She mentioned something about her belonging to some radical student group in Japan during the war years and being arrested and tortured.

chapter forty-seven

It was 2:00 A.M. that same night. The phone in his cottage rang.

"Chappie, I'm afraid." He was half asleep.

"Afraid?"

"It's Milton. He's got a gun and he's running around the back-yard. He says that he spotted Chuck Yeager back there and that Yeager had come to kill him so that the world would never know that he, not Yeager had been the first to break the sound barrier. I don't know what to do. He's out in the backyard waving that thing around."

"Why don't you come over here. He'll get over it in the morning."

"Do you think that's right?"

"He'll be all right in the morning. He'll understand." She agreed to come over.

Shortly, he heard her car pull up in the driveway of the cottage he'd rented. He let her in.

"I'm sorry to bother you."

"Do itashimashite," he said sleepily. He went back to bed. Before he dozed off he heard her in the next room, crying.

They had breakfast in silence.

"I'll drive you home," he finally said. It was Saturday and luckily there were no classes. When they reached their two-story Colonial house they noticed his car in the driveway. She got out of the car and ran up the steps while Puttbutt waited. She rang the bell for a long time. She looked back at Puttbutt. He could tell that she was worried. Finally, Milton Miller answered the door. They embraced. Milton looked down and saw Puttbutt. He waved. Milton was smiling.

chapter forty-eight

They were going over the time lessons. Nanji desu ka. He was having a hard time learning the Japanese minutes. When to put pun and when to put fun. At the end of the class Puttbutt rose with the rest of the students and headed toward his locker. Puttbutt looked good in his blue air force cadet uniform.

"Puttbutt-san." He stopped and was approached by Professor Miller.

"I want to thank you for what you did the other night. Jingo has these episodes. You can't talk to her when it happens to her. Her folks were killed during the bombing over Nagoya. She wakes up. Her gown is wet. She's shaking. I've tried to get her to go and get therapy. Nothing doing. I know that I should exhibit more compassion, but she just caught me in the wrong mood. I'd had a long day with my lawyers and with the five classes I have here. I'm afraid that I raised my voice at her. That's why she came to your house. You understand."

"Sure, Professor."

"I hope that she caused you no inconvenience."

"No, sir. No inconvenience."

"Listen. How about dinner tonight?"

"I have to study, sir. Midterms are coming."

"Aw come on. Jingo's preparing a Japanese meal. Ban-gohan. Seaweed and cucumbers."

"Well, all right." Strange couple, Puttbutt thought.

* * *

When he arrived at their house, Miller was waiting for him. Instead of inviting him in, he put on a gray gabardine coat and a felt hat. Dobbs, maybe.

"I thought that we were eating here."

"Look, we've had an argument. It's best that we go out. I've made reservations. You like seafood?"

"Yes, but . . ." Suddenly a shoe flew down from upstairs and landed at his feet. Puttbutt heard Jingo's voice.

"You're so fucking feudalistic."

"Look we'd better go," Miller said.

chapter forty-nine

He was also having trouble with the syntax. He wasn't used to a language where the sentences ended in verbs. Later he would hear Garrett Hongo, a Japanese-American poet, likening the Japanese sentence to a play in basketball. He decided to stop by Professor Miller's house to get some help. He leaned on the bell. Jingo answered. She was wearing a black silk jacket that hit her at the upper thighs. It was tied with a sash. There was an image of a crane sewn on. She was barefoot. He began experiencing shortness of breath. His insides began to stir as though he had just finished some hot curry goat. She had a Horace Silver ballad on.

"I was looking for your husband."

"My warrior is away at Edo," she said. She was tipsy. He could tell. She giggled as she said Edo.

"Edo. Isn't that the old name for Tokyo?"

"It's what I imagine myself to be sometimes. He's away so often now, with the court case. It's like the samurai brides who had to wait for their husbands to return from the wars. Won't you come in?" she said, ignoring him.

"I don't want to interrupt anything."

"Please. A cup of sake? I've heated some." He followed her to the table in the living room where she had placed some heated sake. She got another cup from the rosewood cabinet. It was one hundred years old. She poured him a cup and then sat in the chair, her knees under her, revealing some comely yellow thighs. His penis began to crawl out of its cave. It began to poke around and swagger from side to side like a black pelican amidst some Canadian geese.

"Colorado Springs reminds me of my home. The snow. The mountains." Sake, like coke, sneaked up on him. Both drugs were like the playmate who put their hands in front of your eyes and demanded that you identify them. "Guess who?"

"Do you like it here?"

"I like it better than Maryland. That's where we used to spend a lot of time when we weren't traveling. My Dad's a major in the Air Force. One of these days he's going to make general. He eats and sleeps war. My mother too. She's with Intelligence. One of the few black women in that field." She looked into his eyes and stared a long time. He looked away. Through the big picture window he could see the afternoon, cusping.

"Well, I'd better get going. We're having midterms soon."

"You're not like the rest of the cadets here. So wooden."

"Thanks." He couldn't prevent his eyes from doing a closeup on the yellow mounds that rose over an unbuttoned top of her jacket. He got up and started toward the door. "Sayonara," he said.

"Please stay. One more cup." He had two, three, four more cups until he got a buzzing in his head. They didn't do much talking. A lot of smiling. He started to leave and she began to sob. She rose and put her arms around his neck. He held her close to him. She felt his hard dick on her stomach. It always had a mind of its own. An anarchist. And in the old days he couldn't keep it under control. She looked up at him and smiled. She got up on tiptoe and his thing was now pressing her between her thighs. She cooperated by opening them slightly. They kissed ardently. One thing, of course, led to another. They fell on top of each other and landed on the floor. He was fumbling for the sash and she was grabbing for the bulge at his swollen crotch. She brought the creature out, held it with her fist and began to churn the thing. He almost came in her hand he was so excited. His throat was strangling from passion as he began to inspect her body. He grabbed a hold of the top of her panties, but his fingers were confused. She pulled them down and over her feet. She put a finger to his lips. She was smiling. He kept thinking silly things and they were giggling and gasping for breath. He thought, for example, which was the most important discovery in the history of the world. Radioactivity, or vaginal lubrication. Before you knew it she was thrashing under him like a fish out of water. Gaia was the goddess of the earth and it was said that if you penetrated her to her core it was as hot as the surface of the sun there. Jingo was very hot inside. Kanojo no naka ni totemo atsukatta desu. He began to jab his thing excitedly between her thighs until he found the place. Oyin ni, as the Yoruba say. Like honey. The greatest pleasures are not achieved without work. And he was working. He pushed into her. Her eyes swelled with amazement. Anata wa okii desu!

"Suppose he catches us." Puttbutt said. He didn't know why he said it. He had gone too far to turn back.

"Huh?"

"I said, suppose he catches us?"

"He's in Denver until tomorrow night." He mounted her and began a long and serious fuck. He was young, green and quick as a jackrabbit on amphetamine. She kept holding on to his balls and gently caressing his buttocks. She was calming him down and reassuring him. Yukkuri, she kept saying, Yukkuri. She kept saying Zehi kite kudasai. Then finally one long IIIII Dessss Neeeee. Every time he tried to get up she brought him back into her. "Mo Ichi do," she kept saying. "Mo Ichi do." He had to pause so that he could achieve the maximum pleasure and so he just leaned in there from time to time and every time he did that her cunt would reward him a gentle squeeze. "Do deshita ka?" she kept saying. He thought that he'd lose his mind. Then she put the thing on him that he would never forget. What the old Yoruba people called the mukulumuke. Nobody ever did that to him. He came and came until he must have squirted enough to fill a half a pint. Finally, he tried to stand and was so groggy he almost passed out. His knees went out from under him. He went to sleep muttering Yata Yata. He looked up at her eyes. She was smiling. "Do deshita ka." He remembered muttering something like subarashikatta, desu.

He awoke on the floor. The day had disappeared and he could see, through the large window, the mountains and the star-flecked Colorado sky. It was snowing. Never before and never again would he experience such peace. He heard Horace Silver coming from upstairs. Señor Blues. He heard some typing. He especially liked the chorus. The trumpet that went: Ta Ta Ta Ta Ta Tata. Ta Ta Ta Ta Ta Ta Ta Ta Ta Ta Ta Ta. Ta Ta Ta Ta Ta Tata. Ta Ta Ta Ta Ta Ta Ta Ta Ta Ta Ta. TatiTa Ta Ta Taaaaata. And then the triplet: Taaataaayatatatata.

chapter fifty

She spent a lot of time at his house after that, whenever she'd find an opportunity to get away. They'd always down a quart of sake and talk about jazz. Talk about Miller. Sometimes Milton Miller would leave the entire week. One morning they were lying on the futon after a night of intense and vigorous lovemaking. She being more experienced than him had taught him a lot over the three months. Being an army brat he had spent most of his time around people who were buttoned to the neck in uniforms. He didn't know about the body other than its use as a killing machine. She had taught him the beauty and pleasure that a body was capable of providing.

He watched her as she rose nude from the futon and went into the bathroom. He heard some mumbling. It was coming from the direction of the window. He wrapped a towel around himself and went to the window. There were three workmen there on three ladders. They were putting on a screen. They had seen Jingo nude.

"Don't you guys warn people before you work on their property?" he asked. The black one answered.

"Look, buddy. You don't have to worry about me. Ain't nothing in there that I want." Then he started to grin and roll his eyes around as he sought approval from his white fellow workers. All three of them laughed. Seeing that he'd delighted his fellow workers, the black repeated the joke. "Nothing in there that I want." Puttbutt didn't see anything funny. He went into Miller's room and took down one of those mean samurai swords. The prize one. He ran down the steps and then out onto the lawn. The two white workers saw him and scrambled down their ladders. The black one tried to get away too, but he stumbled and rolled over on the lawn several times, only to find Puttbutt standing over him. Puttbutt gave him his classical and stern samurai gaze. The black guy was sweating and rolling his eyes like Willie Best. Snot was leaking from his nostrils.

"Look, man, give a fellow a break. We didn't know that you were in there with your woman." Puttbutt lifted the sword over his head as though he were about to strike.

"Please, sir. I didn't mean no harm. I have three little babies. I'll do whatever you ask me to do, but please don't take my life." He was trembling and talking as though snot was clogging his nostrils. Something stank. The fellow had fouled himself, he was so scared.

"Stop it. Stop." Puttbutt turned around. It was Jingo. She was standing in the doorway. Puttbutt started toward her. The man sprang up from the grass and ran, sped up like a cartoon creature.

Puttbutt walked up the slope toward her. He was laughing his head off.

"I was just having some fun. I wasn't going to harm him."

"Get out. You're just like all the rest."

"But . . ." She took the sword from him and slammed the door.

He called her every half hour when he reached his house, but she didn't answer. It was after that episode that Puttbutt became a pacifist. If being a warrior meant losing someone as beautiful as she, then he would study war no more. Like Red Ryder, he'd be a peaceable man, but prepared to fight if finding himself in a life-threatening situation.

chapter fifty-one

A few days later, Miller was late for class. That wasn't like him and the students began to buzz. When he arrived he seemed haggard, and Puttbutt noticed, as he walked down the aisle, that his eyes were glazed. His shirt was open at the neck and his tie was hanging loosely from his collar. As he walked down the aisle he stumbled and had to grab a student's desk in order to support himself. He said "Shit," and stared at the student who occupied the desk. His face was unshaven and his hair uncombed. When he reached the table from which he usually delivered his lectures, he stared out over the cadets. And then, glaring at Puttbutt, he started to speak.

"Today, I will talk about betrayal and adultery in the works of the great playwright of the Tokugawa era, Chikamatsu Monzaemon." At the word "adultery" Puttbutt began to slide down in his seat. The class began to mumble. They didn't know what to make of this remark. They were supposed to work on the Ikutsu counters.

"Like the haiku master Basho, he was born into a samurai family, but unlike his family members he pursued the intellectual arts." He looked down at Puttbutt and smiled ironically. "The message of these plays is similar. Adultery leads to shinju. Suicide and death." When he said that he looked straight at Puttbutt. Awwww shit, Puttbutt thought.

"When a man takes another man's woman, that man and his family are allowed official vengeance from the authorities." He walked from behind the table and stared diagonally toward Puttbutt. "In the old Japan, unlike today's of easy women wearing their muu-muus and fishnet stockings, a day of easier morals, the American Bandstand Japan, there was no excuse for adultery.

"In Chikamatsu's famous puppet theater, *The Drum Waves of Horikawa*, Otane, the wife of the samurai Hikokuro, sick with loneliness for her husband who is away in Edo, sleeps with Miyaji Gen'emon, a man who is teaching her son how to play the drums. A man in whom the family had confidence." He glared at Puttbutt at the word "confidence." "It's her drunkenness that makes her susceptible to this affair, but too much sake is no excuse." He shouted out "It's her drunkenness" and apologized to the students for raising his voice. She told him, Puttbutt thought. Miller walked right up to Puttbutt's desk which was located in the front row, and stared down at him sternly. "She stabs herself with a dagger and her husband, affecting the merciless pose of a samurai, gives her a bite of his sword, and after he is convinced that she is dead, kicks the corpse away.

"When they trap the drum master, Otane's son, her sister and Otane's sister-in-law, as well as her husband Hikokuro, join in on his murder. The play ends with a celebration. Having executed official revenge, they are satisfied." The cadets were baffled. He stood there for a moment and then began to laugh. It was an ugly, creeping laugh. He then started out of the auditorium even though there were forty-five minutes remaining in the lecture. The class was shocked. Puttbutt ran out after him.

"Look, I can explain everything—"

"I have nothing to say to you, Mr. Puttbutt."

"It wasn't her fault. She loves you."

"Get out of my sight, Mr. Puttbutt." He said it with decorum but it was so steely that Puttbutt felt something move in his abdomen. But of course he was used to these male Great Santinis. Refusing to express any sort of direct emotion. Running their household the way they ran their troops. Instead of telling him something like, "Look Motherfucker, I catch you with my old lady again Immona kick yo ass," he worked his anger into a lesson plan about puppet theater in feudal Japan.

chapter fifty-two

He went to his house and began to place calls to Jingo. The phone was busy. It was busy all day. At the end of the day he consumed a cup of sake. Then two. By midnight there was a large empty bottle sitting on his table.

chapter fifty-three

The next day he went to campus and found little clusters of cadets gathered about, talking. When he walked by them, the cadets would stop and give him an expressionless stare. He tried to greet a couple and they turned their backs on him. When he reached his locker he found a note asking him to come to the commandant's office.

* * *

The commandant gave him a chewing out that he never forgot. Something like, "I want your ass out of this school by tonight. You're lucky we won't tell your father." Professor Miller had left a note. He had done this because one of the students was screwing his wife. It was a matter of honor. He remembered that quarrel they had the night they were supposed to have dinner. Jingo saying, "You're so fucking feudalistic." He named Puttbutt. He'd beheaded Jingo and had put a dagger through his stomach. (Beheading is also the ultimate punishment in the Yoruba tradition. The body is condemned to wander through the land of the dead, seeking its head. At the core of both the Yoruba and Shinto traditions is a reverence for ancestors.) Later he found that it was the same sword that he'd used to threaten the black workman.

chapter fifty-four

The bell rang. It was his neighbors. She was with her husband this time. He stared at the floor. He had a full head of what the old race texts called "Negro hair." He was carrying some kind of package. He could tell that the man had shelled out five bucks to get the package wrapped. They stood there for a moment.

"Well, go on, tell him dear," his wife coached him.

"I . . . a . . . well. I know that I haven't been a good neighbor." Chappie didn't say anything.

"I mean, I . . . a . . . well, you never did nothin to me. I guess I'm just a sour sort of guy. But I want to thank you for telling those Japanese to keep me on at Caesar. I wanted you to have this." Chappie accepted his gift. They stared at each other for a moment. The man extended his hand. They shook hands. His wife smiled.

Sirens. The street lit up. The sirens came to a halt outside of his house. They all looked out. It was his father, General Puttbutt. The other car contained his shooting trophies and the medals that wouldn't go on his chest. A soldier opened the door of his car, and carrying a shotgun, accompanied his father. Puttbutt got out and marched stiffly toward his son's house, passing the next-door neighbors as they were leaving. He walked right past his son and sat down. A Japanese man was with him. He introduced him as Ray Tanaka-san, a member of the Japanese consulate in San Francisco. He was a well-dressed man without facial hair; his nails had been manicured. He possessed an "aquiline nose." He could feel his father glowering behind his dark glasses. He turned to the Bass boy.

"Fix us a couple of drinks."

"Will you be having Tanqueray, sir?" The general smiled and nodded. The Japanese-American man declined.

"That's a well-mannered chap you have working for you, Son, is he a college student?" he said as Bass went into the kitchen.

"Yes, Dad. He's over at Jack London." Bass returned to the room with the drinks and sat them before the two. The general began sucking on the gin.

"Young man, have you ever thought of military service? You look like West Point material to me," he said to Robert Bass, Jr.

"I'm thinking about the Peace Corps, sir." The general looked puzzled and then turned to Chappie. "What have you done to this boy?"

"Look, Dad, I have a lot of work to do. Your soldiers arrested Dr. Yamato today and all of the responsibility for running the school has been placed on my shoulders. I wish that you'd permitted us to settle it our way. I think that the show of force on our campus was no different from that which takes place in totalitarian countries. Tanks rolling onto the campuses. Bayonets. I called a meeting of members of the faculty and we'd planned to confront Dr. Yamato. We could have settled the whole thing peacefully."

"I don't know what you're talking about." The general turned to the Japanese man, Tanaka-san, who was frowning, indicating his puzzlement.

"You had Dr. Yamato arrested because of what he was doing to the campus, right? The torturing of the students. The comfort girls. The IQ tests and the naming of the university after war criminals." Tanaka-san and his father were still puzzled.

"They weren't torturing any students. That was just some propaganda that the Amerikaner student branch of the Order of the Boer Nation printed. We had your boy Yamato arrested because he was in on a plot to assassinate the emperor and the prime minister of Japan."

"Whaaaawhaaattttt!!" Puttbutt nearly fell out of his chair.

"Tell him, Ray."

"He was a member of the old Black Dragon group. The Kokuryù-kai. A strange amalgam of militarists, businessmen, gangsters and religious fanatics who wanted to return the Tokugawa Shogunate to power. They included some of the religious extremists in the dojo, the old militarists' group Bushido, the secret business group the Zaibatsu that MacArthur abolished during the occupation, and Japanese mafia, the Yakuza. The Tokugawa ruled Japan for three hundred fifty years until the ascension of the Meiji. They felt that the decline of Japan began with the rise of the Meiji. They wanted to cancel democracy and restore shogun rule."

"Dr. Yamato was into that?" Tanaka-san wore his suit as well as Gregory Peck in *The Man in the Gray Flannel Suit*. Nobody in any movie had ever worn a suit as well as Peck in that movie. Peck and Sidney Poitier must have been influenced by the same director. The shoulders-bobbing walk. The head shifting as though alluding punches. The stiff back. Tanaka-san was slim and had a waistline like Prince. His features were crisp. Tanaka-san was well aware of the rising anti-Japanese sentiment in the United States, which was alarming Japanese Americans like himself into believing that a new internment might be in the wings.

"Into it. He was one of the masterminds behind the plot," Tanaka said.

"Your grandfather was sent to provide backup for Dr. Yamato."
His grandfather, of course, those Do cries. "The ones who punched
out the Amerikaner students." That's why he heard those martial
arts sounds in the background when he met with his grandfather.

"But how did my grandfather get into this?"

He was recruited back there in Detroit when he was with the
Muslims. A Japanese reserve officer named Takahashi was sent to
proselytize them on the basis of some kind of solidarity between the
colored races against the white man. An agent named Naka Nakane
was sent to New York to get blacks there all riled up. Yamato was
the agent who traveled up and down this coast to recruit blacks.
The New York group called themselves the Ethiopian Pacific Movement of Harlem. The ones in Detroit and New York were all rounded
up and sent to jail, including Elijah Muhammad and Robert O.
Jordan, who was known as "Black Hitler." Hoover tried to get Elijah
Muhammad and his group on sedition charges because they saw
Japanese victories as a victory for the colored races. Elijah Muhammad received five years in prison even though he was forty-five years
old. Other proaxis blacks were arrested in Newark and San Diego.
J. Edgar was really paranoid in those days, son. He thought that the
Japanese ambassador in Mexico was financing a black uprising and
they kept threatening the black press, accusing them of being in
league with the Nips." Tanaka-san glared at General Puttbutt. "I'm
sorry, Ray—I . . ." Tanaka rolled his eyes, crossed his legs and
arms.

"It's OK, General. I'm becoming used to it."

"Well, anyway, your grandfather was a martial arts expert and
after the war, Yamato and his friends had him installed in Hawaii
where he was charged with training the muscle for the Black Dragon.
Ray, tell him about Yamato."

"That's just one of his many aliases. Among other things, Yamato
was one of the ancient names for Japan. He was born sixty-eight
years ago in Fukuoka, a hotbed of extreme nationalistic activity,
plots, conspiracies, assassination attempts and secret societies. It

was also a gathering place for down-and-out samurai, which apparently fed the young student with romantic visions of a once-glorious Japan brought low by corrupt politicians and foreign influence. Fukuoka was the birthplace of the Genyosha, a right-wing group that wasn't adverse to using blackmail and clandestine schemes in order to accomplish its ends. They were fanatically opposed to Western influences in Asia and used hoodlums to beat up those who were pro-Western and prodemocratic. During the war Yamato worked for Japanese intelligence. After the war he and other elements of the Black Dragon reorganized. Now they are preparing for a war that they believe will inevitably result from the continued trade competition with the United States. They want to eradicate Western influence in Japan. As with many extremists, the Black Dragon have mystical leanings. A subgroup of crazies known as the Hidari-Gawa. They believed that your grandfather was the reincarnation of Sakanouye Tamuro, the African who defeated the Ainu, a tribe located in the Japanese north. Black Dragon wanted revenge on the Americans. To pay them for the humiliation that occurred when Commodore Perry invaded Japan. They wanted to set things right for the Japanese defeat in the war. Such fanaticism only adds to the hostility that we Japanese Americans are experiencing here at home. Yamato merely helps to perpetuate the stereotype that all of us are scheming, treacherous, and out for revenge."

"Your friend is in deep trouble, Son." Why was he calling him Son. When his father wasn't away on maneuvers when he was growing up, he was holed up in his room, watching Uncle Milty. Yukking it up. Singing along with the Texaco song.

"The Kuroi Ryu was well financed and had penetrated security surrounding the emperor and government where some military types from World War II still enjoy power," Tanaka-san said. "They tried to reach the emperor during the recent coronation, but Japanese intelligence discovered the plot and arrested the conspirators."

"I had to sneak your grandfather out of the country."

"What?"

"Your grandfather. If I hadn't intervened he would have been arrested on the old sedition charges. I was able to get the old man back to Hawaii. He'll be watched. Maybe he'll stay out of trouble. You remember that writer who committed hari-kari."

"Yes, Mishima. What about him."

"The Black Dragon made him sound like a centrist," his father said. He looked to Ray, who continued this strange story.

"Every year they would go into the Japanese countryside and stage a performance of the Kanadehon Chushingura, the theater of revenge that General MacArthur banned during the occupation. It was for them like the Wagnerian pageants at Oberammergau. They wanted to move the capitol back to Kyoto. And they wanted to restore its old name: Heian-kyo. They felt that Japan had slid down-hill since eighteen sixty-nine. That's why they wanted to assassinate the present emperor and replace him with a descendant of the Kuge, the old court aristocracy, a puppet who would do their bidding, an invisible emperor in the tradition of the Tokugawa," Ray said.

"My Japanese teacher was into all of that. And my grandfather was on his side?" So there was no interruption in the line of milita-rists in the Puttbutt family after all. His grandfather had merely served the enemy.

As if reading his thoughts, his father said, "He was working for the wrong side. The world is complicated, Son. Alliances shift. Reality changes. Whether you know it or not, there's real trouble ahead for this Japanese-American alliance that's been going on since the end of the war. We may have to fight them again. There might be another Pearl Harbor. Wouldn't it be funny if the gov-ernment enlisted you to break another Japanese code. Your grand-father rooted for the Japanese during the last war, but why do you think he lives in Hawaii. The Japanese have words for the whites, but they have some names they call the blacks, too. He remains in Hawaii so that his image of pancolored solidarity won't be shat-tered by a trip to Japan. Though they pretended to be into some kind of Asian solidarity bit during the last war, they treated their fellow Asians as inferiors and referred to the Chinese as "coolies." They committed horrendous atrocities against other Asians during World War II. Used bacteriological and biological weapons. Of course, the blame is not entirely theirs. One of the first things that Commodore Perry did when he sailed into the harbor was to put on a minstrel act. The Americans took the disease to Japan, fed it during the occupation and are now aggravating the infestation through satellite TV news." Ray Tanaka seemed annoyed by his father's last speech.

"There were atrocities on all sides. The bombing of Japanese cities by the American bombers. They used napalm on Tokyo. They killed seventy-two thousand people in one night. Not to mention the A-bombing of Hiroshima and Nagasaki. There were also plans to bomb Tokyo with an atom bomb. After the war there was a demand from the American public that the entire Japanese race be exterminated."

"Ray, you're exaggerating and those bombs had to be dropped in order to shorten the war."

"Look, General. A 1944 gallup poll revealed that thirteen percent of the American people favored the extermination of the Japanese. And a Senator Bilbo wrote a letter to Douglas MacArthur urging that the Japanese be sterilized. As for your argument that the A-bombs were dropped to save lives and end the war—the Japanese wanted peace in 1941, and the United States was aware of this fact because it had deciphered and decoded telegrams between the Japanese foreign minister and the Japanese ambassador in Moscow. They were hoping to get Russia to act as mediator to the end of the war."

"Aw Ray, every time I see you we argue about this. Look, if the Americans were so cruel why did they spare Kyoto, the ancient seat of culture and learning. As for sterilizing the Japanese, Senator Bilbo was nuts." There was an awkward silence.

"Do you need me for anything else?" Tanaka asked.

"No, Ray, that will be all." The man from the consulate bade them sayonara and left.

"I'm sorry to have to bring this news to you, Son. I know that you and Dr. Yamato were friends."

"Why should I believe you. Why should I believe anything that's coming from the Pentagon after the lies about Grenada, Panama and Iraq?"

"You're my son, Puttbutt, but of all of the Puttbutts, you're the most chickenshit of the Puttbutts to come down the pike. My own flesh and blood, a fucking . . . pacifist." He said the word as though it were nasty. "Your grandfather is a traitor, but at least the old man went against public opinion and called for a Japanese victory when the American public was hating all of the Japs in existence.

"When you thought that your tenure was automatic, you preached against affirmative action, but when those white people whom you thought were your colleagues denied you tenure, you turned against them and sided with Dr. Yamato in an effort to humiliate them. You don't have no convictions, Son. You're all over the place. A product of this age. Join whatever side that can advance your thing. Signing that petition against the Qaddafi raid when your own mother was in on the planning. And when she was kidnapped by those Arabs, you took the Arabs' side. The Arabs hate niggers worse than the Japs and the white people. Qaddafi used chemical weapons against the people of Chad and is trying to expand his slave trade religion throughout Africa, and you sided with this faggot. You sided with this faggot. Just like that paper you wrote about Othello. I know all about it. Intelligence passed it on to me when you were going to school in Utah. Raving against white people. Then you come to Jack London and let the white people use you against the blacks. But when you didn't get tenure, you got out your beret and started fighting the system again. First they called you white dog. Now they are calling you the black fang."

"You ought to read *Othello*, Dad. It's about a black who carries out raids against the Turks on behalf of white people who despise him and say ugly things behind his back. That's you and Colin Powell, Chappie James and Benjamin Davis. Buffalo Soldiers. But instead of wiping out Indians you're helping to exterminate the yellows and Arabs. Chappie James bragged about killing one hundred Korean soldiers in one raid. From the air, and the Koreans didn't even have the air support. What's so manly about that? As for Davis, he justified the punishment of the black soldiers at Brownsville on the grounds that they didn't follow orders." In nineteen six, three companies of black soldiers invaded Brownsville, Texas after an altercation between a black soldier and a white merchant. President Roosevelt dishonorably discharged the soldiers and disqualified them from future military or civil service. "You guys are Negro Globocops, like that Jewish butcher Kaganovich, who carried out Stalin's orders to collectivize the Russian countryside in the twenties and thirties. He was as bad as the killers they hanged at Nuremberg in 1946. You committed genocide in Iraq. Destroyed the seat of Middle Eastern civilization." The general walked over and lifted his son from the chair. He cuffed him.

"Now you listen here, Chappie. If you weren't living in this country you'd be living in some mud hut, dying of malaria or some other jungle disease or drinking out of the same water that you shit in. You'd have to run around catching food from an airplane, that is, if some friendly Western nation was kind enough to deliver supplies to some desert in which you found yourself. And even if you managed to catch some canned goods, somebody might kill you over some sardines. You fucking intellectuals make me sick. All you can think to do is criticize. Knockin me. Knockin Colin. You know how crazy these white boys are. You saw what they did to Korea. Japan. Mozambique. Indonesia. If it weren't for Colin this hysterical man that they have in the Oval Office would have nuked Baghdad. They would have turned Baghdad into a parking lot. The president was gulping down Halcion like there has no tomorrow. You know, the drug that causes memory loss, depression and amnesia. They had the plans ready. Colin stopped it. That's right. Stopped it. Next to them Colin was a pacifist like you. You remember the last pacifist, JFK and what they did to him. That shows you how much Colin is risking. Besides, why are you taking the moral high road? I know all about that professor at the academy. He took you in his confidence and you paid him back by plugging his wife." Puttbutt felt as though someone had shot him down. His eyes turned away from his father's. "You don't have a bit of backbone. When her husband murdered her you didn't even attend her cremation. What a heartless son of a bitch you are. And your mother. No telling what kind of awful tortures she's undergone. You have shown no concern at all." Puttbutt began to shed tears. Not because he had mentioned his mother, but because his Dad had mentioned her. Jingo Miller. Nagai Kafu would call her his Hikage no hana. Shade's flower or flower in the shade.

He wished that there was some way that she could return from beyond the grave. To come back to him. To send him some sort of message. In those few short months she had given him happiness as no other woman had.

"You're responsible for both of them being dead." That remark got Chappie's attention.

"You're a real disappointment, Chappie. And to think I named you after General Chappie James, Jr., the great Black Eagle, and General Benjamin O. Davis, one of the most capable soldiers in the history of the country." His mother and father honored General Davis. They always talked about the time when the Klan marched through Tuskegee and General Davis sat on the porch in his white uniform to show defiance. He was their role model. General Puttbutt had served with his son.

General Puttbutt arose and, as though reading his mind, said, "You don't know what we had to go through. The Black Eagles. They didn't think that we had the necessities to make first-class pilots. A 1925 War College report said that we had small brains. That we were cowardly and immoral. Even after all of the combat missions in Germany and Italy and the Distinguished Flying Crosses and the Bronze Stars, they still pissed on us. Kept us out of the officer's clubs. Segregated us and our wives in inferior quarters. But we've gone a long ways since then. The armed forces are the most integrated institutions in American life. Yessir. If a black man or woman can't make it there they can't make it anywhere. The greatest equal opportunity employers around." He poured himself another glass of gin. "I have something that the commandant who ran the school sent me when he retired. It's a letter from that yellow slut of yours. I've held onto it all of these years. I think it's time for you to have it." He threw the letter at Puttbutt. It landed in his lap. The general swallowed the rest of the gin and headed toward the door. Momentarily Chappie heard some motorcycles and jeeps start their engines. His father's convoy headed from his block. The helicopter that had been circling the neighborhood clattered away.

chapter fifty-five

Two weeks later Puttbutt was in the kitchen pouring himself a cup of sake. He heard some movement in the laundry room. Somebody was in the house! He went into the drawer and got a kitchen knife. He moved to the laundry room door and slowly opened it. A man emerged from the shadows. He lifted the knife and was about to plunge it into the intruder. His brand of pacifism didn't require one to be murdered in one's house.

"Dr. Yamato. How did you get in here?" He drew the knife back. "I thought that my father and his men had arrested you. They manufactured some wild story about your being in on an attempted assassination of Emperor Akihito. That you were backed by military, business and crime money." Dr. Yamato answered calmly as he strolled into the kitchen.

"Your father is outside of the loop, as they say in Washington.

Do you think that the people who run this country would tell your father what's really going on? The men who run this country are not even known by the average American. Your father doesn't know."

"But they had you arrested."

"They had us incarcerated in one of those federal prisons Putt-butt-san, but mysteriously we were released. The secretary of state offered us many apologies and said that it was all a mistake. We were driven to the Maryland estate of Jack Only, the oil mogul. There we had a number of conversations with the people who are really in charge. The people who run things while the president is out jogging and commuting up to Kennebunkport." He mentioned the name of a general who had been accused of spying on all of the presidents since 1960, and seeing to it that some of their orders that would jeopardize the military industrial complex were counter-manded.

"They agreed with us Puttbutt-san that the Japanese are not cut out for this democracy. Look at the scandals in government and on the Tokyo exchange. There are people in Washington who agree. Who need the kind of government that they can rely on. Like Kuwait. China. One that can curb Japanese business from adventurism. One that can guarantee that American goods will be given a fair break in the Japanese market and that Americans be allowed to have some say-so in the Japanese companies in which they hold stock. We need a government that will treat American business people with respect. We need to end all of the trade barriers that are obstructing the flow of American trade.

"The first thing we do when we take over will be to issue an apology to T. Boone Pickens, who was assaulted with the cries of Remember Pearl Harbor when he was forced to leave a stockholders' meeting in Japan. We will round up the ruffians who did this and have them beheaded. Instead of a parliament, playboy prince and an emperor married to a commoner, we need a firm hand on the sword of the nation. Instead of capitalistic adventurism we need descendants of our ancient families running the economy. A strong leader who will do something about the young people taken to modish Western ideas. How do you say, Michael Jackson. The Jackson family is destroying the morals of Japanese youth. Women loose and powerful. Feminists. All of these things are corrupting our nation. Away with democracy and individualism."

"It happened so swiftly, Dr. Yamato. I mean, they took you from here under arrest and now you're talking about meeting with some invisible American government that's going to put you and your people in power. A few weeks ago you were talking about the Americans apologizing to Japan for Pearl Harbor, and now you're offended by the way some nationalistic businessmen treated T. Boone Pickens?"

"Our society, the Black Dragon, owns too many of your congressmen for the arrest to stick. You know that it was the lowest priority when they assigned your father, a black, to the case. Besides, many of the people in your National Security State agree with us. As for revenge, why does there have to be revenge when a growing number of your people are beginning to switch sides about World War II."

"What?"

"Followers of Adolf Hitler and the Axis that you thought you'd vanquished are arising here and in Europe. Look at the outpouring of affection toward these people by the media and the politicians. There are people in the national security state who are guiding cash to their causes."

"National security state, I don't follow, Dr. Yamato."

"The secret government. You know, the government within a government."

"We only have one government here, Dr. Yamato. The democratically elected government of the people."

"Ha ha. Ha ha ha." Yamato laughed. Yamato actually laughed. "You are naive. It gets its way by working through agents in the governments and private circles of other countries. They will help

us to achieve power. This will be a wonderful deal. Your people
will get what they want, a government where one man makes the
decisions and controls the economy, a state that is a bulwark against
chaos. Instability. As for assassinating the emperor, that would be
crude. Our friends will arrange a suite for him and his wife and their
entourage at the Waldorf-Astoria. They can live out their days
in comfort. Go to Broadway shows. Play tennis. There are some
wonderful Japanese restaurants in New York. We will install our
own emperor. But that's not why I came here. To argue politics. I
wanted to give you the name of a Japanese institute in San Francisco
where you can continue your lessons." Dr. Yamato gave him a card.
"You know enough now to be able to read a Shinkansen schedule
and to order stamps and postcards at the Yubinyoku. You know how
to ask for someone's telephone number and enjoy a meal in a private
home. But there are fifteen lessons to go. You must finish *Japanese
by Spring*." He walked into the hall.

"Shitsurei Shimasu Chappie?"

"Dr. Yamato."

"Yes, Chappie?"

"Dr. Yamato, I'm glad that you got off this revenge kick. You
can't bring back all of the war dead. Besides, the Japanese committed
atrocities in China, and Okinawa. You used people for bayonet
practice in the Philippines." Dr. Yamato ignored him. He became
visionary. His eyes became glazed.

"The restoration of the shogunate will lead to a flowering of art
and culture in Japan unheard of since the days of Tsunayoshi."

"Sayonara, Dr. Yamato." Dr. Yamato left Puttbutt's house.
There was a Lexus parked at the curb in front of the house. Some
men were sitting inside.

"Dr. Yamato." He turned around.

"How do you know that I won't tell?"

"Nobody will believe your word, a black man, against mine.
They'll just dismiss you as a conspiracy nut. This man Oliver Stone.
You see what they did to him. Jack Only knows all about the

assassination. Why he shows all of his visitors JFK's brain. He wanted the people he paid to bring him proof that they'd gotten rid of this communist and lover of Negroes." Dr. Yamato had only lived in the States for a total of five years, General Puttbutt had reported, but he knew his way around. Through the curtains he could see Yamato drive off. First Dr. Yamato was preaching revenge and now he was talking about an alliance with something called the shadow government. Weird. And his father had been used as part of a masquerade.

The lights in the neighborhood were turned off. His neighbors were watching every strange parade that had come in and out of his house. He had outgrown this neighborhood. Tomorrow he would call a real estate agent. It was time to make his move. To the Oakland Hills. To join that colony of the Oakland elites of the business, art and political world, and to leave the low-class riffraff in lower Rockridge.

chapter fifty-six

Dear I.R.

Old man Only came down from the country the other day to tell the Tank the plan for the 1990s. First out, he talked about the "walking TB" and an offensive black bum that he and his chauffeur had to maneuver around in order to enter the building. He spent about five minutes whispering to that throat box that he speaks out of, raving on about how the "walking crap" are reproducing. He wants the Tank to keep up the pressure on the "walking crap." The old guy really looks sick and is so frail that he's got a black chauffeur—the guy who drives Only's old pickup truck—carrying him.

* * *

He praised that lick-ass D'Gun ga Dinza. Guy came from India in 1978 and can hardly speak English, but he's the point man in the fight to wipe out the multikults. He wants old man Only to introduce the caste system in the United States. Says that part of the problem in this country is that the blacks and Latinos expect too much.

Only said that being a segregationist he can do business with Matata Musomi's brand of Afrocentricity. He says that maybe a good solution would be to give Musomi thirty thousand acres in South Carolina. He thinks that maybe a British-trained African like Musomi can control the behavior of these American blacks who have caused American society so much heartache. (Do you think that the people at Jack London know that the black budget was used to bring Matata into the United States and to position him at Jack London.) Only says that those blacks who refuse to go will be turned over to the LAPD or the Burbank Airport Narco Security Department. Old man Only has asked a black to the board, in order to counter criticism that the Tank is racist. He's one of those Puttbutt conservatives you wrote me about. While I'm the token liberal, he's the token black. When some of the directors make racist jokes, he laughs the loudest. Like the other day one of the Irish Catholics on the board—somebody ought to do a study on why so many Irish are attracted to these right-wing tanks; everywhere you look there's some O'This or O'That, just a couple of generations from the slums of Boston, who's always dumping on welfare mothers and black IQ tests when only fifty or so years ago the image of the Irish was that of some poor Hibernian sap with too many kids on the public dole, headin for the poorhouse—anyway, this Irish guy said that if Mandela were in a strong country he'd be a bar of soap.

This Puttbutt conservative laughed the loudest, slapping his knees and carrying on. He said that Mr. Only's plan might backfire. He said after a few weeks of rule under Ice Cube, Matata, Sister Souljah, and the Khan, the blacks might start to get homesick.

*   *   *

As for the multikults, Only ordered a Hail Mary run on them. He says that their influence is growing. He says that he wants to bury them like Schwarzkopf buried the Republican Guard. His latest thing is to pay one hundred thousand dollars to some northeastern monokult historians and "cultural critics" to write vicious attacks against multiculturalism. Their rants are packaged in these pretty books that are published by some outfit in Knoxville, Tennessee. Some of the conservative Jews in the organization are upset with Dinza. He's the mastermind behind the *Koons and Kikes*, that shitty little sheet that these sophomoric right-wing punks are publishing with Only money. The gay Tank members are also nervous. They remembered that in his undergraduate days he had "outed" a number of gay students whom he felt harbored left-wing sentiments. They can't stand the risk of being outed. Considering the fact that they're responsible for some of the most scurrilous antigay propaganda, for them to be outed would be a big embarrassment. Not only for them but for the old man. The old man doesn't know they're here and he uses terms like queer and faggot in their presence, and if anything happens to Only, Dinza's enemies will see to it that his ass is shipped back to India. He's a sneaky, nerdy, nasty little shit. His nickname around here is D'Mon D'Goosa.

I'll be accompanying the old man to California in the late fall. He's going to attend the annual meeting of the Elysian Fields Club. It's this club that brings together some of the country's top business executives, politicians and clergymen. It provides them with an excuse to get up in drag and to romp around the woods and to giggle like schoolgirls. Let's get together when I get there . . . The letter was from one of many correspondents to whom Reed was connected throughout the world. They kept him abreast of the goings-on among the international elect.

chapter fifty-seven

Ishmael Reed had just finished reading the *Tribune*. Puttbutt was flanked by some professors. The headline said, PUTTBUTT DENOUNCES DR. YAMATO. There was a feature concerning an investigation into possible misappropriation of Oakland Arts funds by Matata Musomi. There was a suspicion that funds that were supposed to be directed to Musomi's percussion concerts had gone into Mr. Musomi's life-style. The fancy apartment on Lake Merritt. The downtown office. Then the most shocking story of all. Jack Milch, the white chairperson of the English department and its leading black feminist, had been arrested for keeping his wife and child in prison for ten years. "Dog Mom and Child." It showed Milch's wife and child crawling around on all fours in basement doghouses that Jack Milch had built for them. He had put them on a leash. The neighbors said that they had complained for years about the terrible smell that had been coming from the house. The picture showed Milch being led away by the Oakland police.

Ishmael Reed was reading the minutes of an organization known as Glossos United. They were in better shape than ever and their vision of a Glosso America was in sight. But one thing bothered them. Powerful interests were supporting their ideas. Interests which twenty years before dismissed them with ridicule. They had moved from their shabby office on Sixth Street in Berkeley to an office in a mansion. Where they'd once shared a six-pack or two during their annual meetings held at the office on Sixth Street so poor that it was partially furnished by decrepit movie seats that had been found on the sidewalk in front of a now-defunct movie house, they'd just celebrated an important landmark at the Sheraton Suite at the Sheraton Hotel. The most amazing thing of all, Ishmael Reed found his face in the pages of the leading business magazine. In color.

Ishmael Reed and his fellow Glossos had decided, during an emergency meeting, that they would not stray from their original purpose. That they would stop moving in swanky company. That, being dogged populists, they no longer would associate with cultural bigwigs in the establishment. Ishmael Reed was feeling good about this meeting. Real homey. This was making Ishmael Reed real homey. He wore homey clothes and could eat pork rinds with the best of them. He went around the house humming George Clinton's proletariat song "Do Fries Go with That Shake." He sometimes went around with a tacky beard in order to appear to be a man of the people. He sometimes wore clothes so long that they became ragged and his family would have to go to Macy's to buy him new clothes. He drove an old Toyota that was full of newspapers and cans and unopened letters and manila envelopes and empty grapefruit juice bottles. Homey Ishmael Reed was glad that the board had decided to stop collaborating with capitalistic institutions. Why the next thing you know, they'd be calling upon them to save Western civilization.

The doorbell rang. It was his old friend. He hadn't changed much since he knew him at the University of Buffalo. Medium sized, good manners. He had a habit of pushing back his hair to prevent it from blinding his vision. They shook hands.

"Unbelievable," he whispered, shielding his words with a hand. "You should have seen them. Some of the biggest wheels in the country performing farcical and idiotic shenanigans." He mentioned a former secretary of state. Prominent members of the "Fortune 500." Congressmen, media moguls. "They just admitted their first black member. General Puttbutt. Boy was he happy to be there. Sang at the dinners every night and was so bad only a few members attended the last one." Each year they gathered in California for a week of bacchanal networking.

"Come in," Reed said.

"Wait for the boss."

"What?" Reed looked over his shoulder and a tall black man in a chauffeur's uniform was carrying some faint outline of a human being up the stairs of his white Queen Anne Victorian. Jack Only looked like a giant, craggy-faced cucumber with flippers where legs and arms should have been. A crablike eye peered at him from under a black hat. Behind him was a beat-up old pickup truck. The same one that he drove when he only possessed one old beaten-down oil well. Only and his class referred to the showy Mercedes of the nouveau riche contemptuously as "a Jew canoe." Jack Only had driven the same car for twenty years.

The chauffeur walked past him and carried Only into the room and propped him up in a chair in the living room below a postcard of Main Street in Buffalo that Reed had had blown up. The chauffeur lit Only a cigarette. Then took a chair himself. Reed looked at his old friend. Reed seemed to be saying, what are they doing here? The creature spoke from a box that seemed to be embedded in its throat.

"He wants to know the name of the painting." He was referring to a painting that hung above a desk in the living room.

"It's the Adoration of the Magi," Reed said. "It's by Hieronymus Bosch." The creature stared at him. The creature muttered something else.

"He wants to get down to business." Reed sat down.

"I read him the letter you sent." The eye darted from the chauffeur to his friend and to Puttbutt. Puttbutt had written that Only was wasting his money backing members of the anti-Glosso movement. Reed and his colleagues had decided that they weren't going to help the powerful anymore, but then look at it this way. If the United States went down it would take millions of innocent victims with it. Glossos as well as anti-Glossos. Reed escorted the three into his parlor. On the wall was an ace of spades with polka-dot bow tie and yellow hands, by Betye Saar. Red-lipped smile and white eyes. At the top of the head was the Haitian cross. At the top of a window ledge lay a black plate with a red rooster in its center, an old Russian craftwork from the village of Sitka. Red and black drawings of the raven, which had become the Reed family crest. He thought of the times that he wanted to comment on the foolishness of American business in their support of what amounted to the American intellectual Tokugawa regime. Closed to the world abroad and at home. Limiting the linguistic abilities of Americans with fatuous English Only campaigns. Relating to the world not with trade but with the sword. The Tokugawa treatment of the Christians was similar to that treatment of the Glossos in the imagination of the anti-Glossos. The hibernators. What did Tokugawa intellectual George Will actually mean when he said that the multiculturalists were more of a threat than Saddam Hussein. Was he proposing that they be treated like the Iraqi Republican Guard, buried alive. One contemporary critic of the Tokugawa had compared the cultural suffocation of Japan under the Tokugawa as something like being "buried alive." Like the monocultural American intellectuals, they fought against the introduction of ideas from the outside; the Tokugawa had closed every port but Nagasaki. In 1622, the Great Massacre of Nagasaki took place during the Tokugawa regime of Hidetada. Thirty Christians were beheaded, and twenty-five others, among them nine foreign priests, literally roasted to death, for their tortures lasted between two and three hours. The Glossos wanted the United States to emerge from the American Tokugawa period, a period of repression and censorship in the arts. (The Tokugawa censored woodblocks deemed offensive and were satirized by the Noh theater). The Glossos felt that American civilization should be more cosmopolitan. More Meiji. Since the death of the Kennedy Era (Kennedy rescued Robert Lowell, Hamp Hawes, and listened to Bird) the country had been undergoing one of its periodic puritan interregnums.

• • •

Ishmael Reed hated giving advice to Jack Only. Though he was a modest merchant, he merchandised for the good of society, making available what he thought was quality literature and videodramas to society. He had a neo-Confucian attitude toward merchants. That they contributed nothing worthwhile to society. Since the Reagan Shogunate (high-defense budgets, Star Wars, saber rattling, "make-my-day" posturing) the "Fortune 500" hadn't created a single new job. He had first used the term "multicultural" in the middle seventies, during an interview with the *Berkeley Barb*. A few years before one of Mr. Only's intellectual road salesmen of perfidy, D'Gun ga Dinza, had left India to be groomed for his role as anti-Glossos hatchet man. He wasn't the only one. They'd done the same thing to Little Richard and Chuck Berry. They copped ideas from black scientists, artists and other thinkers. A black man had no patent that a white man was bound to respect. He was beginning to understand why, in Mark Twain's *Huckleberry Finn,* the horses and slaves were advertised on the same poster.

The powerfully built black chauffeur was waiting for him to say something. His boss, Mr. Only, a multibillionaire, was waiting. His friend was waiting.

"Mr. Only, I just received a sheet here from an organization known as Teachers for a Glosso Society." Some static came from Mr. Only's box. Reed looked to his friend.

"He's swearing at you," the friend said.

"Well, if you don't want to listen, Mr. Only." More static came from his box. More ferocious this time. His friend translated. "He's listening. He's listening."

"What I can't understand is why a man like you, a businessman who has to take risks, would align himself with people who probably have less than two hundred dollars in the bank." Ishmael Reed knew that he was probably right. He'd read a profile of a Puttbutt conservative in the *Wall Street Journal.* A black guy, who was getting grants right and left from anti-Glossos as a result of his preaching self-reliance to blacks, was in trouble with the IRS for back taxes. That reminded him of a New York congressman who appeared on C-SPAN. He was lecturing the Japanese on how to conduct business with the United States. He was the most notorious check bouncer in the United States.

Ishmael Reed had told some people at a dinner in Paris that before he listened to a Puttbutt conservative about self-reliance he wanted to know whether he had at least two hundred dollars in the bank. "These people don't have to take risks. They're freeloading off you." The list from the Teachers for a Glosso Society included names of most of those on the anti-Glosso network. "Take, for example. . . ." Ishmael Reed mentioned the name of a prominent anti-Glosso thinker, a Chicago professor who had written one of the fiercest attacks against the Glossos, so strident and ham-fisted that, if a black or a woman had written such a tome, it would have been dismissed as a diatribe.

"He has written that Americans shouldn't study Japanese because Japan is a racist society—ironic coming from him. Meanwhile, the Japanese are studying Yoruba in order to learn the textile secrets of the West Africans." The giant, craggy-faced cucumber shifted its bottom and went into a conference with Reed's friend.

"I had to explain to him that Yoruba was a language spoken by West African people."

"And take a look at this, Mr. Only." Reed took the newspaper article and gave it to his friend, who took it over to the table where Mr. Only was seated and showed it to him. The *Japan Times*: that headline story ACTING BLACK, by Akiko Hanari, "They're hip. They like to dance. They desperately want to appear streetwise. But perhaps most surprisingly in a country that is often criticized for its racism, they want to be BLACK. Black music and fashion have become so popular among Japanese youth that some of them are actually 'turning black' as far as their clothing, music and dance steps are concerned." *Business Week* had reported that they were "vogueing" in Japanese discos. ("Vogueing" was a style of movement invented by the black gay underground and made popular by the movie *Paris Is Burning*). The yellow Negro. The particle yo in Japanese is used to draw attention similar to "the Rapper's" yo.

"Mr. Only. You're losing money listening to people like this. American business will lose out if it can't compete in an increasingly multilingual and multicultural market. The president of Atlantic Bell knows this. While the people on your list are fighting affirmative action, he says that his company gets good ideas because the members of his board of directors aren't from the same background. He says that heterogeneity is the way to go when competing in the global economy. Mr. Only, you're the founder of the old boy's network. You know that some of these guys won't act right unless given a little prodding. You know that they reward themselves with affirmative action perks all the time. Why just recently it was revealed that McDonnell Douglas received a two-hundred-million-dollar advance from the Pentagon without even Congress hearing about it. And what about the S&L scandal and HUD. And what about the United States government putting deposits in drug banks like the BCCI. What kind of message do you think that sends to these black drug pushers on the streets. Mr. Only, admit it. You know that the big boys give each other affirmative action all the time." Reed mentioned the name of a high official in the United States Department of Education who was giving the United States and Texas a bad name with her empty-headed remarks about Afro-American and African culture. She was undoing all of the good work that Baraka Sele, and Nicolas Kanellos, Lorenzo Thomas and others had done to improve the image of Texas. One only had to go to Houston to discover cutting edge trends in dance and music and art.

"Mr. Only, what harm would it do to acknowledge that Egypt was fundamentally an African culture with a number of important black kings and queens, gods and goddesses in its pantheon. Look, just last week I was dining at the Haitian restaurant with my good friend Franco LaPolla and I pointed out a calendar on the wall that was designed by one of your biggest competitors. It said Great Black Queens and Kings." That awful scratching sound came from Mr. Only's box. His friend translated.

"Mr. Only said, no shit?"

"And another one of your rivals is offering people special discount tour packages—airline, hotel, rent-a-car to celebrate Kwanzaa in different cities. Mr. Only, these people on your payroll with their anti-intellectual ideas are losing money. They're denouncing American popular culture when that's one of the few salable products that we export. Last year, Rap music and fashion accessories made more money abroad than automobiles. The American style is a multibillion-dollar business. While the people on your list, like the nazi intellectuals, long for some mythical glory called Western civilization, the authentic European intellectuals are studying our culture, our civilization. My friend Franco LaPolla teaches at the oldest university in Europe. Bologna. And my friend Sam Ludwig, a Swiss scholar, knows more about African-American religion than the mass media intellectuals who keep using that dumb expression voodoo economics. LaPolla teaches a course on American film. He knows every director, actor, and knows the cast of most American films produced. Such is the appeal of American culture. Mr. Only, may I be frank?" The cucumber nodded. His friend gave him a look which told him to be careful. Mr. Only was said to have a mean temper.

Reed got up, walked over to where the chauffeur had propped up Mr. Only and began waving his finger in his face. "Mr. Only, you look dumb when you back questionable sophomoric enterprises like *Koons and Kikes*, and D'Gun ga Dinza, that fake. That Hitler birthday party those punks celebrated at Dartmouth last year brought bad publicity to your cause. Goose-stepping up and down the main street of Hanover. Passing out *Mein Kampf* at Yom Kippur services. Only, you can't afford to back people who spread all of this propaganda against blacks, Jews, homosexuals. You should want to trade with them. You can't make any money with hate, and if the political trend goes the other way, these people will whore their services to some other people. They'll abandon you. Remember, Mr. Only, a neoconservative is not only a liberal who's been mugged by reality, but it's someone who was picking up checks from the liberal establishment in the sixties." There was silence. Finally, Only snapped a frail finger. His friend glanced at Reed. His look seemed to signal that Mr. Only was mad. Reed mentioned another individual who had received Only's financial backing. The guy was drug policy czar and he failed; he was education chief and he failed.

"Would you keep an employee on after he failed at two assignments?" The Department of Education was becoming an oxymoron. A virtual clubhouse of anti-Glossos. A man who had been appointed to the National Advisory Committee on Accreditation and Institutional Eligibility was, in the words of the newspaper article, "a supporter of the extremist David Duke."

"Not only are you backing these anti-Glossos, but you are also a supporter of the General Nathan Forrest Museum. This man not only massacred black men, women and children at Fort Pillow, but was a founder of the Klan. Is there no end to your support of lost causes? These people with their parochial attitudes can't make you any money in a multilingual global economy. They're not even good tax write-offs." Only gave him a mean look. His friend said nervously, "We'd better go."

They left the house and Reed watched as they walked toward the chauffeur-driven pickup truck. His friend didn't even look back. Momentarily the black chauffeur came back in.

"I've been working for this man for thirty years and I never seen anybody talk to old man Only like you just did. Maybe it will do him some good. They talk about black people like a dog. You know, that man who is on TV a lot." He mentioned the name of one of the most pretentious conservatives who pretended to like Bach.

Though his ancestors came to the United States as a result of the Great Hunger in Ireland, you'd think that he had played on the fields of Eton. One of his favorite jokes was that instead of implementing the Great Society programs the government should have bought aphrodisiacs for black women. "He was up at the old man's place the other day. He called Dr. King 'Martin Luther Coon.' He was so drunk he pissed in the sink. I started to strangle that muthah." Ishmael Reed wasn't usually impolite to his guests.

Ishmael Reed thought that if he had been born in Virginia or Alabama, maybe he would have learned to couch his criticism of individuals and institutions. But no, he was born in Tennessee and everybody knows Tennesseeans have strong ideas. The saying about them goes: "Tennesseeans hate their enemies and love their friends." Ishmael Reed was winding up his ninth novel and was beginning another one. *The Terrible Fours.* Scene opens with Nance Saturday having solved the problem the pope has had with his creditors and is about to board the pope's private jet for the trip back to New York. But before that the pope, as a token of his gratitude, rewards Nance with a precious artifact that Mussolini was supposed to have stolen during the invasion of Ethiopia. About an hour later his fax began to ring. A message was coming through. It was his friend. Mr. Only was going to fire all of his dried-up think tank apparatus. Only said that he wanted to shed them like rattlesnake skin and wanted Reed to build a new list from the ground up. He wanted to know whether Reed desired to be a director or maybe chairman of the board of his foundation. Unlike the people who'd wasted his money, Mr. Only had discovered that he couldn't just limit his customers to those who had read Plato. He'd go broke. Ishmael Reed returned a message saying that he'd have to think about it. He was fifty-four years old. He'd studied the violin and played Mozart, Schubert and Bach in grammar and high school. He'd spent the first twenty years of his life reading books by dead white males (and some live ones too). He had read the Greeks and

the Romans, the Germans and the French, the British and the
Spanish. He had traveled to Germany, Finland, Iceland, Italy,
France, England, etc. Ishmael Reed was wondering was there no
end to the sacrifices he would be called upon to make on behalf of
Western civilization. He needed some time off. But maybe from his
meeting a new tactic against the anti-Glossos had emerged. The
Glossos couldn't compete with the anti-Glossos who had infiltrated
the media to such an extent that they had become the electronic
cardinals of a secular religion, Jerry Brown's description of the media.
The anti-Glossos would have to deal directly with the popes who
were their leaders. They would separate these people, who merely
used conservatism as a substitute for a white sheet, from their money.
Maybe the American puritanical and intolerant Tokugawa period
(a period of censorship, of the McConnell Bill that would hold
publishers responsible for harm caused by pornography, of attacks
on the National Endowment for the Arts and on Rap music, of book
banning, and of charismatics posing as intellectuals invading the
campuses, of gender first feminists, Professor Poop, Matata, Afrocentrics, Eurocentrics, of Know-Nothings' reemergence in politics, of
antiabortionists [like their English antecedents holding the belief
that a woman's body is the engine of Satan]) that followed the
assassination of JFK would be succeeded by a Meiji period, or an
American Restoration similar to the one that brought Charles II
back to England from exile to reopen the theater that had been
closed by the Puritans. According to Ernest Wilson Clement's A
Short History of Japan, the Meiji era saw "translations from Occiden-
tal languages, the rise of a newspaper press and of a magazine literature, new styles in fiction . . . new styles in poetry . . . new styles
in prose . . ."

The dialectic to a new Meiji, a JFK-styled Restoration was prophe-
sized by Pearl Buck, who could have been talking about the paranoia
of New-World-Order American Tokugawa Shogunate: "We must
prepare for a future of nothing but struggle and war on a stupendous

scale, particularly for the white man. We shall have to make up our inferiority in numbers by military preparation of the most barbarous and savage kind. We must prepare for super weapons, we must not shrink from chemical warfare on a mass scale, we must be willing to destroy all civilization, even our own, in order to keep down the colored peoples who are so vastly our superiors in numbers and our equals in skills. Is this the future any human being wants to face?" Ishmael Reed and the Glossos didn't want it, and at the beginning of the nineties, there were signs that they might prevail.

chapter fifty-eight

I he *Tribune* carried the story. London Shut Down. New Investors Sought. He was about to make coffee when the phone rang.

"Hi, Son." There was a lot of static on the line, he couldn't make out the voice.

"Who is this?"

"It's your mother." His mother?

"Mom. Where are you?"

"I'm calling from Frankfurt. I should be in Washington in a few days."

"But this happened so quickly. I'm stunned. When did the terrorists let you go?"

"When did they let me go. No, it's when did I let them go."

"I don't follow."

"I'll explain it to you. Can't talk right now. I'll see you in San Francisco in a couple of weeks."

"San Francisco?"

"Yes. Your father and I have just received new orders. We're being transferred to Tokyo. We're going to be assigned to the embassy staff there. They're providing us with a house, a driver and a maid."

"Really?"

"Yes. And we're going to need your help. Your father says that you speak Japanese well enough to get around the country, to make reservations at a restaurant and to buy stamps at the post office. Give it some thought. Listen, I got to go now, Son. They're debriefing me here." Before he could say anything she hung up.

Later he saw his mother on CNN. She was walking down the stairs of an air force plane. She'd lost some weight. She looked trim and without some of the weight she sometimes carried in her face, beautiful even. She was wearing a red, white and blue jumpsuit. Some of the American officials shook her hand. The women kissed and embraced her. Children curtsied. A fife and drum corps, dressed in revolutionary war attire, performed. The American ambassador flew in from Bonn and presented her with flowers. On a split screen they showed his father. He was in Washington. He congratulated his wife for her bravery and her professionalism. They showed some footage of his mothers' captors. They were crawling on their knees and kissing the hands of their American rescuers. So relieved were they to be delivered from "that woman" as they said. They'd captured her all right, but shortly after being seized she had turned the tables on her tormentors and they became her prisoners. They had photos of their ordeal. One showed his mother, sitting at a piano, playing "Onward Christian Soldiers," as the terrorists stood, singing. His mother was smoking a cigarette and had a shotgun lying across her lap. She could have taken her freedom at least a year before her release, but she had vowed not to abandon her captors until they became fine Christian gentlemen. She said that the only reading matter she had was her son's paper on *Othello* that somebody had smuggled in. Oh no, not again.

Puttbutt smelled something burning. He checked the stove. All of the burners were off. The oven. What could it be. He thought to himself. He had studied Japanese at the Air Force Academy and had reached lesson fifteen. With Dr. Yamato he had almost reached intermediate Japanese. On the basis of some elementary Japanese, if elementary was the word for a language that seemed to have been invented for the purpose of keeping out outsiders (the *Christian Science Monitor*'s Jerry Shine writes, "Religious missionaries once considered the Japanese language to be the work of Satan, the devil's language created in hell and made inhumanely difficult to learn in order to frustrate their preaching"), Puttbutt had become the most powerful man on the Jack London campus. Just think what was in store for him when he finished the book! The sky outside turned black. What was going on. And now his mother was requesting his services after vowing never to speak to him again after he had failed at the Air Force Academy. Going to Japan would provide him with an opportunity. He figured that he knew the way to end the tensions that existed between the United States and Japan. He would urge that the Japanese eliminate Kanji. Fire trucks began to send out ear-piercing screams and sirens. They sounded very close. He heard some commotion in the streets. He looked out. The Oakland Hills. The Oakland Hills were on fire. Two hours later a car came by with a loudspeaker, urgent that the residents evacuate. He remembered what Troy had said about the eucalyptus trees and the Monterey Pines that made the Oakland Hills a firetrap, and that the twisting roads made it difficult for the fire trucks to access the hills. A policeman came to the door and asked him to evacuate. He packed some clothes, the last two copies of *Japanese by Spring*, and Jingo's letter.

April 21, 1969
Dear Chappie,
   I told Milton about us. It hurt him very much. I didn't want to continue practicing our deception. It was wrong. These years have been very hard for us. I saw our love wither as Chuck Yeager consumed more of his time. He would mumble, "Chuck, Chuck" sometimes in his sleep and while doing so would cling to me

tightly. His den was covered with pictures of Chuck Yeager. I never told you this, but once he traveled to the town where Chuck Yeager lives and camped out overnight, trying to get a glimpse of Chuck Yeager. Being a military man he refused the recommendations of our friends that he seek professional help.

It may be hard for you to realize this, but Milton Miller wasn't always like this. I remember him as a handsome young officer who worked with General MacArthur's staff. He was very good to me and to my family. We lost our home and our possessions during the bombings and he made it possible for us to receive meat and fresh vegetables, which were difficult to obtain in those days. I loved him. We had a good life. It began to collapse after he broke the sound barrier. Nobody could convince him that Chuck Yeager accomplished it first. It is a tragedy. He is downstairs turning over things. We just had a violent argument. I don't know what is going to become of us. I don't know how he's going to take the fact that I cheated on him. He is more Japanese than the Japanese, he thinks. All of this samurai nonsense about honor and loyalty. I love you.

Mo Sugu

P.S. I hate to tell you this, but both Milton and I agree on one thing. You'll never get your particles straight.

epilog—Olódùmarè regained?

At the end of October, Ishmael Reed ran into Chappie Puttbutt and his parents while lunching with a friend at the Washington Square Bar and Grill in San Francisco. His father was congenial enough, but he didn't seem to pass the inspection of his mother, who regarded him coldly. While they were chatting, some of the patrons approached the table and asked Mrs. Puttbutt for her autograph. There was a jeep full of soldiers parked outside of the restaurant and customers had to present ID in order to enter the establishment. When he approached the table where Chappie and his parents sat, he thought he saw a man go for his gun, but after seeing Chappie greet Reed warmly the man relaxed. They told Reed that they were about to leave for Japan. Chappie's enthusiasm for Japan was still very high. Reed, however, was beginning to see signs of trouble for Japan's continued prosperity. The Japanese leadership swaggering, making jokes about the abilities of Americans, the quality of their goods, the management style of their executives, meant that they hadn't learned much from World War II when they wanted to establish an economic sphere that the Japanese thought would stretch from the coal mines of Manchuria to the oil fields of Indonesia, which was the way powerful white nations solved their scarcity problems. The Japanese were acting white. Had gone too far. Didn't know their place. Were uppity. Were, in the words of Lee Iacocca, one of the participants in the Bush trade trip, "beating our brains out."

It was only a matter of time before the US would humiliate Japan the way the uppity colored men were traditionally humiliated, even Colin Powell, the so-called chairman of the Joint Chiefs of Staff who, excluded from the loop, learned of important Gulf War decisions by watching television. Then, as now, they were attempting to establish a coeconomic sphere in Asia with Japan as its leader, as they had in the 1930s despite warnings from Cordell Hull and other diplomats, incensed that the Japanese had abandoned Wilsonian principles of interdependence (hindering the West's exclusive divine right to gobble up Asia's resources) in their attempt to establish hegemony over Asia, which meant that they were acting like a white nation. The Japanese thought that since they had sat as equals with white men at the 1920s Paris Peace Conference, they could do what their white brother nations could do. Roam the world plundering the resources of inferior nations. Formosa. Korea. Manchuria. China. They made the same mistake that Adam Clayton Powell, Jr., made. He thought that since he smoked cigars with his white colleagues he could get away with the same kind of perks as they. They made the same mistake that Marion Barry made, who must have known that cocaine was the recreational drug of official and media Washington, and that even one of the men who was in on his entrapment enjoyed a hit from time to time. He, like Japan, thought that he could do what the big boys did (the Anglo-Japanese Alliance [1902 and 1905] must have really swelled the Japanese head).

But the whites never saw the Japanese as equals. Oh sure, Jack London congratulated Japan for its devotion to materialism and to development and lauded its industrialization of China (London also believed that after the disastrous land war in China that a smitten Japan would retreat to its islands) but this was like patting a bright child on the head, which is the way the Western nations viewed Japan. A child like the other third world nations, only a bright child. Mimicking the Western style. And as soon as Japan became too uppity, the West would take it away from them again. As a nation of islands, Japan was vulnerable to attacks on its merchant marine industry. Dependent upon other nations for its raw materials, it was vulnerable to embargo. It was the embargo on oil and rubber that forced Japan's hand. The result was Pearl Harbor.

Reed knew that if Japan's prosperity continued, the white nations were sure to take it away from them by one means or another. There was an eerie similarity between the economic issues confronting Japan and the West in the nineties, and those which led to conflict in the 1930s. William Lockwood wrote: "The flooding of Japanese goods into foreign markets after 1931 brought frantic outcries in the West. Most other countries, including Japan's major industrial competitors, were struggling in the slough of depression. This was indeed one of the reasons for the ready appeal of Japanese manufacturers. Their cheapness enabled them in some degree to tap levels of consumer demand below the reach of higher-priced European and American goods. But they also cut deeply into established markets, especially those of Lancashire and elsewhere, as in the United States. Though they remained small in volume, their unsettling effects spread uncertainty and alarm just when governments were attempting to put a floor under prices and wages, or at least to reserve shrunken markets for home producers." As was the case in the thirties, nineties economists and politicians were alarming the public with Yellow Peril warnings, were calling for protectionism. The media, which served big business, and the status quo, were raising a lynch mob against the Japanese just as they daily raised resentment against blacks and Latinos.

• • •

There were other indications that Japan's prosperity wasn't sure. Moody's Investors had cut long-term credit ratings for Japan's four main security companies and blamed this move on the continued weakness of Japanese stocks, agency France-Presse reported. The *Wall Street Journal* reported that sagging economies and saturated markets were jeopardizing financial prospects for two of Japan's leading technology companies, Sony Corporation and Hitachi Limited. In April of 1992, the Japanese stock market would plunge to its lowest level in six years. Economists were using terms like "downturn" and "credit crunch" to describe the condition of the yen. The *Japanese Times* was reporting that the average Japanese worker was complaining about his standard of living and was angry about being sacrificed so that a few people at the top could enjoy prosperity. The Japanese were complaining about being worked to death, indicating that the kind of civil turmoil that had occurred frequently in Japan's history might be in the offing. The unwillingness of a new generation to accept the life of their parents was a sign that even a new antidevelopment antigrowth dropout generation might emerge. That there might be a call for a strong leader, a Charles I type leader, a shogun who would defy or even end the diet that had been afflicted by scandals, just as Charles I, who went to his death invoking his divine rights, defied the English Parliament.

Reed's gloomy assessment of Japan's continuing its prosperity without Western nations challenging that prosperity didn't alter his respect for the Japanese, regardless of the silly and primitive racist attitudes of some of its leaders toward black Americans. As Quincy Troupe said, when asked why he'd moved to San Diego to live when there were crackers in San Diego: "There are crackers everywhere." Troupe was right. There were white, yellow, red and brown crackers. Black crackers, too. As a black man he could identify with Japan. The destiny of the Japanese and his African ancestors had been affected by the arrival of ships manned by the Portuguese during the fifteenth century. Admiral Perry's ships arriving in Tokyo had changed the history of the Japanese. The Japanese and the African Americans had another thing in Common. Both were being blamed for the decline of the United States. And just as economic embargoes were used against yellows, they were also used against blacks. The eighties curtailment of social programs amounted to an economic embargo against an enemy nation, cutting off assistance to those who needed it the most. Though they were considered hotheads, those who used the term "genocide" in describing the cutback on food stamps, health care and subsidized housing were correct. During the years of the Reagan Shogunate, black life expectancy had declined. Historically, when whites moved among yellows, blacks and reds, death always resulted, according to Matata. He called them Death's Earth Angels, who had been evicted from the Garden of Eden, not by God but by the serpent, Damballah. Reed believed that racism was learned. That racism was a result of white leaders of Western nations placing little value on nonwhite life, or indeed, projecting violent impulses upon those who lived under constant fear of white terror. For example, "the black community" was blamed for the actions of four men who beat a white truck driver senseless on the first night of the 1992 LA riots. The white media regarded the beating of the white trucker as a "symbol" of the LA riots, not the majority of black and Latino men who were killed as a result of the riots. Others noticed the way that whites exalted white life over "other" life. The nightly reports of the air bombardment of Baghdad conjured up memories of the US bombing campaign against Hanoi during the Vietnam War. It invited comparison with the American air war against Japanese cities during World War II. "Once again, it seemed, US bombers were pounding largely defenseless Asian cities" was the way that an article in the *Japan Times Weekly* read. The citizens of Hanoi, Tokyo, Nagasaki, Hiroshima and Baghdad must have also been struck by the irony of the American political and think tank leadership imputing all of the violence to the "inner cities." As for the comment by the officer who inflicted most of the beating of Rodney King comparing blacks to gorillas (Los Angeles chief of police Daryl Gates said that the black men were vulnerable to the choke hold because of their anatomy; Douglas MacArthur believed that "inferior races" succumbed to wounds more easily than the Anglo-Saxon), that's how the American media depicted the Japanese during World War II. They were monkeys swinging from trees. The comments of United States elected officials also suggested that little value was placed upon yellow, black, brown and red life. Responding to charges by Japanese officials that the Americans were lazy and illiterate, Senator Ernest Hollings (D–SC) was quoted by the Associated Press as saying that "you could draw a mushroom cloud and put underneath it *Made in America by lazy and illiterate Americans and tested in Japan.*" An aide for Hollings said that the senator's comment was an "appropriate metaphor" in view of the US-Japan trade war.

After the Los Angeles City Council ratified a white male affirmative action deal by rescinding an agreement that would have awarded a contract allowing Sumitomo to build a mass transit system in Los Angeles—the contract went to an unqualified American firm, an example of white male protectionism—an Asian-American Los Angeles city councilman complained that anti-Japanese hostility was becoming so intense that he feared the internment camps would be reopened. Both the yellows and blacks were subjected to pressure by white-led governments. Gai-atsu. Japan's relationship with the United States had been defined by noun plurals: "restrictions, encirclements, barriers, pressures and concessions," from the time of the Treaty of Kanagawa (July 11, 1854) to the demand that Japan adhere to the Wilsonian prescriptions—(A) Equal access to raw materials, (B) World interdependence and (C) Nonviolence. These pressures continued, from the warnings to Japan about expansionism (a process that the white nations reserved for themselves) from Cordell Hull, through Japan's economic strangulation by Western nations, to the humiliating postwar occupation by a white shogun.

*   *   *

The name of one treaty was telling. The Treaty of Limitations. Black men knew about limitations. As a black male in the United States, Ishmael Reed could understand limitations. The history of blacks in the United States was a "history of confinement." It was significant that the places that most Americans were comfortable with the black male presence were all enclosures, basketball courts, football fields, jails. That was the only playing field where the majority of white Americans enjoyed black men, and even that playing field wasn't level. There were few black men in the front office of the sports industry. According to *New York Newsday*, March 4, 1992, former Mets player Darryl Strawberry accused reporters of glossing over the failures and personal problems of white players and emphasizing the failure and personal troubles of black players during his 7½ seasons with the Mets.

But Japan thought that since they had swallowed the nineteenth-century gospel of "development," had "evolved" from a feudalistic society to a "modern technological state," that they could do what their white brothers did. The Hollings remark, though considered frivolous, meant that powerful whites still considered extermination an option for dealing with the resurgence of the Japanese quest for a coeconomic sphere.

A little over six months after their meeting, California suffered another fire as devastating as the one that struck the Oakland Hills. This fire resulted from a jury verdict that was announced in a Simi Valley courtroom. Ishmael Reed felt lucky to have gotten away from the suburban verdict that acquitted the four policemen who viciously beat Rodney King, a motorist whom they had stopped for speeding. Blacks and Latinos said that such police brutality happened all the time, only this time a video camera was there to capture it. But while the majority of white Americans disagreed with the verdict and accused the Bush administration of not doing enough in the inner city, under 25 percent of whites agreed with blacks and Latinos that the criminal justice system was oppressive against blacks and Latinos. Reed didn't know which was worse, the verdict, or the suburban "analyses" that followed the verdict. White male editorial opinion makers spinning out the dogma that blamed the whole thing on the black underclass, even though people from all races participated in the riots and looting, and lecturing black people about their lack of morality and values, the line promoted by a CBS analyst and senior editor for *Newsweek*, Joe Klein . . . the author of some black pathology merchandise called "Tribes" blamed the rioting against Korean stores, by a small group of blacks, on blacks being jealous of Koreans, yet neither he nor other black pathology careerists, those who were making a handsome living by turning out books, op-eds and articles that blamed everything on blacks, had an explanation for why whites burned down Korean stores. A probation officer who was on the street at the time said that he saw youths wearing yarmulkes looting liquor stores. The man who was on the street said that those who thought the riot to be black were laboring under a misconception. The media only saw black.

Ishmael Reed had read novels about the media class and the blame-everything-on-black-greed class and knew that they were downing all of the poontang, government subsidies, in one form or another, and coke they could lay their hands on. And then there was the dopey vice president sounding off about family values when a blond lobbyist charged that this goofy Ken doll was grabbing all over her bod during a weekend retreat and even the newspapers were printing stories about his alleged dope dealer being held incommunicado so as not to embarrass the vice president when he was campaigning for the job as the nation's number-one pillar of morality. Brett C. Kimberlin, a prisoner, told the El Reno *Daily Tribune* that he had sold marijuana to Dan Quayle on fifteen to twenty occasions between 1971 and 1973.

Things hadn't changed since Civil War diarist Martha Higgens recorded that the planters, who had black concubines and mulatto children, viewed themselves as model husbands and fathers. For them, all the vice was going on among the underclass down in the slave cabins. It was this immorality, the word that William Wells Brown used to describe the custom among slave owners to practice polygamy with white and black women, that maybe drove Martha Higgens to opium.

Ishmael Reed told a Freiburg newspaper that this analysis—the Moynihan analysis—reminded him of the nazi media discussing the Ostjugend, who were blamed for crime and accused of coming on to Aryan women. It was Jewish males who were Willie Hortonized in Germany, something that neoconservatives have forgotten. Their right-wing logic went something like this: the four cops beat Rodney King because they were dismayed by the black underclass. They said, "Hey, there's a member of the black underclass, let's rehabilitate him." (The use of the baseball bat by white racist fascists was becoming an international habit. The German fascists were wearing baseball caps and beating foreigners with baseball bats. Standing before a department store on a wealthy Nuremberg street, Ishmael Reed witnessed a fashion show which included men and women in baseball outfits. Black and white women models paraded before two black male models who were gyrating their hips to the music of Michael Jackson. His host said that LA Raiders T-shirts were popular.)

A "research fellow" from the William McKinley Institute located at Stanford, a senile dweeb, who gets paid for recycling lazy Moynihanisms, blamed the riots on "seriously dysfunctional society of damaged people." If Ishmael Reed ever saw Jack Only again he would bet Jack Only that if he made a surprise visit to these think tanks that were recipients of his money, he'd find most of these "research fellows" asleep in their club chairs, with copies of *Barron's* on their laps. Or in their expensive private restaurant doing "research" on some young coed waitress's legs. Or doing some "research" on some California zinfandel. The left-wing analysis was equally lazy. These hoodlums and punks who looted and burned black, Korean and Latino stores, for them, were "revolutionaries."

They were part of some kind of *intifada*. One of the professors who dominated the so-called analysis after the riots said that these people were "revolutionaries" because they wore Malcolm X T-shirts. The biggest crack dealer on Ishmael Reed's block wears a Malcolm X T-shirt. Ishmael Reed wrote an opinion about the verdict and the aftermath only to be told by the newspaper to which it was sent that the piece was "scattered."

Reed had been wary of going to Germany because he had seen a "60 Minutes" documentary that gave the impression that neonazis and skinheads had taken over the place. The only nazi he encountered was an American policeman who boarded Swissair in Zurich for the flight to Los Angeles. This man was trying to affect the look of the "silver fox": blow-dried white hair and mustache. The "silver fox" kept staring at mongrelized Ishmael Reed (African, French, Irish, Cherokee) and his mongrelized daughter Tennessee (African French Irish Cherokee, Russian, Tartar), members of the mongrelized Western Hemisphere majority. His Berlin hosts put him up in an estate that Joseph Goebbels had stolen from a Jewish banker. As he was walking up the path toward the place on his first night in Berlin, he thought of sunken-cheeked Goebbels bringing his hand slowly down his face in disgust as he gazed at mongrelized Tennessee and Ishmael Reed approaching this mansion overlooking Wannsee, carrying their bags. Ishmael Reed never slept better.

The silver fox was sitting two rows ahead of Ishmael Reed and at one point he and another policeman—they'd attended some kind of law enforcement conference in Zurich—stood up in the aisle and started chatting. The conversation turned to Rodney King. His fellow officer was a moderate. He thought that the fact that the one cop would be retried for excessive force was a positive development. The silver fox, however, staring at Ishmael Reed, said that if Rodney King had surrendered he wouldn't have been beaten, because the two people who were traveling with King cooperated with the police and weren't beaten. (That's a lie. King's companions were beaten.) With such thinking the silver fox could get a job as a "research fellow" at the McKinley Institute. He could get an article published in the *American Lawyer*, where staff writer Roger Parloff concluded in the June 1992 issue that "the jury acted not just plausibly but properly." A Latina who served in the jury said that her fellow white jurors made up their minds about the four policemen's innocence even before viewing the evidence. Before even viewing the video-tape.

When Carla Blank returned to her seat Ishmael Reed said, so that the policeman could hear, "There's a fucking fascist on this plane who believes that Rodney King got what he deserved."

In his sermon about Olódùmarè, Sànyà said that anger causes cancer. By getting angry, according to the principles of Yoruba, Ishmael Reed had lost. The "silver fox" had won. He had precipi-tated a burning of energy inside Ishmael Reed. Racism was a cancer-causing agent.

When the "silver fox" got off the plane a ragged-faced elderly white woman told the "silver fox" and his companion to "keep everything under control." The "silver fox" was wearing a little black nazi cap, black leather jacket and shorts. He could have been a member of the Village People, but the Village People were putting everybody on. This sucker was serious.

Ishmael Reed had taken nine planes and was taking his jet lag cure. Pigging out on movies. He had rented *Hangin' with the Home-boys*, about two black guys and two Latino guys in a night on the town. He kept studying the younger Latino actor's face. It bore a resemblance to John Garfield's face. It had become a sort of game with Ishmael Reed, studying an actor's face and, in his mind, casting this actor in a movie about the life of an actor or performer from a former period. Ishmael Reed believed that Queen Latifah would make a terrific Bessie Smith.

Saturday night, the night before Olódùmarè's resurrection—Olódù-marè being a proper name for Ọlọ́run, Ọlọ́ for owner, run for heav-ens, Owner of the Heavens—Ishmael Reed had rented a movie called *Shattered*. It was about a man who was suffering from amnesia. This guy wakes up in the hospital after a terrible car accident. His face is so messed up that his wife has to provide the plastic surgeons with a picture so that the surgeons can reconstruct a likeness. So this guy spends most of the movie trying to find out who he is. He keeps staring at his head. It is like a Yoruba parable. At the end, he finds that the head he has is that of the husband he has cuckolded and there is a suspenseful scene where he lifts the husband's body from the formaldehyde (the blond wife, the villain, is so dumb that she thinks that the corpse has been placed in a barrel of chemicals that will dissolve it) and discovers that he and the husband have the same head. Then, during a flashback, he realizes that, contrary to what his wife, or his lover, rather, has told him, he didn't murder the husband, but she murdered the husband and he helped to deposit the body in the barrel of chemicals and after they drove from the scene, he suffered a pang of conscience and wanted to go to the police. But she told him that it was too late for that because he was in over his head, so to speak. She gets hysterical and they struggle for the steering wheel which causes the car to go over a cliff. These people are Marin County types and so the homes are lavish and the cars expensive. A red Porsche gets almost as much play as the minor characters.

That night Ishmael Reed has a recurrent dream. In this dream he is visiting his dead grandmother. He has to leave because for some reason he can't remain in what appears to be a cottage. He identifies it as the cottage that these rich Germans, the Grotes, in Chattanooga, Tennessee, at 480 South Crest Road, on Lookout Mountain, provided for her. She was one of their maids and cooked for them. She used to take him there. He remembers playing with white kids in some spacious kitchen. He remembers that the huge white house had elevators, connecting the floors.

In this particular dream he is sitting around a campfire with some friends including someone who is very close to him. They decide to leave the camp, but first Ishmael Reed has to go to a small cottage that's located down a hill from the campfire. He's left something. But he knows that his grandmother is there. Maybe his stepfather is there too. A man with Hollywood good looks. He died in April. Ishmael Reed climbs a fence and is halfway down the slope when he finds himself sinking into some tall grass. He interrupts his journey and heads back toward the campsite which is being broken up. (Ishmael Reed has been in California for twenty-five years and has never gone camping. Where this image comes from is not known.) Escaping from the mud and tall grass he reaches the fence only to find that hands have grabbed his shoulders and are dragging him back. He gets away.

He's in the bath, thinking about this dream, when Òdún Sànyà calls. He reminds Ishmael Reed that he is going to begin his temple this morning, June 7, 1992. Covering himself with a towel and dripping wet, Ishmael Reed gets the directions. The temple will be held at Eastmont Mall in East Oakland. Reed downs a few cups of java. In honor of this ceremony, Ishmael Reed decides to wear a double-breasted black linen coat, white sneakers and pea-green pants. This is something that he must see. Something rarely seen. Ògún will resurrect Olódùmarè, a god who lies dormant in the African-American experience. A god with whom African Americans lost contact after the breakup of the Yoruba empire and the slave trade which the people at Whittle Books blame on what they refer to as "African chieftains." Ishmael Reed has visited the enormously rich churches of Europe. But for Olódùmarè's resurrection Sànyà has chosen a community center hall of a shopping plaza.

Though the descendants of Africans who survived the Atlantic crossing—the Olóṣun—still worship Yèyeṣun, or Òṣun (Olódùmarè's daughter), Olódùmarè, the omniscient, omnipresent, omnipotent, is all but forgotten by the African diaspora. Sànyà blames the despair, Onnu, that exists among all classes of African Americans on their lost connection to Olódùmarè.

. . .

Ishmael Reed reaches Foothill Boulevard and makes a wrong turn.
Eastmont Mall is a large place. Fast food stores, clothing stores,
Taco Bell, Mervyn's. He parks near Taco Bell. He doesn't know
where the community center is, and so he goes into a liquor store
and asks directions of a droopy-eyed clerk, who gives them to him.
She says Woolworth's, but she means Mervyn's. After walking some
distance he runs into one of Sànyà's friends who directs him to
entrance E of the Eastmont Mall. It is located next door to Mervyn's.
The service doesn't begin until 11:00 A.M. There are about twenty
people present. All over Oakland people are worshiping a god who
is illustrated as having a white beard and whiskers and looks like
Thor, a northern European ice god. Ironic, because a piece of jewelry
that Ishmael Reed saw in Iceland, an irreverent item showing an
upside-down Christian cross, was called Thor's cross.

A curly haired kid in the front row is playing with a Batman doll.
Some are dressed in the traditional outfit—'Agbádá', 'Àwọ̀tẹ́lẹ̀ and
Ṣòkòtò'. Some of the teenagers are dressed in hip hop clothes. While
some Americans are dressed in traditional Yoruba outfits, some of
the Nigerians wear Western clothes. There are about 50 percent
men and 50 percent women. For some reason there is a small delegation from Sacramento. Sànyà sits on the platform with a woman
dressed in white, the color of the Ọlọ́ṣun, the worshipers of Olódùmarè's daughter. Olódùmarè and his daughter in the same room,
one invisible, the other represented by a woman in white. Sànyà
has reunited Olódùmarè with his daughter. He noticed the women
in white at his stepfather's funeral. His stepfather belonged to the
A.M.E. Zion church, a church founded by Africans in 1820. They
left the main Methodist church which humiliated them by insisting
that they sit in the balcony during the services. It was his stepfather's
homegoing, which was the word the minister used—the homegoing
of a man who had given so much to the church, who had raised
thousands of dollars, who had taught Sunday school for over thirty

.

years—that was Ishmael Reed's homecoming. When the minister described him as "a warrior for Christ" Ishmael Reed imagined him armed with Ṣàngó's ax as he lay in the coffin. It took a funeral of someone close to him to make him realize that the church that he rebelled against in his teenage years, a church that he thought was too Western, was based upon the Yoruba model and had maintained the Yoruba social organization. It took becoming a Yoruba Fellow in his fifties to make him see things that were invisible to him in his teens. That his disagreement with the A.M.E. Zion Church of his parents was largely aesthetic.

The Ọlọ́ṣun at his stepfather's funeral wore nurses' uniforms. In a puritan country, Africans had to use camouflage in order to preserve their faith. Had to behave like chameleons. He remembers seeing for the first time, from his uncle's back porch, the Ọlọ́ṣun walking in procession down to the Tennessee River to greet the goddess Ọ̀ṣun. The river goddess. Now he could imagine this scene being played at plantations throughout the south. The overseer asks, What are you niggers doing? Reed could see them answering, we're going down to the river to "baptize" boss. He could see the puzzled overseer, mounted on horseback, remove his plantation hat, scratch his head and say something like, Well, good. The overseer is probably the great-great-grandpappy of the "silver fox" that Ishmael Reed saw on the plane from Zurich. A contemporary overseer with the mentality of the indentured servant, bent upon preventing the blacks from escaping from the plantation. He was wondering what Ishmael Reed the fugitive was doing away from the plantation. His stare was saying, nigger, what you doing here in Switzerland. Who let you out of Ginny. Show me your freedom papers. The overseer might have been Irish. The kind of Irish like the ones on the talk shows, the ones running for president, the think tank right who believed that they had to still perform their plantation duties. Be Paddy Rollers. Keep third world people from bothering the Brits. Ishmael Reed also knew that there were progressive Irish. Abolitionists. Labor leaders. JFK. The one who whetted Frederick Douglass's appetite for freedom. The ones who kept William Wells Brown engaged so that his illegal escape on a boat wasn't detected. Ishmael Reed, Adrienne Kennedy, Alex Haley were among the millions of Yoruba-Americans who had Irish ancestry, and so, obviously, the Irish and the blacks have collaborated on more than tap dancing. And though some journalists describe the LA riots as the first instance of a multiracial uprising, they forget that it was the slave Caesar and his girlfriend, Peggy Kerry, described as an "Irish beauty," who were the ringleaders in a plot to burn down New York in in 1741. Both were executed.

Ishmael Reed had gotten a good laugh when he told his German audiences that for Pat Buchanan to assert that he wished to prevent Western civilization from being buried in the landfill of multiculturalism, and for him to say that his idea of Western civilization was the culture of the British, after the bondage in which the British had held his ancestors for eight hundred years, was like Ishmael Reed saying that his idea of civilization was the confederate model and that American schools should adopt Jefferson Davis's idea of education.

Blacks had to hide their religion beneath the garb of Christianity, had to keep their thoughts to themselves (when the Obeah people were getting under the colonial skin in Jamaica, a law was passed forbidding a black to even think of harming a white person), had to conceal, and to deceive and so there was nothing contradictory about raising a god in a shopping mall. But Ògún Sànyà was threatening to go public with his church. No more deception. No more speaking in codes. That would be the test. Were blacks ready for Olódùmarè, were whites? The whites, browns and blacks seated at this service were.

The only accessories for the service are two jars which lie on a table covered with white cloth. On each side are candles. One jar is filled

with earth and stones. Another is filled with water. Sànyà uses them
to demonstrate the elements that are essential to life. The Yoruba
hold the earth to be sacred. According to one legend, recorded by
G. J. Afọlábí, "Olódùmarè sent a chameleon down from heaven to
find out whether it was safe to walk on the liquid surface below.
The chameleon returned to report that it was unsafe. Then Olódùmarè sent Ọbàtálá, a deity, to raise up a solid portion to form the
lithosphere. Olódùmarè put metal and sand in a white cloth and
gave this to Ọbàtálá with a fowl and a pigeon. In performing the
task, Ọbàtálá poured the sand with metal in it on the liquid surface.
The fowl and the pigeon descended to spread the sand in many
directions. Land surfaces intermingled with water surfaces. The chameleon was again sent down to examine the solidity of the surface.
He reported favorably. Then Ọbàtálá with Ọ̀rúnmìlà as counselor
was asked to run the earth."

Also sitting on the platform is Professor Crabtree of Jack London
College. This European American is dressed in traditional Nigerian
fashion. While Sànyà's outfit is yellow, Crabtree wears a blue and
white pattern. Sànyà perhaps includes this European American in
the service for the same reason that the hymn "O God, Our Help
in Ages Past" by Isaac Watts or William Croft was chosen. He wants
to show the universal appeal of Yoruba. Given this stance, Ishmael
Reed decides that the North American "Afrocentric" faction that
preaches racial hatred is probably heretical. One that is based upon
hurt, anger and revenge. Sànyà promises to use Native-American
and Eastern texts in future meetings. (Milton would be appalled.)
And then, in this community room, in the Eastmont Mall, a small
gathering of people invoke a god who has been lost in the misty past
of Yoruba America. Crabtree leads a song of praise for Olódùmarè.

Àwá Dé O, Ọlọ́run

Àwá dé o, Ọlọ́run; Àwá dé, Ẹlẹ́dà̀ wa
Ìwọ l'ó l'oǹí àt'ànà̀; Ìwọ l'ó l'ọjọ gbogbo
Ọlá rẹ kárí ayé; Ìfẹ́ rẹ kò l'abùkù

Ìwọ l'ó l'òní àt' àná ; Iwọ l'o l'ọjọ gbogbo
Gbọ́ tiwa, Ọga Ogo ; Sọ wá d'ọtun Èdùmàrè
Ìwọ l'ó l'oni àt' àná; Ìwọ l'ó l'ọjọ gbogbo

After the song to Olódùmarè, Sànyà explains that Yoruba people
were worshiping Olódùmarè thousands of years before the birth of
Mohammed and Christ. (Being a democrat and a populist, the
worship part worried homefolks Ishmael Reed. Sànyà wanted Reed
to participate in the meeting in an more active way, but Reed begged
off, saying that he was not a religious person and just wanted to
observe. "But you are spiritual, Ishmael. You are spiritual." Reed
still begged off.) But after the Great Severance, the wresting of
millions of people from Africa, the diaspora had lost contact with
Olódùmarè. Sànyà likened it to a loss of phone contact with this
deity. He was suggesting that the phone contact be repaired so that
the diaspora's direct line to Olódùmarè be restored. "We are not
connecting with this energy," he says.

Sànyà talks about how he arrived in Los Angeles from Yorubaland
twenty years before and how, for over twenty years, people had been
urging him to begin a temple. He said that at the occasion of his
birthdate, in 1991, he meditated over whether it was time to start
the temple. Sànyà ended the ceremony with a discussion of the
importance of the head in Yoruba philosophy. He left his listeners
with a Yoruba saying about the head. Orí.

Orí agbe ní í ba'gbe munó
It is the head of the bird that is dyed indigo
Orí ẹja l'ẹjǎ fi i la' bú
It is the head of the fish that bursts through the turbulence of
    the Ocean
Orí ahun ní í gbè f áhun
The tortoise has to discern danger with its head

Ki' órí bá mi ṣé
Let my head work for me

Sànyà says that without a head the person is unknown. That besides there being a physical head there is also an "inner head." He says that Yoruba philosophy is determinist. That one chooses one's head from the heads mass produced by Olódùmarè, and once one has chosen one's head one is stuck with it. And that whatever fortunes occur to an individual during a lifetime depend upon the head one has chosen. After the dismissal prayer, Ishmael Reed leaves the Eastmont Mall to return his film about a man moving through life with another man's head. The wrong head. A dead head. Orí búrú. *Shattered.* Captain Video is located a block from Lake Merritt park. After depositing the film, Ishmael Reed decides to take his daily walk around the lake. This walk clears his head. His head doctor is Lake Merritt. When he heard the Rodney King verdict, Ishmael Reed first called Cecil Brown to tell him the news. Cecil said "Please don't tell me that, please don't tell me that," and hung up. Lake Merritt accepted his rage and his anxiety. Ọṣun resides there. Like raising a god in a shopping mall, Yoruba doesn't require a fancy lake.

They are holding the Festival of the Lake and so he has to park near Broadway. Ninety-eight thousand people will attend this year. Food stands are set up in the park. African: Le Saloum Catering, Red Sea Restaurant; Cajun: Louisiana Cajun Lady, New Orleans Catering, T.J.'s Gingerbread House (T.J. dresses in the Ọlọṣun style); B.B.Q./ Soul: Pearlie's Special Recipe, Ribs-N-Things; Caribbean: Other Woman Catering; Chinese: LIAO's Food; Filipino: Lumpia, etc.; German: East European catering; Greek: Phaedra Foods; Indian: Sabina India Cuisine; Indonesian: Dutch East Indies Restaurant; Italian: Didomenico's Gourmet Pasta; Japanese: Ta-Ke Sushi Restaurant; Latin American: La Cocina Mexicana, Cafe De La Paz; Native American: Intertribal Friendship House; Thai: Thai Stick.

They have entertainment. Pete Escovedo, Dance Brigade, the Gospel Hummingbirds, Chilean Folk, Nueva Cancion; Nicaraguan
Folk, Duo Guardabarranco; South American folk, Altazor; Brazilian
Jazz, Bough; Country Western, California Cowboys; South Filipino
contemporary music and dance, Kulingtang Arts; Japanese, Taiko
Ensemble; Afro-Venezuelan Percussion Ensemble, Groupe cam-
pana; Ghanaian & African Highlife, Hedsoleh Soundz.

They dance. Sun Eagle Drummers & Fancy Dancers, Zydeco Flames,
Salsa, Charanga Tumbao Y Cuerda, Cuban Salsa. Soca/Calypso/
Reggae. Kotoja, Modern Afro Beat. Flamenco. Traditional Flamenco. Rumba Flamenco. Vietnamese Music Ensemble. Oakland's
multicultural population is streaming into the park. Ishmael Reed
walks toward them. Cambodians, Laotians, Vietnamese, Chinese,
Japanese, Africans, Latinos (there are parts of Oakland now that
resemble Mexico City). A white man wears a Malcolm X sweater.
Vendors have set up stands selling "African" clothing. Shirts, sweaters, dashikis. There is a lot of Malcolm X clothing for sale.

This is the way the United States would look in twenty-five years.
You could see it already happening in Oakland. You could see it in
the Los Angeles airport, which now resembles a meeting at the
General Assembly of the United Nations. The Filipino Americans
and Latinos move through the airport with their black walks. (The
Anglos get the first generation. The second generation belongs to
the souls.) The East Indian women wear their saris. In the battle of
multiculturalism, California has fallen to the enemy.

Ishmael Reed was thinking about the ceremony he had witnessed
earlier. Maybe Sànyà was on to something. If, of all of the indexes
of a nation's health, the condition of the children was the most
important, then the United States was deeply troubled. Black male
children were killing each other. White children and Native American children were killing themselves. Millions of children were

mired in poverty and had no health care. Olódùmarè and his daughter would have their work cut out for them. As this thought was abandoning his mind, he was walking toward the Camron Stanford House, a Queen Anne Victorian mansion, where, in 1880, a reception was given for Mrs. Rutherford B. Hayes. Just then a beautiful black butterfly with yellow spots collided with his chin and flew away.